"ONE OF THE GENRE'S
BRIGHTEST NEW STARS!"*

ᘓ

Praise for the novels of
EILEEN WINWOOD
Winner of the
Regency Plume Award of Excellence . . .

"DAZZLING . . . An outstanding achievement in
romantic fiction, this beautifully crafted tale offers
a myriad of pleasures . . . Sharp, witty dialogue spices
a wonderfully sensitive love story and brings to
highly memorable and intelligent life two totally
unforgettable lovers. Rare treasure indeed!"
—*Romantic Times**

"Spellbinding . . . impossible to put down!"
—*Rendezvous*

Now the award-winning author of
Garden of Secrets *presents her newest,*
most unforgettable novel . . .

So Reckless a Love

Titles by Eileen Winwood from The Berkley Publishing Group

GARDEN OF SECRETS
NOBLE DECEPTION
WORDS OF LOVE
A WORTHY ENGAGEMENT

SO RECKLESS A LOVE

EILEEN WINWOOD

DIAMOND BOOKS, NEW YORK

For Abby, who taught us
to believe in miracles.

This book is a Diamond original edition,
and has never been previously published.

SO RECKLESS A LOVE

A Diamond Book / published by arrangement with
the author

PRINTING HISTORY
Diamond edition / March 1995

ISBN: 0-7865-0079-4

Diamond Books are published by The Berkley Publishing Group,
200 Madison Avenue, New York, New York 10016.
DIAMOND and the "D" design are trademarks
belonging to Charter Communications, Inc.

PRINTED IN THE UNITED STATES OF AMERICA

10 9 8 7 6 5 4 3 2 1

PROLOGUE

Anglesey, Wales
Spring 1816

GWYNNA RAISED THE DAGGER TO THE MOON. THE WHITE CLOAK that hooded her newly shorn hair fell back as she lifted her face to the silvery radiance. The steel blade, sharpened on the stones of the ancient tomb, glinted with the light of battle.

She was ready.

Tears filled her eyes, but her voice was firm as she began to recite the words handed down over the centuries:

> *"Eryr digrif afrifid*
> *Owain, helm gain, hael am ged,*
> *Gore wirfab, (gair or ofod)*
> *Grufudd Vychan glan ei glod . . ."*

She savored the sound and feel of the language of her mother's people as it rolled off her tongue. Then, in her father's language, she repeated the paean to the warrior prince:

"Thou delightful eagle Owen, with thy bright shining helmet—generous in bestowing riches—thou are the brave and ever conquering son of Gruffydd Tychan of noble renown."

1

A large cloud suddenly obscured the moon, but still she recited, the wind off the mountains lifting her cloak and stirring her spirit as it must have once stirred the ancients.

"When thy toils pressed heaviest upon thee in besieging yonder walls, thy ashen spear terrible in battle, in the strong attack its head was steel . . ."

Drops of rain tingled on her skin, but she ignored them. The stiff wind threatened to take her words, but she raised her voice defiantly against its keening whine.

"The strength of thy arm, shoulder, and breast caused splinters and flashes of lightning to sparkle from the steel. There the armies were driven before you by twos, and threes, and great multitudes . . ."

Now the rain pummeled her face. The white cloak that had billowed out behind her clung limply to her slender frame. Still she chanted, her voice strong and firm:

"Thou, that art descended from illustrious ancestors, shalt be immortal. Thou that art a wise and able warrior, equal to a two-edged sword, steer the ships to Britain; thou art clad in garments as white as flakes of driven snow, and thy onset in the field of battle is terrible."

Her voice soared as she flung the last lines to the mountain before her:

> *"A'r gwiw rwyfg a'r gorefcyn*
> *A'r glod i'r marchog o'r Glyn."*

"May due authority, success, and praise attend the Knight of Glyn!"

Thunder crackled overhead, as if Prince Owen himself were echoing her battle cry. Gwynna took the heavy dagger and laid it upon the stone altar. Carefully, deliberately, she ran her finger over its deadly blade. When the blood came, she allowed the drops to spill upon the gray stones. This was for the ancients. They were not warriors like Owen, but they would understand her sacrifice.

Finally Gwynna pulled out a single rose from her pouch and placed it at the entry of the ancient tomb.

"Megan Glendowr Owen," she crooned. Then, more softly, she added, "Mother." Her whisper evaporated in the wind's moan.

She sat back on her knees. Was it only her imagination, or was that her mother's spirit swirling around her? Despite the storm's cruel chill, there was something warm and comforting about this place.

"I will find him, Mother," she promised fiercely. "I will make him pay for your pain. For mine. And I will make him help me rout the evil from this island."

A bolt of lightning suddenly split a gnarled oak tree not twenty feet from her. The tree erupted in flames, and the acrid scent of burning wood assailed her nostrils.

Gwynna retrieved her dagger from the altar and plunged it into the scabbard at her waist. Then she turned to the tomb and smiled. Owen was with her. The ancients were with her. Her mother was with her.

The battle was joined.

CHAPTER I

London

GIDEON TRAHERNE DODGED THE PURPLE OSTRICH FEATHER JUST AS
its turbaned wearer nodded vigorously, sending the plume
straight for his eye socket. His superbly deft movement was
born of an oppressive number of recent nights in the
company of matchmaking dowagers like Lady Hereford-
Smythe. Despite his best efforts, however, the feather
grazed his cheek. Gideon frowned. Perhaps his reflexes
were slowing.

"Oh, I do quite understand your discomfort, Your Grace.
Perhaps you think it is too soon to begin thinking about your
choice of a bride. I know how devoted you were to *dear*
Elizabeth." As the woman nodded knowingly, her beady
eyes bored in on him like those of a bird of prey.

Wretched woman. Gideon ignored her remark and forced
himself to study the weaving feather. If he were not careful,
it would blind him. One end of his mouth curved upward.
That would scare away the matchmakers. Who would want
a blind duke?

"Her poor mother had such hopes for a match between
you," Lady Hereford-Smythe purred. "But life *does* go on,
to be sure. And you do have obligations, now, *Your Grace.*"

Ah, there was the rub. Blind or no, a duke was a duke.
And an unattached one was prime husband material. The

4

devil take his father's despicable cousin for dying without producing a more willing heir than Viscount Gideon Traherne. Gideon sighed. The devil *had* taken him. That, of course, was the problem. There was no use hoping that dark angel would give him back when he realized what a cold, mean-spirited curmudgeon he had on his hands. At least William Traherne would give the devil his due.

The woman was staring at him, her parted lips revealing a toothy grin reminiscent of a crocodile's the instant before its jaws gaped to snare dinner. She gestured to a young woman who seemed to be hiding behind her skirts. He knew what was expected. An introduction, a dance. Perhaps he would take the chit into supper. The obligatory flowers the next day, the afternoon call. He could almost feel the parson's noose around his neck. His pulse quickened with the familiar surge of battle. At least Napoleon had not hidden his nefarious intentions behind a bunch of ostrich feathers.

The new Duke of Claremont pulled out his bejeweled quizzing glass, pausing to brush an imaginary speck of dust from the lapel of his midnight-black evening coat. He frowned, taking an extra moment for an ostentatious inspection of his coat sleeves. Finally he turned his attention to Lady Hereford-Smythe. He peered through his glass at the dowager, sparing not a glance for the timid creature who hid behind her skirts. His eyebrows arched elegantly, but with the suggestion of boredom. He said nothing, simply continued to favor the woman with his most haughty gaze. Finally his hazel eyes slid languidly from the ladies to a spot across the room.

"Egad!" he drawled, eyes widening.

Lady Hereford-Smythe hesitated. "Is something wrong, Your Grace?"

From his lofty height Gideon turned to look down at the

woman. His sandy brows furrowed in momentary perplexity, as if he had scarcely recalled her presence. The purple ostrich plume bobbed uncertainly, brushing the tip of his nose. Gideon brought a handkerchief to his face and coughed delicately.

"You will excuse me, madam," he said in a peremptory voice. "I see that Lord Fairchild has arrived."

An expression of confusion crossed Lady Hereford-Smythe's face. Then she smiled knowingly. "You must not let us detain you, Your Grace. I collect that you have important business with his lordship."

"Yes, indeed," Gideon agreed, dismissing her with an idle wave of his quizzing glass. "He has most urgently requested the name of my tailor."

With that, His Grace slid quickly away and melted into the crowd, leaving Lady Hereford-Smythe gaping in open-mouthed outrage.

"What is it, Auntie?" came the soft, terrified voice behind her.

"His Grace is excessively puffed up with his own consequence," Lady Hereford-Smythe replied acidly. "I should never consider such a bumptious fop proper husband material"—she turned to her niece and smiled—"were he not so *very* handsome and so *exceedingly* wealthy."

"UNREST IS ALL AROUND, Claremont. Just last week there were riots in Suffolk and Norfolk, of all places."

Gideon emitted a bored sigh. "There have been riots in the country for years, Fairchild, courtesy of Ned Ludd. I fail to see why I should be concerned about an unruly mob in Norwich."

The Earl of Fairchild shook his head. "These are no scheming Luddites. They couldn't care less about the machines. In Bideford the kickup erupted at the quay over a cargo of potatoes. The rioters do not want crops shipped abroad. They claim people are starving here."

"Nonsense," Gideon replied dismissively. "These riots are but cover for those who want to reform Parliament. Can you conceive of the notion of universal suffrage? I have no patience for such foolish ideas."

Lord Fairchild frowned, although he nodded. "Of course. But we cannot dismiss the uprisings, and now I am afraid you must also deal with these matters. Have you forgotten your new position?"

Gideon sighed as he surveyed the ballroom. Across the way he could see Lady Hereford-Smythe's beady eyes searching the crowd. The woman was indefatigable. "Not for a moment, unfortunately. What is that to anything?"

"Damnation, man. If you had bothered to respond to any of the Home Secretary's emissaries, you would know by now that the Duke of Claremont is also Lord Lieutenant of Cheshire. In addition to those responsibilities, you have extensive holdings throughout North Wales. Both areas are ripe for unrest at the moment."

She had spotted him. The crocodile grin appeared instantly on her face. Gideon ran a hand through his tousled blond hair. "So?"

Lord Fairchild looked at him in disgust. "These disturbances are your business now."

"Oh, surely not, Fairchild," Gideon drawled. "I warn you, I am not inclined to dirty Weston's best by undertaking to break up potato riots."

Lord Fairchild's face was growing red with anger. "Acquiring a dukedom has made you too high in the instep, Gideon," he said with a huff.

"On the contrary, Fairchild," Gideon replied smoothly. "The rarefied heights have always been my milieu. The dukedom only complicates things, if you must know." He eyed the earl mournfully. "Alas, I shall have to give up Wednesday nights at Almack's. The price on my head is simply too high. The ladies now assume that I am in urgent need of a wife to help me spend my money and preside over my dukedom. When I was simply a viscount, I could move about at will. But now . . ."

He broke off as he saw Lady Hereford-Smythe marching determinedly through the crowd, dragging that unfortunate niece of hers. Gideon looked around, but only a potted plant offered any cover, and it was woefully scraggly.

"I suppose what I hear is true, then," Lord Fairchild was saying. "You have not even lifted a finger to deal with your new responsibilities. Why, I could scarcely credit the reports that you have refused to meet with the late duke's solicitors, but now I see they must be true." He shook his head. "That is no way to go on, Claremont. You must deal with your affairs. It is quite urgent, I'm afraid. The old duke took so little interest that the area is now ripe for conflict. There is even talk of revolution. The Home Secretary is very concerned . . ."

"Fairchild, I do beg your pardon," Gideon interrupted, his eyes on the approaching dowager. "Perhaps we can pursue this matter at another time."

Lord Fairchild glowered. "The Lord Secretary is weary of these dodges, Claremont. You served your country well in the effort abroad, but now it is time you turn your attention to your responsibilities here. You have obligations, you know."

That word again. Gideon's smile was brittle. "I hope the Lord Secretary does not expect me to drop everything and set off for some godforsaken corner of the country, Fairchild," he said. "Why, I would miss the height of the season."

"It would not hurt you to visit your new estate, at least,"

Lord Fairchild snapped. "And perhaps if you did not find it too terribly inconvenient, you could manage to look into the welfare of the people who have the misfortune of being your responsibility."

Lady Hereford-Smythe was scarcely a carriage length away. Gideon edged to the door that led out to the terrace. "I doubt they have anything approaching an adequate tailor in the country," he muttered, "but perhaps the climate might be invigorating. London *is* becoming a shade uncomfortable at the moment." His voice grew fainter. "Wales, did you say?"

"Cheshire!" Lord Fairchild snapped. "Claremont, where are you going?"

"Fresh air, Fairchild," came a disembodied voice from the terrace. "Nothing better for one's health."

And, though the terrace was a full fifteen feet above the ground, the new Duke of Claremont jumped nimbly down to the courtyard below.

THEY WERE A MOTLEY GROUP, eerie figures marching in the night, silhouetted against the inky horizon by a thin sliver of moon. Several torches flickered off to the side, held aloft by faceless members of the outlaw band. An occasional barked command caused the figures to turn abruptly and march off in a new direction. The thick scrub grasses of the moor muffled the sound of their boots, but Gwynna could hear their grunts from her position on a slight rise above them.

She hugged her arms around her against the chill. There had scarcely been a spring this year, and now, on the cusp of summer, the cold seemed unusually penetrating. Perhaps it was just the strange spectacle below that was making her shiver, for she had always loved the night. At home night was a peaceful retreat, a place of solitude where one could stand on the beach, breathe in the salt spray, and ponder the great snowcapped mountains rising beyond the serpentine strait. But here, in this land beyond the mountains, the night was a sinister place of forbidding moors where strange men marched in the darkness, drilling in secret for unknown battles to come. She felt a thrill, along with a tingle of fear.

A nervous giggle erupted nearby, drawing her attention. "Be quiet, Anne," she commanded sharply, "or they shall find us out!"

The giggles subsided, and the plump, brown-haired young lady at her side suddenly looked fearful. "Oh, Gwynna! Papa would be furious if he knew I was here. He says it is dangerous even to speak of the Society. What would he do if he knew we were spying on them?"

Gwynna frowned. "They shall not find us out if you keep quiet. But I do wish you had not worn that white frock. It is ever so noticeable."

Anne shrank against the hillside, wriggling farther behind the small bush that served as their cover. "I did not think of that," she said unhappily, glancing at Gwynna's dark cap, breeches, and brown shirt. "Perhaps I should have dressed as a boy, too."

Gwynna tried to imagine the buxom baronet's daughter in breeches and rough-woven shirt. She shook her head. "There is no need for that," Gwynna replied with a smile, "although I have discovered in my travels that it is very freeing, somehow, to be thought a male."

Anne stared sadly at the figure beside her. "I wish you would let me tell Papa about you," she said. "I cannot bear to think of you sleeping in that old shack night after night. He could help, you know. Not that he knows the duke. No one does. He is said to be positively ancient, and lately I have heard rumors that he is sick. But who knows? He has been shut up in that drafty castle of his for years. No one sees him."

Gwynna's eyes returned to the marchers on the moor. "I am grateful for your help, Anne. What a stroke of luck that it was you, and not your father, who found me. I should not enjoy a decent meal were it not for the food you smuggle out to me each night. You have been a good friend. But it is time for me to leave. I must see the duke."

"You will not tell me why, though."

Gwynna's eyes hardened. "That is a private matter. I am sorry."

Anne stared at the resolute figure. It had been ten days since she had found Gwynna Owen hiding at the edge of her father's property in an old cottage fit only for the snakes and some errant chickens, the roof having long since crumbled and the walls gone to mold and moss. Anne's dog had picked up an intruder's scent, and when Anne hesitantly followed the animal, she found a slight, weary young woman dressed in a boy's worn breeches. She claimed to have traveled, mostly at night, from somewhere to the west—an island, it seemed, jutting out into the Irish Sea.

Anne shook her head. Gwynna could scarcely be much older than eighteen, her own age, but a world-weary air set her apart from any other young woman of Anne's acquaintance. She had resisted Anne's efforts to pry from her the reason for her journey, but Anne suspected that her new friend had some personal troubles. Was she fleeing a lover? A violent father? Did she even have a family? Why was she so intent on seeing the duke? Whatever the reason, Anne prayed that Gwynna had the sense to give up her disguise before long. Darkness and Gwynna's slender figure had doubtless helped her pass herself off as a boy at night, but her high, delicate cheekbones and brilliant sapphire eyes would give her away by day. And her thick, close-cropped red hair looked unnatural, although it must have been magnificent unshorn. Anne sighed and pulled her cloak more tightly around her against the cold.

"Perhaps we should be leaving. Papa will be looking for me soon."

"Just another minute." Gwynna was staring intently at the figures on the moor. Here in Cheshire, at least, the people were not accepting the food shortages without a fight. If only there was a little more of this sort of gumption on Anglesey. She closed her fist around the hilt of her dagger. "What do you know of these men, Anne?"

The young lady eyed her nervously. "It is not wise to speak of them," she whispered.

Gwynna turned to her friend. "Nonsense!" she retorted briskly. "They are just men, after all. They are clever to organize in this manner, for the government would never countenance such meetings in the open. But I do not think we have anything to fear from them."

"'Tis said that what they are doing is treasonous," Anne insisted in a wavering voice. "Sedition is the word Papa used."

Gwynna scoffed. "Your papa is a rich man, Anne. He has nothing to gain by siding with these folk. You must see that it is not in his interest to encourage the freedom of association among disgruntled members of the lower orders."

Anne said nothing, but Gwynna noticed the mutinous light in her eyes. "I meant no insult, Anne," Gwynna added gently, "but I doubt you have ever been truly hungry. If you had, I think you would sympathize with these people, as I do. Sometimes it is necessary to rebel, to speak out. The forces that rule are not always good."

Anne shook her head fearfully. "The way you talk, Gwynna, it is so strange. It makes me afraid."

Gwynna laughed. "The Welsh have a saying: '*An Lavar*

koth yu lavar guir, Bidh dwrn rhe ver, dan davaz rhehir, Mez din heb davaz a gallaz idir.'"

The words had an odd, lilting sound that mystified Anne. The people across the mountains had always seemed strange and foreign to her. Gwynna smiled as she softly translated: "'What is said of old will always stand, too long a tongue, too short a hand; but he that had no tongue lost his land.' So you see, one must speak up to redress a grievance, even if you do not think you can do much about it."

"What is that from?" Anne asked.

"It is a bit of ancient wisdom from the Druids. They lived on our island long ago. They were very wise."

"This island of yours sounds very unusual. Tell me more."

"It is a lovely place. Sometimes I think it is paradise, but then reality intrudes, and I see only evil." Gwynna's voice had taken on a hard note.

"Evil?" Anne echoed uncertainly.

Gwynna laughed, trying to banish her tormentor's image from her mind's eye. "You must think me a madwoman. It is hard to explain. One day . . ."

Footsteps crunched behind them, and Anne gave a little shriek.

"Eh, Billy!" came a rough voice. "What have we here? A pair of young lovers, eh?" Anne and Gwynna looked up into a leering face so dark that it appeared to have been smeared with coal dust. It was impossible to see the man's features, but Gwynna knew he must be one of the marchers.

"Stifle it, man, else you'll have the dragoons down on us. Let's have a look." Another face, also blackened, peered from behind the first man. A smile slowly spread over it, exposing a coarse set of rotting teeth. "Just a scrawny lad and his wench. Pretty thing, too. What're you doing out here, missy?"

Despite his disguised features, the lust on the man's face was unmistakable. Anne shrank against the scrawny shrub. Gwynna met the man's gaze head-on. "We are taking the night air like yourself, sir," she said in a gruff voice. "We have no more desire to bring attention to ourselves than you do," she added pointedly.

This last comment was met by loud guffaws. "Seems the lad's trying to scare us, Bill. Ought not to stand for that."

"Watch out, Davey," the second man said with a broad smirk. "The lad has spunk."

The first man growled at Gwynna. "Watch your tongue, lad, unless you want Miss Pretty here to come to grief."

With that, Anne burst into tears, which only provoked more laughter from the pair. The men were so close that Gwynna could smell the sweat and thistledown on their clothing. She looked past them to the moor below. None of the other marchers seemed to have noticed that these two ruffians were missing. It was pointless to hope for rescue from that corner in any case. But there was no escape here, either; that was certain. No one with good intentions traveled these moors at night.

One of the men reached into his pocket and pulled out a length of rope. "If yer nice, laddie, you'll keep quiet and save your neck and your ladyfriend's, too. If yer lucky, we'll even let you watch us with the wench here."

Gwynna's face was expressionless. Suddenly she made a quick movement. The uncompromising metal of her dagger glinted in her hand. The men stared at the ancient weapon, then burst into laughter.

"Look at that old piece of tin, Bill. And the look on the lad's face! Ready to die, he is, for his wench's honor."

"Let me know when yer finished with this upstart," his friend said. "I will just have me a bit of sport." He crushed Anne against him, his hands moving roughly over her body.

Anne's scream split the night. With lightning speed, Gwynna lashed out with her knife. But the other man grabbed her wrist and twisted it like a feather, and the dagger sliced harmlessly through air. Gwynna's knees buckled as the burly man kicked her from behind. She fell to the ground, the knife slipping from her hand. She stifled a groan of pain as she glared up at them.

"Two fine manly specimens you are," she said disdainfully, "hiding your faces and bullying people half your size in the middle of the night." She gestured scornfully toward the moor. "I give your revolution precious little chance if the rest of them are the likes of you."

Her assailant looked down at her menacingly. "And just what do you know of any revolution, laddie? I don't remember mentioning it myself."

Gwynna's heart hammered in her chest. It was clear from the dangerous glint in his eyes that he did not intend to let them go. As Anne whimpered against the other man's chest, Gwynna's assailant reached for his rope and snapped it taut. She could almost feel the rough cord around her neck.

He seemed to read her mind. "Aye, laddie," he said, his eyes glittering, "'twill make short work of that scrawny neck of yours. Then there'll be no more talk about revolution."

"An utterly boring topic, in any case," drawled a voice.

Everyone jumped. Gwynna could scarcely believe her eyes. A lone figure on horseback surveyed them with an air of extreme ennui. Under brows arched in aristocratic boredom, his eyes evinced only idle curiosity at their plight. The wind ruffled his fashionably tousled sandy hair, giving him a slightly rakish appearance at odds with his drawing room demeanor. His horse was a magnificent roan with an elegantly appointed saddle of highly polished leather. Its silver trim gleamed brightly in the moonlight, imparting a princely air. The rider himself looked to be about thirty. He was tall and fit, dressed in a dark blue coat with gleaming brass buttons, leather breeches, boots with a deep turnover top, and a stiff cravat tied in the most extraordinary manner.

Gwynna had never seen a London dandy, but she supposed this man was the epitome of the breed. He cut a strange figure out here on the moors, but he was eyeing them as if they, not he, were the strange sight.

"It is as I suspected," he murmured sadly, almost to himself. "No one around here has the slightest idea of how to dress."

The two ruffians were dumbfounded at the apparition. "Must be a madman," muttered one.

The horseman favored them with a smile. Then, as if noticing their circumstances for the first time, he cocked his head. "Pray, is there some trouble here?" he asked, his baritone rich and highly cultured. "I should not like to ruin my best travel clothes by embroiling myself in any local dispute. I am not," he added placidly, "precisely familiar with country ways."

Gwynna eyed him with open contempt. This man was no rescuer, but a pretentious fop. The two men exchanged glances. The man called Bill scowled. "No trouble at all, yer lordship," he said with a smirk. "Jest having a little fun."

The horseman's face grew puzzled, then cleared. "Ah, some eccentric game, I expect, that requires grown men to gad about with coal dust on their faces and tussle with two young persons in this desolate wilderness." He elevated his brows. "It shall take me a while, I'm afraid, to learn how to go on here."

The men touched their faces, as if suddenly recalling their disguises. They shifted uneasily. "We keep to our own business in these parts, mister," one man growled menacingly.

The horseman nodded. "So I have heard," he said. "Unfortunately, people here do have the reputation of being exceedingly unfriendly. Which is why," he added almost apologetically, "I always take precautions against inhospitable dispositions."

Gwynna could not have said how the gleaming silver pistol came to be in the horseman's hand. One minute it was not there; the next it seemed to appear from thin air. The horseman's composed, polite demeanor did not change. He merely remained atop his great horse, gazing at them benignly, the pistol pointed directly at the two men. Something about the way he held the weapon told Gwynna he was an excellent shot.

Their assailants did not remain for further conversation. After a quick glance at each other, they turned and raced off into the night. The horseman eyed their fleeing forms, then shook his head. "Such manners," he opined, rubbing the pistol barrel idly with the tip of one elegantly gloved finger.

With an exhausted cry, Anne collapsed into the bush that had earlier served as their hiding place. "It is all right," Gwynna said, putting an arm about her. "They are gone. I do not think we have anything to fear from *this* one."

The horseman arched his brows eloquently. "I am honored at your high opinion of me, boy. Nevertheless, it seems that, however unfitting, I have been cast in the role of knight-errant. Your mistress appears to be a trifle indisposed. I suppose I must volunteer my services to help you get her to her home." His brows knitted together. "She *does* have a home, I trust?"

Gwynna looked up indignantly. "Certainly. You need not trouble yourself about us. We shall manage."

"Oh, no!" Anne cried. "What if those horrible men come back?"

"My sentiments precisely," the horseman said, dismounting. "Come, boy. Let us help your mistress up. She can ride in front of me. You, however, will have to walk."

In short order, Anne was tossed onto the roan. The horseman mounted behind her and, with a flick of his elegant wrist, set them off across the hills in the direction that Gwynna indicated. Scant minutes later, he deposited Anne about twenty yards from her father's large manor house.

"With any luck, I shall slip in the side door, and Father will not notice my absence," Anne said tearfully, giving Gwynna a hug.

The horseman's brows arched in disapproval, but he said nothing until Anne entered the house. Then he turned to Gwynna.

"What sort of groom lets his mistress wander off across the moor in the dark of night?" he asked in haughty reproof. "Had it not been for the risk to the young lady's reputation, I would have insisted on informing her father of your lapse. A groom of mine who behaved as you have would have been turned off in an instant."

Gwynna lifted her chin defiantly. "I am not her groom. And I do not see how it is any of your concern."

The horseman's brows rose even higher at such impertinence. "Unfortunately, boy, I have only recently learned that everything in this area appears to be my concern." He gave a sigh.

"How so?" she demanded scornfully.

"You see," he replied in a bored voice, "I am the Duke of Claremont."

Gwynna gasped. "That is impossible!" she cried.

The horseman frowned. "I assure you, young man, it is quite possible," he said disdainfully. "Though why it should affect you so, I am at a loss to guess."

Stunned, Gwynna sank to the ground. She squinted up at

him in the darkness. His eyes under those arrogantly arched brows were unreadable.

"You are too young," she murmured, shaking her head in wonder. Her world was suddenly in shambles. She clutched the hilt of her dagger, trying to draw from its solid strength.

"Too young for what?" he demanded imperially.

"Too young to be my father."

The expression of idle boredom abruptly fled from Gideon Traherne's face.

CHAPTER 2

IT WAS GALLING TO HAVE TO ASK DIRECTIONS TO ONE'S CASTLE, especially from an upstart stable lad who was clearly raving mad.

"What sort of duke doesn't know the way to his own estate?" muttered the boy as Gideon set the lad in front of him for the ride to Claremont Castle. The imp clutched that rusty dagger but offered no resistance to Gideon's instant decision to take him to Claremont. That was fortunate, for he meant to get to the bottom of the boy's wild ramblings this very night.

Gideon recovered his equilibrium quickly. Most likely the lad was dropped on his head as a babe, which would explain his nonsensical talk.

"One who is not obliged to explain himself to whelps like you," Gideon responded as he nudged Captain off into the night. He was more than ready for the comforts of a duke's bed, not to mention savoring the other luxuries of his new castle, starting with a glass of the duke's finest brandy. *His* brandy, he amended with some satisfaction. Then he would deal with the lad.

They rode in silence after that. Gideon could almost feel the boy trembling with some strong emotion. Anger? Possibly. Fear? Gideon didn't think so. He had never met a servant quite like this one, but then he had never had the occasion to engage one in extensive conversation.

He frowned. He was quite sure he had not fathered any offspring. The lad did not look a day over fourteen, so perhaps it was possible.

Nonsense. He had been a precocious youth, but not *that* precocious. The boy was right. He was too young to be his father, thank God. Although it would be novel, perhaps even pleasant, to have a son and heir. But if he recalled matters correctly, it was necessary to have a wife for the whole thing to work out properly.

Not that he hadn't taken the first step, however unplanned. The ceremony in Vienna had been a bit rushed, perhaps, and not up to the shade of elegance that Elizabeth would have expected, had she been in her right mind, which she assuredly was not. She had been prostrate with grief and feverish from the plague that had carried off her parents, and so had offered no objection to the beady-eyed, rather questionable man of the cloth Gideon had plucked from the streets. It was not precisely how he had once envisioned his wedding day.

Had that really been a year ago? When he was still a diplomat, still a lowly but contented viscount? He shifted his body awkwardly to move away from the stable lad's soft, rounded backside.

One year. A year of secrecy, for the *ton* still thought their betrothal had ended in Vienna after the death of Elizabeth's parents. He sighed. He had existed in purgatory since then, married but without a wife, a bachelor to all eyes but his own.

Gideon halted Captain before a gloomy stone structure. The state of his marriage was a problem for another time. For now there was the matter of this strange lad and his entirely too appealing backside. He arched a brow, wondering whether he was losing his mind.

He dismounted and stared at the building. Surely this

could not be his castle. A sinking feeling, however, told him otherwise. He heard the lad's light, hurried footsteps behind him as he strode toward the great door, which rose a good twenty feet above a set of crumbling stone steps.

The structure itself was as big as a cathedral and far less inviting. Stone turrets rose unsteadily into the air from one wing that appeared to be the oldest part of the castle. A relatively newer wing jutted off to the right from the main structure, but even it was old and decrepit, probably cobbled together by masons a hundred years ago. Gargoyles that once had stared proudly off toward the horizon now looked up from the ground where they had fallen, their dead stares bleak and unwelcoming. Claremont Castle was an uninhabitable, rotting pile of stones.

"Good God," Gideon muttered.

No welcoming torches blazed. No lights glowed through any of the windows. The boy stared uncertainly at the overgrown brambles that had nearly overtaken the entryway steps. "Do you suppose anyone is here?" he ventured.

Gideon scowled. "Why did you not tell me my castle was a wreck?" he demanded.

The lad surveyed him coolly. "It seems strange that you did not know its condition yourself."

Gideon stared at the youth. Prickly child. Evidently no one had bothered to teach him any manners. Not that one needed them in this godforsaken place.

"And anyway," the lad was saying in a gruff voice, "I have never seen the castle. I have been in Cheshire for less than a fortnight."

Now *that* was a piece of dubious information, but Gideon put it from his thoughts as he surveyed the huge relic that was now his. He viewed the prospects of spending the night here with as much enthusiasm as he did spending another moment in the company of this surly lad. It served him right, of course, for being too impatient to wait for his baggage coach, his valet, and the rest of the entourage that was supposed to travel with such an important personage as a duke. But when his carriage had rolled into the mud and broken a wheel near Litchfield, he had refused to wait for the repair. The urge to flee London was too great. Now his folly was clear. There appeared to be not another soul here, without or within.

He lifted the ancient knocker. It sounded with a lordly thud on the massive door, and he could hear its echo deep inside the cavernous castle. No one came to let them in, however. He knocked again, more insistently. It took a quarter hour of this exercise, the boy glaring suspiciously at him all the while, before a small peephole opened and a fogged voice demanded, "Who dares to disturb our sleep?"

"Your new employer," Gideon returned imperiously. "Open the door!"

There was silence at first. Finally the great door creaked open on its enormous hinges. An elderly man in a dressing gown and nightcap was huffing and puffing alarmingly with the effort of pulling the long chain that controlled the infernal contraption.

"Good God, man!" Gideon quickly stepped inside and relieved the servant of the chain. He pulled the door shut, and it closed with a great boom that echoed through the hall like a cannonball ricocheting off the walls. It was some time before Gideon's ears stopped ringing.

"Thank you, sir, er, that is—" The man broke off, breathing heavily, his eyes wide. "Did I understand you to say that you were . . ." He hesitated.

"The Duke of Claremont," Gideon said with a heavy sigh. "And you are . . . ?"

"Rowland, Your Grace," he said, bowing deeply. "I am afraid that we were not expecting you."

"Obviously not."

It was impossible not to notice the dust and cobwebs that draped the tables and chairs in the great hall. Some of the furniture was in holland covers, but much of it was not covered at all. "It appears that you rarely expect anyone," Gideon added dryly.

"Oh, no, Your Grace. We never do."

Gideon arched a brow at this response. "Tell me, Rowland, do I have a study?" he said irritably. "And a bottle or two of brandy? A place to wash and a bed in which to lay my head? Or am I, perhaps, expecting too much?"

Rowland bowed. "Regrettably, Your Grace, Mrs. Carson, the housekeeper, will have to prepare a bedchamber. But," he said as he looked up hopefully, "I believe I can find a bottle of brandy."

"Then do so at once," Gideon commanded, saying a silent prayer of thanks for at least that civilizing amenity.

"Yes, Your Grace."

Gideon fought back a sneeze as Rowland led them into a dust-covered study and brushed off a chair upholstered in cracked claret leather. The man hesitated, then lifted the covers off a second chair, eyeing the boy with curiosity.

"You will also prepare a room for my, uh, servant," Gideon said, wrinkling his nose in distaste at the boy's attire, which looked even more tattered in the meager light of the candles that Rowland had fished from somewhere.

The butler nodded and left the room. Gideon surveyed his surroundings with a pained expression as the boy laughed derisively.

"A fine homecoming for a duke—*if*, in fact, you are a duke."

Gideon pulled out his quizzing glass and haughtily subjected the lad to careful scrutiny, a gesture that he saw with satisfaction put the lad ill at ease. There was something strange about this boy that he could not quite discern. His eyes were a luminous blue and oddly familiar; in a girl they would have been quite appealing. His cheeks were ruddy from the outdoors, but the cheekbones were delicate, almost fragile-looking. The impression of fragility was belied, however, by the defiant manner in which the lad was looking at him, his arms crossed over his chest. A strand of reddish hair poked out from under that moth-eaten cap he had pulled tightly on his head. Gideon idly waved his glass.

"My pedigree can be of no concern to you, boy," he drawled, "but what, precisely, was that nonsense you were repeating earlier? It dealt with your paternity, I believe. Although why it should interest me, I cannot imagine."

Gwynna stared at him defiantly. She had never seen such a conceited coxcomb. It was unthinkable that she might be related to such a man, however distantly. But she had come here on a mission, and her dislike of him was beside the point. If this man had inherited the dukedom, it meant that her father was dead. She swallowed tears of disappointment and sorrow. She would never see her father, never bring him to justice. Instead she would have to deal with this infuriating Englishman.

"I collect that you have recently come into the title," she said, vowing never to "Your Grace" this man. "My father was the previous Duke of Claremont, William Traherne."

Gideon eyed her in patent disbelief, with a haughty stare that had been known to reduce wayward servants to a state of trembling.

"Indeed," he replied, his tone dripping with sardonic amusement.

He was pleased to see the lad shift under his gaze. He might be a duke without a habitable castle, but at least he could still manage an upstart stable boy. But the lad's next words caused him to reconsider that rash conclusion.

"Yes, much as it displeases me, Englishman, I fear we are related," the boy shot back. With that outrageous declaration, the lad flopped into a chair.

Gideon remained standing, a look of distaste on his face. "*If* you have a connection to the late duke, which I doubt, it is obviously not on the right side of the blanket," he declared haughtily. "Such impertinence as you have displayed can only be a sign of excessively low breeding."

At those words the boy leapt up and threw himself at Gideon, his face contorted in rage. "How dare you! My mother was as fine a woman as your own. She would never have lain with a man out of wedlock! How dare you insinuate otherwise!"

A series of blows landed on Gideon's chest, and he wrenched the boy's hands tightly behind him just as the lad prepared to launch another assault. The boy gasped in pain. Gideon stared at the delicate face and the sapphire eyes that now were brimming with tears. He stared again, hard.

Something was not quite right.

Holding the lad's arms with one hand, Gideon pulled off the scruffy cap, exposing an unruly mop of close-cropped reddish hair. He held up a candle to illuminate the small face. Thoroughly bemused, he studied the delicate features. Then the truth dawned.

Bloody hell. Instantly he released the slender arms and stepped back.

Gwynna stared at him, uncomprehending, as he crossed the room, poured a glass of brandy, and drank deeply.

"It is not enough that I must contend with a dilapidated castle, barely fit for the rats that no doubt prowl its corridors by the hundreds," he muttered darkly into the dust-covered wainscotting. "Now I must needs have a girl on my hands."

Gwynna blinked in surprise. "You know?"

He turned. "You may have fooled two dim-witted thugs in

the black of night, but that disguise of yours does not bear up under scrutiny. Whatever else I am, Miss . . . er . . ." He looked at her expectantly.

"Owen. Gwynna Owen."

"Miss Owen, then. Whatever else I am, Miss Owen, I hope I am able to identify a girl."

"I am not a child," she corrected. "I am twenty, to be precise." She shot him a defiant glare.

Gideon stared at the excessively boyish figure, the unfashionably ruddy complexion, the unattractively cropped hair. "Twenty," he repeated numbly. The sapphire eyes blazed at him.

A woman's eyes.

Gideon gained the door in two long steps and threw it open. "Rowland!" he shouted.

It was a maddeningly long few minutes before the elderly servant appeared.

"Yes, Your Grace?"

"Do I have a secretary? A man of business somewhere nearby?" Gideon demanded.

"Mr. Busby, sir. He served the late duke for thirty years. Though we have not seen him since His Grace's lamented passing."

Gideon arched a brow. "You will have him on my doorstep before breakfast," he ordered. "In the meantime, you will send to London for my solicitors."

Rowland hesitated.

Gideon eyed him regally. "Well, what is it, man?"

"Begging your pardon, Your Grace, but there is no one to send on such errands until young Jim comes in to do the marketing for Mrs. Carson. And that is not for another three days."

Gideon emitted a heavy sigh. He stared at the elderly retainer. "Are you capable of managing a large staff, Rowland?"

Rowland puffed out his chest. "I should say so, sir. Why, in the old days, we had a staff of fifty here. I remember—"

"Rowland," Gideon interrupted softly. He closed his eyes and said a prayer for patience.

"Yes?"

"You have my permission to hire a full staff in the morning. But first you will send someone—anyone—to fetch Mr. Busby. Do you understand?"

Rowland bowed creakily. "Perfectly, Your Grace."

Gwynna watched this exchange, wondering how things could have turned out so badly. She had prepared herself to face an eccentric duke, a crotchety old man who nevertheless might have had some lingering softer feelings for her mother; a man who, as he approached death, might have wanted to set things right. That man she was prepared to confront, to throw his sins in his face if need be. Instead, here was this elegant dandy, a man of insufferable airs, who cared only for the cut of his clothes. He would have no use for anyone but himself.

In other circumstances she might have found him attractive. He was tall and muscular, like the men of Anglesey. But unlike those men, who did an honest day's work for their living, this duke arrayed himself in finely cut garments that seemed to have no other purpose than to dazzle an audience and proclaim their quality. His tousled hair was a deep golden shade that reminded her of the sun as it gleamed off the ocher of Parys Mountain. His eyes were a magnificent hazel that ran to green and bronze like the mountain's rich copper ore. She must be homesick. There could be no other reason for seeing the charms of her island in this fatuous coxcomb.

She felt a surge of despair. She might well have cajoled an old duke facing his Maker, but she would never persuade this self-centered man that she was entitled to his name and fortune. He was no fool—she had seen that much out on the moor. He would never believe her.

"Now . . ." The rich baritone intruded into her thoughts, and Gwynna saw that the duke was pouring himself another brandy.

"I should like some as well, please," she said.

His brows rose in that supercilious manner that was becoming quite familiar. He said nothing, however, and surprised her by pouring her a glass. He even brought it to her, and Gwynna fought back a shiver as their fingertips touched.

He frowned. Gwynna hastily took a drink. The amber liquid burned as it trickled down her throat, and she felt a warming sensation throughout her body. It was most satisfying, she decided. She took another deep gulp, barely stifling a cough.

Gideon watched this display with fascination. He had never seen a woman down a glass of brandy with such determination. For that matter, most of the women of his acquaintance professed a distaste for the stuff. Elizabeth thought it was positively vile.

Elizabeth. That thought brought his wandering attention back to the matter at hand.

"If you have quite satisfied your thirst"—his brows rose consideringly—"I believe it is time to hear your story."

As she drained the glass, her tongue shot out to capture an errant drop, provoking in him an unexpected warmth. Gideon frowned anew. *"Now,* if you please," he commanded, resolutely banishing the unwelcome sensation.

Gwynna put the glass down and wiped her mouth with her shirtsleeve. Belatedly she realized that he was probably used to more refined manners. The daughter of a duke undoubtedly behaved with more decorum. She sat a little straighter in her chair and fixed him with a direct look.

"I am from Anglesey," she said. "The late duke liked to summer there. That is where he met my mother. Apparently he meant to build a summer home on some land he owned near the sea." She looked down. "But he never did."

"Anglesey?" His brow furrowed, then cleared. "Ah, yes. That island with all the ruins. The end of the Dublin road, is it not?" He yawned. "Never traveled there myself. All those mountains in between, you know. Not one for such exertions."

Gwynna could barely contain her contempt as she met his bland gaze. It was quite clear that one who shunned even a little exercise would never lift a finger for her. How did he manage to appear so fit? she wondered. Artifice, no doubt. She had heard that these dandies were skilled at it. She could not bite back the retort that came to her lips.

"It is not necessary to cross the mountains to get to Anglesey, only to sit back like any lazy Englishman and allow the horses to take you along the coast road around them. I imagine that even one such as yourself could manage that chore." She eyed him defiantly. "Seeing Anglesey is far worth the small effort it takes to get there."

He did not rise to the bait, but merely continued to watch her with that disconcertingly smug expression. "I believe you were going to enlighten me as to your family history."

Gwynna forced down her anger, knowing that it would get her nowhere with this man. He was only going through the motions of hearing her story. He cared nothing for her circumstances. She took a deep breath. She had not come so far to let a condescending duke intimidate her.

"My mother and the duke fell in love the second summer he spent in Anglesey." His brows arched skeptically, and Gwynna suspected that he disdained that emotion as beneath him. "They were married secretly," she continued, "at the place where they met—one of the Druid tombs near the strait." She swallowed hard. "Or so I am told."

He remained impassive. "How utterly charming," he said in a bored voice.

Gwynna ignored this comment. "They kept the marriage a secret because my mother's family had no use for the nobility." She could not keep the contempt from her voice. "Her family worked for their daily bread and could not understand anyone who did not. The duke returned to Cheshire, perhaps thinking to give my mother time to accustom her family to the marriage."

"And how is it that you are so knowledgeable about the duke's thoughts?" His hazel eyes glinted scornfully.

Gwynna flushed. "I do not know, of course."

"Of course," he murmured.

"But I have given the matter much thought," she insisted. "It is the only reasonable explanation."

He arched a brow. "I can think of other possibilities," he said pointedly.

Flushing, Gwynna fought her anger at his knowing look. "My mother discovered after he left that she was with child," she said.

"Ah." He nodded sagely.

Gwynna wanted to slap that infuriating look from his face. Men were despicable creatures. "When she mustered the courage to tell her father, there was an enormous row," she said evenly. "Meanwhile, the duke's return to Anglesey was delayed. At all events, my mother's father did not believe her story. He turned her out."

"What an endearing family," he observed dryly.

Gwynna reddened. "I cannot pretend that my grandfather behaved well," she said. "Still, he is the only family I have ever known. You see, my mother was walking at the tombs one day near her time and fell. She cracked her skull and did not recover. I was born just as she breathed her last."

Gideon drew a sharp intake of breath. He might have known that she would devise some heartbreaking tale. He steeled himself against those enormous blue eyes and the small, fragile-looking face. "And the marriage lines," he prodded in a silky voice, "what of them?"

She met his direct gaze. "I do not have them."

"Of course," he murmured with a sigh, walking over to the decanter of brandy. "In fact, you do not know the truth of any of this—not the marriage, not the ceremony at some moldy tomb, none of it. Is that not correct?"

Gwynna bristled. Anyone would have been skeptical of her story; still, his insults were infuriating. "I have searched for the marriage documents, you can be sure. I can only conclude that the duke kept them, for what reason I cannot guess."

"I see."

He was eyeing her thoughtfully. Gwynna could no longer contain her fury. "I am certain that a man like you cannot begin to understand why someone would wish to keep such a marriage secret," she said angrily. "But—"

"You know nothing about me."

His sharp tone took her aback. For a moment his eyes seemed to burn with unusual intensity. Then Gwynna decided her imagination was playing her tricks. Yes, for now he was propped elegantly against the mantel, looking every inch the idle aristocrat, his face a blank mask.

"It is late," he said, and he sounded genuinely weary. "We will not resolve this tonight. I will have Rowland show you to your chamber, wherever that may be. Unfortunately I cannot promise that the accommodations will be of the first stare. We will resume this discussion in the morning."

Gwynna stood up, feeling like a wayward child summarily dismissed after being caught awake past her bedtime. But there was nothing else to do. She walked to the door.

"Miss Owen." His rich baritone gave her name an elegant sound she had never heard.

"Yes?"

"I realize this situation is somewhat . . . unorthodox. But if you have any intentions of capitalizing on it, I would advise you to think again."

She stared at him in confusion. "I do not understand."

One of his brows arched skeptically. "I am speaking of compromise, Miss Owen," he said in a pedantic tone. "You are a young woman sleeping under my roof, such as it is, without benefit of a chaperon. I regret I cannot offer you something more respectable. But if, in order to solidify your claim to my name, you intend to try to insinuate at some future time that I took advantage of you, I would advise against it. I cannot be trapped into marriage, nor will I offer to soothe any of your offended sensibilities—if you have any, that is—with my gold."

Gwynna's mouth dropped open. Her fury was such that it was some time before she could speak. All the while, he continued to look at her, the picture of aristocratic arrogance.

"I assure you, Englishman," she said, her voice suffused with scorn, "I have no designs on your person. I seek only that to which I am entitled."

His fingers drummed idly on the edge of his desk. "Ah. And that would merely be my name and my money."

She flushed.

"You do not deny it, I see."

"You are hateful," Gwynna declared fiercely. "It is not like that at all."

He merely arched his brows and gave her a speaking

look. Gwynna slammed the door behind her with a thud that resounded to the rafters.

ALOYSIUS BUSBY MAY HAVE been in his seventh decade, but he was as fit as an ox. And so, when young Jim Crowley presented himself at the door shortly after dawn with a summons from the new duke, he did not hesitate to strike out for Claremont Castle on foot. After all, it was only five miles. Nor was Mr. Busby a fool. He knew that such a peremptory summons could only mean a matter of great urgency, and so he gathered the various papers that he had been holding for just such an occasion.

When he was shown into the duke's dust-covered study, Mr. Busby looked around him eagerly. He had not been in this room for a dozen years. The late duke preferred to conduct his business, when he paid attention to such things, from his sitting room upstairs. Perhaps this was a sign that the new duke meant to put things in order. Mr. Busby looked up hopefully when the door opened and His Grace entered the room.

The new Duke of Claremont was quite simply the most elegant man Mr. Busby had ever seen. His top boots were polished to a fare-thee-well, the leather gleaming like a freshly poured claret. His tailor was obviously a superb artist; his attire showed him to advantage, but the task needed no artifice. The man looked fit as a fiddle. His Grace carried himself with the demeanor of a man long accustomed to his position of privilege and power. His face was intelligent, however, without a sign of fatuousness. His eyes were sharp and his mouth firm; Mr. Busby would have wagered that His Grace was awake on every suit.

He wasted no time in trivialities. After a polite greeting, the duke sat behind his desk and fixed Mr. Busby with a hard gaze.

"What can you tell me of a Miss Owen from the island of Anglesey?"

Mr. Busby nearly jumped from his chair. Now the reason for the urgent summons had become apparent. He cleared his throat.

"Just before his death, Your Grace, the duke had initiated proceedings to become Miss Owen's guardian."

This comment drew only an elevation of those aristocratic brows. Mr. Busby took this as leave to continue. "The proceedings were never completed," he said, "the duke having succumbed to an inflammation of the chest, as Your Grace knows."

The duke's eyes narrowed. "Did the duke acknowledge a familial connection to Miss Owen?"

Mr. Busby shifted under the force of those penetrating eyes. "Not precisely."

The duke rose. "Come, man," he said impatiently. "Let us not mince words. Miss Owen has arrived here to lay claim to the Traherne name and, presumably, some of the Traherne fortune. Is there any basis to her claim?"

Mr. Busby hesitated. "I do not know," he said at last.

An ominous silence greeted this response, and Mr. Busby hastened to fill it. "I never saw any documents that would verify such a claim. I can only tell you that the late duke sent a small annual sum to Miss Owen's grandfather. He gave me no explanation, as was his right, of course. Then, five months ago, he summoned me to dictate a letter to his solicitors directing them to take steps to secure Miss Owen's guardianship. The papers were prepared for his signature, but they arrived the week following his death. I returned them to the duke's solicitors." He hesitated. "They did not inform you of the matter?"

The duke shot him a sharp look. "I have not yet seen the solicitors, a fact that now appears exceedingly unwise of me. Nevertheless, the woman is on my doorstep, and I must deal with that now without benefit of their advice. You say you have seen no marriage papers?"

"No, Your Grace." Mr. Busby paused. "The late duke was a very private man," he said. "Although I served him for thirty years, I knew nothing about his private life. In his later years he was a complete recluse."

He eyed the duke cautiously, wondering if perhaps the man would think such a comment inappropriate. But the duke revealed nothing of his feelings in the matter. He did, however, massage his temples, as if his head ached. "Did he ever travel to Anglesey?" the duke asked tersely.

"Yes. He used to spend the summers on the island, even bought some land there. Anglesey was one of his favorite places. But he stopped going there about twenty years ago. In the last decade of his life, he never went anywhere."

"I see. After the duke's death, I assume you collected his papers."

"Yes, Your Grace. They are in the desk there, along with the account ledgers. The duke spent almost no money, however, in the last years. He lost interest in the running of his various estates."

"One imagines they are all in a similar condition," the duke observed dryly.

Mr. Busby nodded cautiously and pulled out some documents. "I took the precaution of cataloging his papers, Your Grace."

The duke took the papers. "I assume there is not even a hint of any marriage." The secretary shook his head and watched as the duke yanked the tattered bell cord, only to have it come apart in his hand. His Grace sighed in frustration, then rose and crossed the room to open the door.

"Rowland," he said loudly into the hallway, "send Miss

Owen to me." He turned to Mr. Busby with an exasperated
look. "Did the late duke not believe in bell pulls?"

Mr. Busby was taken aback. "I cannot say I ever thought
of the matter, Your Grace."

"Never mind," came the muttered response. In silence the
duke perused the documents Mr. Busby had given him.
After a few minutes the door swung open.

A slender figure fairly flew into the room, and Mr. Busby
could not help but stare. The young woman's reddish hair
was cut so short that it gave her a boyish appearance, though
she looked decidedly feminine—if comical—in an ornate
dress that looked to have been fashioned during the last
century. The blue taffeta creation was trimmed in a profusion of lace. Its plunging neckline gaped dangerously, and
the little tufts of lace at the bodice did nothing to hide the
delicate roundness of the young lady's bosom.

"I shall not wear this monstrosity," she declared heatedly,
her deep blue eyes shooting fire.

Mr. Busby cleared his throat, but neither the young
woman nor the duke took any notice of him. In fact,
something very odd had happened to the duke. The moment
the young woman entered the room, he underwent a
transformation. His brows arched skyward in an expression
of extreme hauteur, and the keen look in his eyes was
instantly veiled by one of bored arrogance.

"Indeed," His Grace agreed dryly. "I believe I much
preferred you as a boy."

The young woman clenched her fists at her side. "You,
sir, are a stuffy, pompous—"

"Miss Owen," His Grace interrupted in a bored voice,
"this is Mr. Busby, the late duke's secretary." The woman
whirled around in surprise. "He was just explaining that
while he had discovered no proof of your claim to the

Traherne name, it was apparently the late duke's wont to send money to your grandfather."

Her eyes widened in surprise. "I did not know that. My grandfather never mentioned it." She swallowed hard. "He died six months ago."

The duke seemed unmoved by this statement. "Is there any clergyman in which your mother might have confided?" he asked. "*If* there was a wedding, someone must have performed the ceremony. And recorded it."

Her eyes blazed. "There are few trustworthy clergymen on Anglesey," she declared vehemently.

The duke rolled his eyes and sighed. "Then I very much fear, Miss Owen, that we shall have to see this island of yours."

Mr. Busby looked at the duke in surprise. He saw that Miss Owen was scarcely less amazed. *"We?"* she echoed in a stunned voice.

The duke rose, signaling that the interview was at an end.

"Yes. You and I, Miss Owen. We shall leave for Anglesey in five days. I believe that will give you time to arrange a suitable wardrobe. I agree that this antique gown Mrs. Carson found among the attic trunks scarcely becomes you. Anything—even from a village seamstress's needle—is bound to be an improvement."

She stared at him, dumbfounded. He pulled out a quizzing glass and surveyed her ill-fitting gown disdainfully. "But I rather think," he added in a haughty voice as he eyed her figure mournfully, "that we cannot hope for miracles."

Her face turned beet red, and her fists clenched at her sides.

"You, sir, are a pompous prig," she declared. Mr. Busby nearly gasped in shock at such a daring insult, but the duke merely nodded benignly.

"Miss Owen," he drawled complacently, "I have never pretended otherwise."

CHAPTER 3

GWYNNA SAT AT THE WINDOW OF HER CHAMBER, WATCHING DAWN stalk slowly across the moors. The sky still had that hazy look it had worn all spring, as if millions of dust particles were hovering in the air, preparing to blanket the land. Now, as the sun's rays broke over the horizon, the orange brilliance was tempered by the eerie dancing dust. Gwynna had never seen anything like it, nor had she experienced anything like the chill of this strange summer. On Anglesey there was even talk that the ancients, their spirits angered over the Crown's virtual theft of the oat crop, were responsible. But here, on the Cheshire moors, the sunrise looked just as strange.

Gwynna sighed, her mood as uneasy as the swirling wind and dust outside. She had slept very poorly these four days at the castle. Her room was dank and musty, and she was uncomfortably aware that the Duke of Claremont's chamber was next to hers. Under normal circumstances, she supposed a young, unmarried woman would not have been given a chamber next to the duke. But the servants had thought Gwynna a boy, and his personal attendant at that. There was much dithering between Mrs. Carson and Rowland when her sex was revealed; however, Gwynna suspected that there were few other habitable chambers in the castle, and she was not surprised when no change was made in her accommodations.

They were leaving tomorrow. In the space of four short days, she had acquired a new wardrobe, much to her dismay, as well as a respectable title: ward to the duke. Claremont had put it about that he was her temporary guardian, charged by a commitment to her late grandfather with the task of conveying her to Anglesey and overseeing the settlement of her affairs. That story was to avoid jeopardizing either of their reputations. But the duke had made it clear to her that his "guardianship" was for appearance's sake only; he would not legitimize her connection to the family without some sort of proof.

Gwynna knew he intended for the upcoming trip to expose her as an imposter. When their search of records on Anglesey produced nothing to document her claim, he could then conveniently denounce her as a fraud. There was apparently no hope of finding papers in the castle that might verify her mother's marriage. Then again, it was impossible to find anything in this pile of stones. Moreover, the duke had summoned a team of workers from the nearby villages and set them to making repairs. One could hardly move about for the work being done.

Gwynna nervously fingered the dagger, her talisman from the past and only weapon for the present. Could it help her best this infuriating man? At the moment she felt ill prepared for the task. She had been off balance in his presence from the very beginning. During these few days, she had deliberately kept out of his way, spending her time out on the moors while she pondered how to deal with him.

He was such a strange man. Insultingly arrogant, the kind of nobleman her grandfather had always scorned. One look down his angular nose made her feel like a mere insect, as did his disconcerting habit of subjecting her to ostentatious inspection through that quizzing glass. She had to admit that those hazel eyes were intriguing enough, when they were not filled with acute boredom. And his lean, muscular body was certainly something to admire, when it was not draped languidly in a chair in a pose of extreme ennui. But while his finely textured baritone was mesmerizing—especially when he said "Miss Owen" in a way no one else had ever done—it could be maddenly patronizing, as if she were the veriest joke to him.

Now he was taking her home, to Anglesey. But did she belong there? Or anywhere? That monster Evans never let anyone on the island forget that her claim to legitimacy was unproven. Gwynna's mouth thinned into a grim line.

Evans was a fiend, but it was her father, William Traherne, who was responsible for her plight. He was to blame for her mother's death, for the stigma that had followed Gwynna throughout her life, for the easy assumption that men made about her own morals. Whatever her mother had felt for him, Gwynna had only anger and resentment. He had not been there to help her mother withstand her grandfather's harsh judgment. After her death, he had not bothered to visit the island, had not even acknowledged his own daughter. The land he had purchased sat idle and abandoned, when it could have provided employment for those who desperately needed jobs.

She heard sounds through the door leading to the duke's chamber. She had been surprised to discover that he arose early, for she assumed that dukes and the like slept at least until noon. Perhaps William Traherne, in his younger days, had been like this man: handsome, wealthy, polished. Perhaps that was what her mother had seen in him. Gwynna turned away from the sounds in the duke's chamber and studied the horizon again. It was beautiful. And lonely.

She raised her dagger to the sun's fledgling rays. It felt heavy and leaden in her hands. Owen's spirit seemed far away. Gwynna tried to feel her mother's presence, but in this drafty castle there was only an uneasy feeling of gloom.

"'Thou art secure and undaunted like steel,'" she chanted, caressing the blade.

But the words rang hollow.

"I DID NOT APPROVE THAT COLOR." He was frowning.

His comment caught her off guard. She put down her soup spoon and stared at him. "What?"

"It is all wrong for you. That red hair needs something more vibrant. That gray is positively funereal. Saps the life from your cheeks."

Gwynna pushed back her chair abruptly. "This is too much, sir! You have ordered my life these past four days. It is too much that you insist on choosing my clothing as well. I would rather travel as I did before—as a boy—than to subject myself to such intolerable interference. I do not need a new wardrobe, anyway."

He arched a brow. "I did not choose *everything* in your wardrobe, Miss Owen. You somehow managed to persuade the village seamstress to concoct that perfectly dowdy gray frock. Furthermore, you cannot traipse around in breeches. You make a perfectly dreadful boy. Anyone with an ounce of sense would see through that disguise in an instant."

Gwynna eyed him defiantly. "*You* did not, not at first."

His eyes slid away from her to his dinner plate. His fork speared a piece of stringy mutton. "Perhaps that is because it was dark when I first had the honor of making your acquaintance and that of your untidy companions, who, as I recall, were intent on rather nefarious activities." He toyed with the mutton. "And perhaps," he added with a distasteful glance at their surroundings, "because I was later shocked senseless by the horror of discovering that I had inherited the country's most dilapidated castle."

Gwynna shot him a contemptuous look. "This castle is a

fitting irony for one of your stripe, Englishman." She tossed her napkin on the table and rose. "You will excuse me. I have lost my appetite."

He eyed her impassively. "Very well. We shall adjourn to the drawing room." He frowned. "No, not there. The workmen have turned it inside out. My study, then. I have something to say to you in private."

Fighting off a sense of alarm, Gwynna followed him from the small alcove that served as their dining area, the vaulted rafters of the enormous dining hall presently being a haven for cobwebs, spiders, and a great number of bats. In his study, the duke poured a brandy and offered it to her. Surprised at his charity, she took it. He poured himself a glass as Gwynna eyed him suspiciously.

"Miss Owen, I do not wish to insult you," he began.

"That, Englishman, is a bold-faced lie," she retorted.

He paused mid-sip. His face remained impassive, but there was a gleam in his eyes. "I take it you are finding your visit here a trifle difficult?"

Gwynna drew a sharp breath at the copper lights in his eyes. Odiously charming man. She would wager that his smile was breathtaking.

"Not at all," she said with mock sweetness. "Your condescending arrogance, insufferable airs, and withering indictments of my appearance have not been in the least off-putting."

His rich laughter caught her by surprise. Well, she had her answer. His smile *was* breathtaking. She stared at him, wondering at the strange quickening of her pulse. When his laughter subsided, he drank deeply of his brandy and eyed her speculatively. Gwynna took a gulp of her drink.

He moved toward her, halting a few feet away, the veiled look returning to his eyes. "Miss Owen," he began, his tone censorious, "you have refused the maid I hired for you from the village. I wish to know why."

"I do not need a maid," Gwynna replied tartly. "I am accustomed to doing for myself."

He arched a brow and looked pointedly at her gown. Without thinking, Gwynna found herself smoothing her wrinkled skirts. "Yes," he said, "I can see that." Before she could fling him a biting retort, he continued: "Does it not occur to you that propriety dictates that a maid accompany us on our trip tomorrow?"

Gwynna waved her hand in dismissal. "I am not concerned about propriety. I assume you will have your servants. A duke does not travel alone." She frowned, recalling how she had first encountered him, a solitary rider on the moor. "At least not in the normal course of things," she amended.

His eyes narrowed. "My valet has only just arrived from Litchfield with an inflammation of the lungs from shepherding my baggage coach through several days of a chill rain. He must remain here to recover." He paused. "I, too, can do for myself." At her dubious look, he added, "My dear Miss Owen, my cravats owe nothing to my valet. They are my own creation, and they are the rage of London at the moment."

She scoffed derisively, but he ignored her. "My coachman and a few outriders are not considered sufficient chaperons, Miss Owen. You must have a maid, another female, at the very least. Even though I have put it out that I am your guardian, that will only take us so far. There undoubtedly are some who would think ill of your reputation should we arrive on your island with no chaperon in sight."

"I have no reputation," she replied curtly. "You forget that I am widely thought to be a bastard."

A muscle tightened in his jaw. "Very well," he drawled,

"if you care nothing of your reputation, perhaps you would care to think of mine."

She blinked. "What do you mean?"

"Surely you know that under ordinary circumstances I would be honor bound to marry you if the slightest question were raised about the propriety of our arrangement."

Her mouth fell open. "Whyever should you?" she asked in surprise.

His eyes narrowed thoughtfully, and his brows rose. "You sound like the veriest innocent, Miss Owen, and perhaps you are. But you will pardon me if I retain some skepticism. I have lately found myself the subject of rather relentless efforts to drape me in the parson's noose."

Now it was Gwynna's turn to arch her brows. "How dreadful for you," she replied dryly. He shrugged.

"Miss Owen, I cannot ignore the fact that my wealth and title make me an inviting target. Unfortunately, whatever assurances you may offer as to your lack of interest in such things do not give me confidence about your noble intentions. That is why I wished to warn you."

"Warn me?" Gwynna echoed.

"Yes. You see, I already have a wife, although that fact is not generally known. Therefore, it is useless to try to entrap me."

Gwynna stared at him, thunderstruck by the nonchalant manner in which he had delivered this announcement. In his bland tone he might as well have been discussing the weather. In her shock she all but forgot his insulting assumption about her intentions.

"Married?" she echoed, her mouth dry. *"You?"*

He frowned. "You find that difficult to believe?"

"Yes." Gwynna could not imagine the woman who would endure his oppressive airs. No, that was not it. A lady from his own world would probably enjoy being married to a supercilious pink of the *ton*. What *was* impossible was to imagine him enslaved by love, or by any passion. He was so aloof, so remote.

Silly girl, she chided. Love was not a requirement for marriage, not for one such as he. In his circles, marriages were bloodless unions arranged with considerations of property, politics, lineage, wealth. Gwynna took a deep breath.

"Where is your w-wife?" she asked, mortified as the word caught in her throat.

He looked uncomfortable. "At a country retreat near London. A convalescent home, actually. My wife is recuperating from a prolonged illness."

Gwynna wondered what sort of illness had befallen the poor woman. Her imagination began spinning all manner of dark possibilities. Who knew what went on in the duke's coldly arrogant soul? Had he made his wife ill? Driven her mad? Gwynna could well imagine that living with the Duke of Claremont might be intolerable. She was filled with curiosity. "How long have you been married?"

"A year." He set his glass down with a thump. "Your questions are impertinent, Miss Owen," he declared in his haughtiest voice. "I have no wish to discuss my marriage, which, as I say, is not generally known. I merely intended to warn you against any devious scheme you might have devised. And to spare you the trouble."

Gwynna rose indignantly. "Your insults are unwarranted and insufferably conceited, Englishman," she declared, her color high. "I can only repeat that I have no designs on your person."

The man obviously thought very little of women. Were all the ladies of his circle such connivers, then, scheming for his title and position? Perhaps they were driven to such demeaning behavior by his maddening arrogance and contemptuous airs. Gwynna suddenly felt sorry for all those young women competing for the duke's attentions, not knowing that he was secretly married all the while. How he must laugh to himself every time he leveled that damned quizzing glass at them.

Gwynna had a sudden desire to give him a taste of his own medicine. She drew herself up to her full height, arched her brows, and with what she hoped was a hauteur that equaled his own, deliberately allowed her eyes to survey him from his sandy hair to the tip of his toes. As his brows shot up in surprise, she walked slowly around him, noting the well-defined planes of his face, the solid breadth of his shoulders, the leanness of his torso, the muscular curves of his broad thighs, and the sinewy muscles of his calves—all of which were shown to perfect advantage by the excellent tailoring of his buff pantaloons and fawn waistcoat.

But rather than put him in his place, her bold scrutiny had another effect. A slow smile spread over his face, and a disconcerting light danced in his eyes. Gwynna felt a strange current kindling between them. With horrifying certainty, she realized that he had misread her daring gesture entirely. Where she had intended only scorn, he saw an invitation. Gwynna felt her face grow red. She was no good at this game.

"No designs on my person," he repeated softly, the rich baritone sending a tingle through her. "I think it is you, Miss Owen, who have told a bold-faced lie."

Angrily Gwynna took a step forward. "You are the most insufferable man I have ever met," she said fiercely. As she stood facing him, her chin set defiantly, she became uncomfortably aware that he, too, had taken a step forward. The gleam in his eyes made her pulse race. There was a sudden thundering in her head. An all too familiar panic rose like bile in her throat.

Frantically she averted her gaze, only to realize in horror

that it had settled on his sensual mouth. She swallowed hard. They were so close that she could hear his breathing. Unlike her own, it was even and calm. She wanted to run, but somehow her legs would not move. As he closed the inches between them, she braced for his crude assault, cursing her carelessness in not bringing her dagger downstairs for dinner. He would pay for degrading her with his lust. For now she knew she would have to endure it. Eventually, though, she would have her revenge.

What he did next was outrageous, but not at all what she expected. Slowly he brushed a fingertip across her mouth, so softly that her lips parted in wonder as his perfectly manicured thumb gently smoothed her lower lip, then paused to repeat the exercise. That copper spark in his eyes blazed as he held her chin lightly but firmly for his inspection. His gaze moved from her mouth to her eyes and up to her hair before settling again on her mouth. His eyes were unreadable, but Gwynna had no trouble discerning his intentions as his mouth descended to hers.

She waited for the familiar feeling of revulsion, the sense of violation. To her amazement, however, the touch of his lips brought only pleasure. It robbed her body of its fight.

His kiss was quite simply the most extraordinary thing she had ever experienced. Gentle at first, like the dawn breezes off the strait, his lips brushed across hers, teasing and tempting them into a pleading state of readiness. Then stronger, like the moody afternoon winds off the mountain, his mouth began its slow plunder. Now tumultuous, like the storms that blew in from the west, his tongue invaded her willing mouth. The whirlwind that swept over her turned her knees to mush, but his arms were there, lending her their strength. Gwynna leaned into him, her body a wretched mass of breathless, aching desire. She could not imagine why the fear did not come, why she found herself returning the pressure of his lips, why her wayward tongue was engaging in the most brazen sort of behavior, why she was pulling him even closer.

Gwynna had no sense of time as this incredible exercise continued; she only knew that she was on the verge of some enormous disgrace, some cataclysmic capitulation to his arrogant power. He was shaming her, with all of the masculine weapons at his command. Still, she could not manage to move so much as her little finger in protest.

Owen, Owen, where are you? The thought echoed inanely in her head. But *he* would not help her against this stuffy Englishman's skilled assault. Owen had been a man, too, after all. And such was her inability to resist that when she felt the duke's hand on her breast, she could only sigh in pleasure.

The sound seemed to rouse him. Slowly he lifted his head and put her from him. His face was still unreadable, but Gwynna was pleased to see that at least his breathing was as ragged and uneven now as her own.

Gwynna jumped back. "You are disgusting," she said rather too loudly, her voice sounding thick to her own ears, like that of someone who had been drugged.

In response he merely arched one eloquent eyebrow.

"I have no interest in your person," she rushed on, babbling like an idiot. "And I do not care one whit whether you are married or not. Nothing about you concerns me in the least."

Again he did not reply. The hazel eyes met hers. Copper fire burned there for a moment, then a veil of boredom slid down.

"I am most happy to hear it, Miss Owen," he said smoothly. With a dismissive elevation of his brows, he took another sip of his drink. But as Gwynna fled through the door, he lifted the glass to her in a silent toast.

CHAPTER 4

GIDEON CLOSED HIS EYES AGAINST THE PICTURESQUE LANDSCAPE outside the carriage window. He did not need his superb vision to tell him that the young woman across from him was studiously avoiding his gaze.

What a nuisance. Barreling through Wales on a wild goose chase, looking for proof of a marriage that doubtless existed only in that fertile imagination of hers. If his cursed cousin *had* fathered the little spitfire, it most assuredly had not been in holy wedlock. William Traherne had been a blight on humanity, but Gideon doubted the man would have abandoned his wife when she was expecting his child and possible heir. The only answer was that there had been no marriage. It was nothing short of amazing that his parsimonious cousin had sent money to his bastard child. A lot of men would not have done even that, and he was quite certain William Traherne had had no tender fatherly yearnings. But why, at the last, had his cousin tried to set himself up as Gwynna Owen's guardian? A bitter taste filled his mouth. If ever there was a man less fit to fill such a role, it was William Traherne.

Thank you, Cousin, Gideon muttered silently, *for dumping the matter on my plate*. He crossed his arms on his chest. The irony of the situation was not lost on him. He had left London to avoid entanglements and had run headlong into some he had not even imagined.

Gideon sighed. It was nearly dusk. They had gotten a late start, due to Miss Owen's decision to take an early-morning walk alone out on the moors. He had finally found her sitting on a rocky outcropping at the edge of the castle property, waving that rusty knife of hers about and reciting some Welsh poem about a prince's bloody death in battle. Her eyes had shot daggers at him when he interrupted her ravings.

Since then she had said scarcely a word. She had avoided his gaze, apparently reluctant to engage it after last night. Drat the woman, anyway. *He* was not the one responsible for that amorous interlude in his study. If she hadn't looked at him with those limpid sapphire eyes that left him unable to think clearly . . .

Gideon gave a snort at his own folly. He had only meant to teach her a lesson—that her feminine wiles were no match for an experienced man of the world like himself. And he had been right. She had melted under his kisses like one of Gunther's ices in summer's heat. But he had learned something, too. To his great surprise, this scrub-faced, scruffy imp had ignited his passion like a spark to dry leaves. It had taken every ounce of his control to put her from him, especially after her enticing moan of pleasure when he caressed the soft curve of her breast.

That was another irony. She was not at all the sort of woman he normally found attractive. Too scrawny by half. Too sharp a tongue. Not like Elizabeth, a woman of cool beauty and gentle sensibilities. Elizabeth would never groan like that in her life.

He sighed wearily. It was disconcerting that he kept forgetting the existence of his wife. It would surely be easier to recall that he was married once he had enjoyed the delights of his marriage bed. But after a year of waiting for his wife to recover from her grievous ordeal, that possibility still seemed remote. Oddly, that fact didn't bother him as much as it seemed it should. He had stopped at the convalescent home on the way to Cheshire and been told by a defiant young doctor that Lady Elizabeth Throckmorton—she continued to use her maiden name in the interest of preserving the secrecy of their marriage—was unavailable. Whatever that meant. Since it was his money paying for her recovery at such expensive leisure, Gideon might have thrown the silly cub out on his ear. But at the time, all he had felt was an immense relief. He had turned and left without a word.

No, he was not eager to take up the shackles of married life. Women saw marriage to a man of wealth and title as their ultimate achievement, the trophy affirming their desirability and worth. Most women, anyway. Perhaps Elizabeth would be different. They had been friends for so long that it had seemed strange to contemplate an intimate relationship. But he was weary of this purgatory, weary of the secrecy, weary of relegating his sensual pleasures to the occasional tryst with an opera dancer.

He tried to summon an image of Elizabeth, her pale blond hair coiled smoothly in place, submitting to his kisses as Miss Owen had last night. He tried to imagine her mouth opening to his, eagerly receiving his tongue and surprising him by offering her own for wild exploration. He tried to imagine her feverishly pressing her breasts to his chest.

He could not.

Instead he could only summon a picture of a slender young woman with unruly red hair, her jewel eyes blazing with confusion and passion as her full lips parted for him.

He opened one eye a slit. She was still looking out the window, clutching her hands tightly together. Probably had that dagger hidden somewhere on her person. Bloodthirsty lot, these Welsh.

It was not tucked into her bodice. Her boyish build would

never have hidden such a heavy relic. That must mean it was strapped to her leg. But he had caught a glimpse of her trim ankles as she stepped into the coach, and had not seen anything other than the smooth, creamy skin of an exceedingly enticing pair of legs.

Higher up, then. She had probably strapped it to her thigh. Not so easily accessible, but better than nothing. An image of Miss Owen lifting her skirts to retrieve her dagger came suddenly to mind. Would she fumble with the blade and require his assistance? Or would she draw the knife from its scabbard with ease and plunge it deep into his chest while he sat mesmerized by the sight of those creamy thighs?

Gideon cursed inwardly and abruptly shut his eye. The woman was a temptress of the first order. The sooner this journey was over, the better. He resolved to keep as far away from her as possible. For his own sake, for what he owed Elizabeth. All he had to do was remind himself that Gwynna Owen was probably a liar and almost certainly a fraud. And he must forget about those sapphire eyes. It should be easy. He had become quite adept at keeping the fair sex at bay.

"I need quite a lot of money."

The words intruded into his thoughts, and this time Gideon opened both his eyes. The sapphire gaze was somber and earnest as it met his. "I beg your pardon," he said politely, thinking he had not heard her correctly. "I seem to have dozed off."

"It's as much the money as anything," she rushed on awkwardly. "I need quite a bit of it."

His eyes narrowed. "Let me understand, Miss Owen. Are you saying that you are less interested in claiming the Traherne name and more concerned with relieving me of some of the Traherne fortune?"

"I do not care about your name," she said contemptuously. "I am an Owen. There is no better name in all of

Wales. I simply want to remove the stain put on it by William Traherne, to vindicate my mother. I myself intend always to remain an Owen. But I must have the money." She gave a toss of her head. "After all, I am entitled to it as William Traherne's daughter."

Gideon had rarely heard such a bald admission of greed. Apparently she was having second thoughts about this journey, realizing that when her claim was proven false she would receive nothing. Now she was evidently offering to save him the trouble of the trip and drop her claim to legitimacy in exchange for money.

"How much do you require?" His voice dripped with cynicism. He detested extortionists.

She shifted nervously on the seat across from him. "Several hundred pounds. More, perhaps." She bit her lip.

Gideon's brows shot skyward at such a paltry sum. Either she was desperate to end it now, or she was a complete amateur. "Why should I agree to such a thing? Other than the fact that you believe you are entitled to it, of course." The sarcasm fairly dripped from his words.

She glared at him. "There is always the possibility that giving me money might bring you pleasure," she shot back. Then, on a softer note, she added, "You might find the experience rewarding."

He blinked in astonishment. Her face was a picture of fierce determination as she continued: "Even such a stuffy lord as yourself might come to see that a small sum can bring a great deal of pleasure."

Of course. Now he understood. She was offering herself to him. It was the only thing that made sense.

The reason for her bold gesture last night suddenly came clear. She had dangled the bait before him in his study; now she was setting the price. Perhaps he should have expected it, but he found himself oddly disappointed. He fixed her with his haughtiest gaze.

"I think not," he said shortly, and had the satisfaction of seeing her flush, whether in anger or embarrassment, he could not tell.

"But you have not heard me out," she protested. "How do you know you will not like—"

"Miss Owen," he said repressively, "kindly do not pursue this line further. I am not interested in purchasing your body to silence your claim to my name. I do not suffer extortionists, regardless of the lure. We will go to that infernal island of yours or be damned trying."

She stared at him, her expression one of profound amazement. It was some time before she spoke. "I never . . ." she began, her face flushed beet red. Then, incredibly, she broke into peals of laughter. "It is too much! You truly are filled with conceit!"

Gideon stared. Never would he have imagined that those eyes could dance with such mirth or that her soft mouth could be so appealing as it twitched in laughter.

But even as he was pondering these facts, the carriage slowed. The steady clattering of hooves grew more uneven. When the vehicle rolled to a stop, his coachman opened the door.

"Beggin' your pardon, Your Grace, but there be a great number of men up ahead blocking the road. Some wagons of corn look to be the cause of the trouble. 'Tis likely a farmer trying to get his crop to the dock. The crowd won't let him pass. We might bluster our way through, but I wouldn't answer for the consequences."

Gideon got out of the carriage. They were still a safe distance away, but he could see the dust up ahead and hear angry shouts. He looked at the sky. They had little more than an hour until darkness. He cursed his preoccupied brain for not stopping sooner to find accommodations for the night. Damn the woman, anyway. On the other hand, he mused, it was an ideal opportunity to put into practice his new resolution to keep the enticing Gwynna Owen at bay.

"Egad," he drawled with a bored elevation of his brows. "I have no desire to go marching into the middle of that mob."

"Do not tell me the great duke fears a few disgruntled villagers," she said contemptuously from the carriage doorway. The laughter was gone from her eyes; he was pleased to see that there was only disdain on her face. He gifted her with one of his most condescending looks.

"My dear Miss Owen, I should be remiss in my duties were I to march us into the thick of battle. It is my duty to protect you. Besides . . ." He allowed his gaze to travel down his aristocratic nose and rest upon her flushed cheeks. "Besides," he repeated, "I have no desire to dirty my carriage, risk my perfectly matched bays, or allow my new boots to be scuffed with the exertions of combat."

He turned to the coachman. "Take us back to that field we passed a mile or so back. Some fresh air would not be unwelcome at all events, just as long as there is no mud to blacken my boots. You may send one of the outriders back to look for an inn for the night."

She glared at him but did not speak. When they reached the field, she bolted from the carriage and stalked over to sit under the branches of a large oak tree. Gideon could feel the heat of her contempt from thirty paces. but he merely arched a brow and returned her a benign look. In this manner they passed much of the next hour.

When darkness descended without any word from the rider, a second rider was sent after him. A third man was dispatched up ahead to see if the mob had dispersed and whether an inn could be reached safely in that direction. He reported that while the earlier disruption had cleared, there were roving bands of armed men over the next few miles.

Gideon sighed audibly at this news. Then he took out the provisions they had taken in the carriage, spread the lap blanket on the ground, and gestured for Gwynna to join him in a cold supper. With a mutinous look, she sat down on a corner of the blanket as far away from him as possible. Without a word, she picked up a piece of cold chicken. He watched her in amusement. She rose so easily to the bait. At least the journey would not be boring. He cleared his throat and began to speak in his most pontifical tone.

"I have a strong aversion to sleeping on the ground. It is positively ruinous for one's clothing." He paused to allow that point to sink in. "Unfortunately that appears to be what fate has in store for us tonight," he added mournfully. "I can only imagine what such a prospect does to the delicate sensibilities of a woman such as yourself."

Scorn shot from her eyes. "I have slept out of doors many times. It took me several weeks to get to Cheshire from Anglesey on foot. I had no roof over my head until I met Anne."

"Ah, yes. I had momentarily forgotten your boyish masquerade. But then, you put that off quite easily, did you not? Or so it seemed last night." Gideon found he quite enjoyed seeing her shift disconcertedly on the blanket. The blackmailing little thief.

She said nothing, and he arched his brows. "It may be impolite of me to offer such an observation," he continued, "but your ways are rather bold, are they not? Is that how women are reared on that island of yours?"

"I was raised to take care of myself," she returned shortly, "and not to suffer fools."

Touché. Gideon stifled a grin as he watched her tear into the last of her chicken and run her tongue over her lips to catch an errant morsel. He felt vaguely guilty as she reached unabashedly for another piece. He had only to look at her slender build to know that such meals had not come easy for her. But then, she was a thorough opportunist, was she not? He banished his guilt.

"I gather that you prefer to take things into your own hands, Miss Owen," he observed dryly. "Rather like that mob up there."

She cocked her head and studied him appraisingly. "I believe that all of us have a duty to throw off oppression. That corn was undoubtedly bound for the Continent."

"Oppression?" He eyed her incredulously. "Surely, Miss Owen, a man who harvests his corn has the right to sell it, regardless of whether it is consumed here or abroad. That mob would stop him, deprive him of his livelihood. *That* is oppression. That is what you have conveniently forgotten."

"You speak with the silken tongue of the rest of your class," she said heatedly. "You wish to preserve things as they are, even if thousands suffer. But the old ways are not necessarily the best. It is the duty of the oppressed to throw off the yoke."

Dusk had banished the light, so he could not see if her cheeks were flushed with the passion of her speech. But he would wager that they were. The little revolutionary. "Seditious talk, Miss Owen. Pray, what is it that oppresses you?"

"On Anglesey we have the bounty of the sea, so we do not starve—at least in the normal course of things. But the Crown takes our precious oats for shipment abroad. Now the price at home is so high no one can afford to buy. Many people are going hungry." She looked at the sky, where the stars had begun to wink through the clouds. "It is all because of a few men who care only for their own power." She shot him a sharp look. "Those men are evil indeed, but far worse are those whose complacency allows them to tolerate evil."

He arched a brow. "I take it you have decided that I fall into the latter group, Miss Owen."

Her chin rose defiantly. "Only you can answer that, Englishman."

Gideon yawned. He put his hands behind his head and lay back on the blanket. "I do not get involved in politics, Miss Owen. Or in local affairs."

"Yes, conflict is a rather messy thing," she said scornfully. "I can see that you do not wish to involve yourself in anything that might tarnish those impeccable clothes you wear so well."

He had asked for that. He was pleased to see that she had read him perfectly. Oddly, his satisfaction was only fleeting. In fact, he felt positively out of sorts.

"You wound me," he said lightly.

She shook her head. "I seriously doubt whether anyone can do that. After all," she added, her voice filled with sarcasm, "you are the Duke of Claremont, the epitome of position and wealth, a nonpareil . . ."

"Bloody hell."

Her head shot up at his sharp tone. He sat up abruptly, trying to master his sudden anger. Her lips parted slightly in confusion, and he found he could not take his eyes from them. Little minx. He rose to his feet.

"Sartorial splendor notwithstanding, Miss Owen, I am simply a man," he said curtly. "But not a simple one. You would do well to remember that." Then he turned on his heel and walked away.

THE FACE IN HER DREAMS was always the same, a rubbery mask of contorted rage and laughter. The bushy eyebrows framed a demented pair of eyes that gleamed at her with feverish intensity. Even during the services, when she huddled protectively against her grandfather, the fiery eyes sought her out with their demonic message. In the midst of his fervid ravings, his pious urgings, she knew that his true message was as black as his soul.

"Daughter of Sin. Shapen in iniquity and in sin did thy mother conceive thee."

His acrid breath stung the back of her neck as he leaned closer, his exhortations a dark caress: "Repent, Daughter of Sin. Let God free you from the stain of your conception."

They were always alone when it came to the next part, in her grandfather's house with her grandfather lying sick in the next room. Her tormentor's hands were around her shoulders, kneading them feverishly as his eyes burned into hers. "Repent, sinful woman. Open thy heart to the cleansing power of God's emissary." His hands snaked down her shoulders to imprison her arms at her sides. His face drew nearer, his black eyes gleamed, and his great slashing mouth gaped wickedly as it descended to hers. His hands fumbled with her clothing.

"Save thy mother's soul," came his fierce, ragged whisper. She opened her mouth to scream, only to find his thick, thrusting tongue robbing her of speech. She could not push him away; he was too strong. Monstrously strong. No one challenged him. Only a slip of a girl. And now she was paying the price.

"Stop it!" she shrieked, knowing what always came next. But her head hit something hard, and she groaned in pain. She kicked out, flailing against him. The strong arms tightened around her, shook her. Her feet felt something solid. She kicked again with all of her strength.

A loud oath, completely devoid of pious invocations, woke her. Gwynna opened her eyes to see the Duke of Claremont, his hazel eyes glinting angrily, mere inches away. He was shaking her like a rag doll.

"Damn it, woman, come to your senses before you punch a hole in my lungs."

Gwynna eyed him groggily, wondering why she found that angry voice so comforting. Then she understood: she had had the dream again. Angry or no, the Duke of Claremont's rich baritone was nothing like the feverish rasp that haunted her sleep. She shivered.

He frowned. "Are you ill?"

She shook her head. He released her, and she pulled the lap blanket around her, yelping as her elbow hit the side wall of the carriage. For all its spaciousness, the carriage offered precious little room for sleeping. She would rather have made her bed on the ground, as the duke had, but he had insisted that she sleep in the vehicle's protective confines.

"It was just a dream," she said dully. "It comes sometimes."

He arched a brow. "Not that I am overly familiar with such things, but I believe you were quoting Scripture. A tussle with your conscience, perhaps?"

Gwynna sat up angrily at his dry tone. The man's smooth demeanor was unaltered by the fact that he looked only just to have awakened himself. His sandy hair was rumpled from sleep and that exquisitely sewn shirt of his was open at the neck, but he still seemed the epitome of cultured elegance and poise. Whereas she seemed always to be at loose ends in his presence.

"Nothing plagues my conscience, Englishman," she snapped.

"Then you are to be envied, Miss Owen," he replied, his mouth quirking in a wry expression that Gwynna found most disconcerting. She fumbled for the blanket, but he took it from her.

"Allow me."

He draped the blanket around her shoulders, then sat back

on the seat across from her and subjected her to an unnerving silent scrutiny. A thin ray of moonlight offered scant illumination, but Gwynna could see the gleam in his eyes. It penetrated the short distance between them, pierced the midnight blackness in a way that the paltry light of a few stars and the barest sliver of moon could not. Outside, all was eerily quiet. Gwynna felt as if they were the only two people for miles. As her eyes met his, she nearly gasped at the intensity that burned there. She could not avert her gaze. It was as if an invisible cord bound her to him. Her breathing quickened, and suddenly she felt uncomfortably warm. Just as the feeling threatened to overwhelm her, he stretched out his legs and yawned, breaking the spell.

"The cold is unusual for this time of year," he said blandly. "I understand that a volcano is to blame."

She stared at him in confusion, dumbfounded at the sudden shift in mood. *"What?"*

"I do not know if I truly credit it," he continued in the idle tones of the drawing room, "but some scholars believe that an eruption halfway across the globe is responsible. Surely you have noticed the sunspots, Miss Owen. You strike me as a very observant woman." He smiled benignly, his eyes veiled in politeness, as if discussing the weather in such circumstances were as natural to him as breathing.

Gwynna eyed him cautiously, uncertain how to respond. The man certainly knew how to keep her off balance. Very well. She would play this game. She took a deep breath to clear her mind. "On Anglesey it is said to be the *derwydd*— the Druid spirits—who are responsible for the excessive cold. They are said to be angry that the people are not allowed to keep their crops. They have exhorted the heavens to kill the crops, so that no one may have them."

He eyed her curiously. "And do you believe in such things, Miss Owen?"

"I believe in the power of the ancients—in the power of many things." She shifted uncomfortably on the seat. This was a very strange conversation.

"Oh?" He cocked a brow, then leaned forward, his hands on his knees. "What other things?"

Gwynna felt a surge of anger. If he wished to make sport of her island ways, so be it. "In the power of all spirits. In the power of good. And of evil."

"Ah. Good and evil. I take it that it is the latter that dominates your dreams. I wonder why."

Gwynna lifted her head defiantly. "There are evil men on Anglesey, just as there are evil men everywhere," she said evasively.

He was looking at her consideringly. "And just who is the evil man who torments your dreams?" he asked.

She was surprised at his perceptiveness. "He calls himself a man of God," she said bitterly. "In truth, he is a power-hungry, selfish buffoon." She shivered again, recalling the voice of her dreams, the feel of those hands on her.

But, no, those were not Evans's hands. They were the duke's, and they were touching her arms, ever so lightly. "Miss Owen," he said with unexpected gentleness, "you need not continue."

She was surprised at his soft tone, but she lifted her chin. "I am not one of your delicate society females, sir. I am perfectly able to face down my demons." Her hands balled into fists. "*Especially* my demons."

His large, well-shaped hands covered her fists. Gwynna looked at those perfectly manicured fingers, knowing that they put her rough, nail-bitten ones to shame. But as she was reflecting on this rueful fact, his hands began to knead hers, rubbing them between his. Warmed by the sensation, she swayed toward him, wondering if he had the vaguest notion what he was doing to her insides.

"Your Grace," she began awkwardly, startled to hear his title on her lips for the first time. "I want to thank you for interrupting my nightmare. I— Well, it is a dream that often plagues me."

He said nothing for a moment, his fingers making idle circles on her wrists.

"You are a most unusual female, Miss Owen," he observed. "Fierce and warlike one moment, frightened by your dreams the next. First you offer yourself to me like some Covent Garden strumpet. Now you act as though you have never sat with a man alone in a carriage at night. I wonder what you intend to do next."

Gwynna flushed. "I did *not* offer myself to you," she insisted heatedly. "It was your insufferable conceit that led you to put such an interpretation on my remarks this afternoon. I was foolish enough to think you might receive some pleasure from seeing your money put to good use, from seeing the happiness it brought others. I can see now that you have no use for anyone save yourself. You are the most self-centered, arrogant man I know."

She expected some witty, biting retort. Instead he merely continued to watch her gravely from those unreadable eyes. His fingers trailed up the sensitive inside of her arm to rest on her shoulders. Then, in a gesture that seemed as natural as life itself, he brought their lips together.

Gwynna knew she ought to be outraged, but instead she heard herself moan. His mouth was firm and gently demanding as it covered hers, and when his lips moved to the delicate pulse point of her neck, she reveled in the feel of his rough chin on her tender skin. Her nerve endings were raw with desire. She groped for his shoulders, her fingers moving to the open part of his shirt, and felt him shiver as her hands touched his bare skin. She could not seem to stop, not even to ponder why she did not feel repulsed by these intimacies. As her trembling fingers continued their exploration, Gwynna suddenly felt him disengage her hands and set her away from him. He looked chagrined.

"Miss Owen, you are very adept at this sort of thing," he said ruefully, "but I do not think it wise to remain here long enough to test the remainder of your skills."

Gwynna was mortified. He had made her sound like the veriest harlot. Her face flushed. "Go to the devil," she retorted.

His brows shot skyward. He shook his head mournfully. "Whether or not I am deserving of such a fate," he drawled, "I have the distinct impression that you, Miss Owen, will be my Charon." He executed a mock half bow.

By the time Gwynna found her half boot and hurled it in his direction, he had disappeared through the carriage door.

CHAPTER 5

THIS WAS PARADISE.

Gideon inhaled deeply, savoring the salty air as it filled his nostrils, entered his lungs, tingled the pores of his skin. His senses felt gloriously alive. All around him was deep blue-green. Before him silvery rock plunged with stark grandeur into the white foam that churned against its well-worn crevices. Sandy beaches, smoothed by the constant lapping of the sea, stretched for miles between rocky coves sculptured by time and tides. Farther inland, verdant meadows swept up from the rocky shores.

Behind him were the mountains of the mainland, snow-capped still, rising on the horizon like gentle giants standing sentry over the island. Gwynna Owen's island. Home to mysterious Welsh spirits and warriors, evil clerics, and ancient superstitions.

She was standing at the dock as the coachman led the horses off the ferry. There had been an uneasiness between them since the night of her dream. As they neared Anglesey, she had seemed increasingly nervous, shifting in her seat and biting her lip. Now that they were on the island, however, she seemed almost buoyant. Her brilliant eyes reflected the glory of the sea as she stood proudly erect, staring across the serpentine strait at those magnificent mountains.

They were indeed stupendous. It made his soul swell to

see those snowcapped giants peer at him through misted blue veils, their summits secret to all but the most intrepid explorers. He could only guess at what Miss Owen felt. No doubt she had stood on this spot many times, perhaps waving that dagger of hers about, exhorting the spirits of those great hills.

Gideon gave himself a mental shake. In another moment he would be believing in Gwynna Owen's ghosts. He turned to her, only to be struck by how that unruly red hair blew all around her face in soft curls. Uncropped, it might be almost as magnificent a sight as those peaks across the water. Gideon frowned. He would have to guard against such thoughts. His resolve had already slipped—he had nearly lost his control the night of her dream. Even his inane chatter about the weather had not helped. The more time he spent with her, the harder it was to envision her as a greedy temptress. There was indeed something knowing about her eyes, something worldly and sad. But there was something else, too. A fool might have called it innocence.

"Come, Miss Owen," he snapped, irritated at his wayward thoughts. "I am more than ready to satisfy my palate at this inn of yours. Let us be off."

She turned to him, a half smile on her face. "You will not persuade me, Englishman, that even you are unmoved by this." She made a wide gesture that encompassed it all—the mountains, sea, rocky harbors, and smooth beaches. There was a softness in her eyes that he had not seen before. Whatever villainy lurked in her heart, she loved this island, drew strength from it.

Damnation. He would be talking to her Druid spirits next. Gideon arched his brows.

"I have no doubt that the island air will be positively ruinous to my boots," he replied in a bored tone. He moved toward the carriage, feeling her contemptuous look at his back.

The Bull's Head Inn in Beaumaris was no better or worse than others of its ilk, although it possessed an enormous door, and a certain charm that doubtless came from standing on the same spot for more than three centuries. Conversation in the convivial taproom came to a halt upon their arrival but resumed after a few moments. They shared a meal in a private parlor, then set off by carriage through the town's neat, regular streets and down a winding lane.

In a low meadow at the edge of town, they passed an old, unfinished castle with gray walls reflected in a water-filled moat. When Gideon expressed surprise at its relatively good condition, Gwynna sniffed scornfully.

"Your King Edward thought to intimidate us by building this pile of stones. He meant to show us his power, to force us to acknowledge our subjection to his might. Did you know that he erected the heads of Welsh warriors on stakes at the castle walls?" The color was high in her cheeks. "He was a fool. The only thing Beaumaris Castle represents is the stubborn folly of Englishmen."

"I see." He could almost see her on the battlefield, banishing the vengeful Edward with her dagger. "You Welsh prefer war, then?"

She eyed him disdainfully. "Not at all. We love peace. But we crave sovereignty. Surely you do not think we like having our home known as 'Englishmen's Island'?" Her eyes glinted angrily. "Your Edward stole the principality and set his own son up as Prince of Wales after finagling to have the babe born at Carnarvon. What a joke! A mewling English infant offered to fill the mighty Llewelyn's shoes."

His brows rose. "You Welsh helped put the Tudors on the throne—Henry himself was a Welshman. I should think that fact would have gotten rid of such resentments."

This statement was met by a laugh of incredulity. "A true Welshman would not have banished our laws, our customs, our language, as the Tudors did," she said derisively. "No, the last true Welsh prince was the Knight of Glyn."

Gideon frowned. "Who?"

"Owen Glendowr." She said the name proudly, and her chin rose defiantly, like a soldier ready to fight to the death for his sovereign.

His brow cleared. "Ah, the bloodthirsty tyrant who cut a swath through England, fomenting rebellion and burning towns until he mysteriously disappeared—a rather ignominious end for a warring hero, do you not think?"

He saw that her eyes were filled with surprise. Doubtless she thought he had never even opened a history book.

"Owen was a visionary," she insisted, her voice filled with passion. "He would have set up a free Parliament and given us independence from Canterbury . . ."

"And murdered all the Englishmen, as well as any poor Welshman unfortunate enough to have adopted English ways." He waved his hand as she tried to protest. "I have studied history, too, Miss Owen. Your Knight of Glyn was a ruthless tyrant."

Her eyes narrowed. "You may know history, Your Grace, but you know nothing of truth. Only what your English teachers chose to tell you. Owen Glendowr was a brave and honorable man. I am proud to be descended from him."

His brows rose anew at this revelation. "Your pedigree becomes more interesting by the moment, Miss Owen."

"I shall carry his sword to my death, Englishman," she said fiercely. "And there, beyond the clouds, beyond the reach of fools such as yourself, Owen will be waiting for its return."

Without a word, she reached under her skirts and produced the heavy dagger, her motion so quick and fluid that

Gideon was startled when he saw her holding the blade between her hands. Her eyes looked him a challenge as she lifted the dagger for his inspection. Studying it closely for the first time, he noted that the blade appeared to have been recently sharpened to within an inch of its life. The hilt bore two encrusted red stones, and many more indentations where stones must once have been. It was badly tarnished, and he could not begin to make out the words engraved there.

"It has been passed down through our family," she said proudly.

Four centuries old? Not bloody likely. Either she was a madwoman, or this was part of her strange masquerade. His brows rose in sardonic amusement.

"Very impressive, Miss Owen. Pray, are you preparing for war?"

She smiled, a fey sort of grin that was most unsettling.

"Yes, Your Grace," she said softly. "That is it exactly."

THE WHITE CLAPBOARD COTTAGE was still there, exactly as she had left it. Grandfather's possessions were still in order, including the stark bed on which he had spent his final days. Her own bed looked singularly lonely, covered with a thin, solitary quilt and waiting forlornly in the tiny room that had been her refuge for nearly twenty years.

"There is little point in this exercise," she muttered over her shoulder. "I have searched every corner of this house. There are no marriage papers."

"Nevertheless, you will not mind if I satisfy my own curiosity."

Gwynna merely shook her head, and the duke wandered off, presumably to search through her grandfather's last few possessions. They were meaningless to a man like Clare-mont, of course. He would care nothing for the rock collection that they had gathered when she was a little girl, carefully arranging and categorizing each stone. He would ignore the lute that sat in a corner of Grandfather's room, the instrument that had soothed his last days. He would not notice the gnarled walking stick that her grandfather had used as he and a little girl with red curls hiked over every square inch of the island.

Gwynna sat on her bed with a sigh. David Griffyth Owen had been a man of silence; they had seldom had a conversation of more than a dozen words. He had rarely mentioned her mother, and he had said nothing at all about William Traherne. Whenever she broached the subject, he had only cast her a stoical look and shaken his head. She did not blame him, not now, although there had been times when it angered her that her questions went unanswered.

She did not understand why her mother never produced the marriage papers that would have satisfied her family. Or why no one had ever claimed to have witnessed the ceremony at the tomb. The only witnesses had been those who came across the couple there the next morning, as they lay wrapped in each other's arms. *That* story Gwynna had heard for years. But she had yearned to hear her mother's story from her grandfather's lips, not from the idle gossip of others. She had craved to hear him speak of her as a little girl, to learn about her dreams and treasures. Gwynna felt sure her grandmother, had she lived, would have told her many of these things; but she had died when Gwynna was a babe. And so Gwynna had grown up in a house of silence.

Sitting alone in her room, staring at the worn planking that she had scrubbed clean many times, Gwynna realized that she felt no anger at the silence, only sadness. During her grandfather's illnesses, when he had lain pale and silent on his spartan bed, his eyes vacant windows of pain, she had come to understand that some things were too painful to be spoken of. She had come to see that David Owen was a grieving husband and father who could not share his grief and so would be forever burdened with it. Still, sometimes she wished . . .

"I see the prodigal has returned."

With a start, Gwynna looked up. A pair of coal-black eyes burned down at her from a great height. The man himself towered over the bed, his shadow engulfing the tiny room. A frisson of fear rippled along her spine, but Gwynna's chin was defiant as she rose to face the towering giant. He was dressed, as usual, all in black. The devil's color.

"You are not welcome in this house."

The man shook his head reproachfully. "Gwynna, Gwynna," he said in a deep, sorrowful voice. "Your grandfather would be wounded to hear you say so. I was his dear friend, his counselor. In his hour of need, he sought me out. As you must also." He moved toward her. Inside, Gwynna cringed, but outwardly she did not flinch, even when one of his great hands moved toward her shoulder.

"My grandfather is dead, Evans. This is my house now. I repeat: you are not welcome here."

The hand rested on her shoulder, and the black eyes glinted at her like pieces of coal bound for some ungodly inferno. "Your grandfather had hopes for us, Gwynna," he whispered softly, his voice taking on a mesmerizing, sing-song quality. "It was his dying wish that you erase the stain on your soul by uniting with me in that holiest of states, that of sacred matrimony. He knew it would be your salvation. You know it, too." His hand tightened on her shoulder, just enough to send chills down her spine. "Come," he whispered. "You must not fight God's will."

"What do you know of God's will?" she retorted contemptuously. But he only watched her, eyes blazing. His other hand eased around her back and slowly pulled her to him. Just as he brought his face down to hers, she dodged and tried to wriggle free. "I am not worried about my soul, Evans, but you ought to be worried about yours," she bit out. "It is as black as midnight, for you are the devil's own spawn!"

His two black, bushy eyebrows came together ominously, and he jerked her roughly to him. "Gwynna Owen, thou art willful and defiant," he growled. "I will punish you for your sins of pride and blasphemy, as I did once before. Then, perhaps, you will no longer fight me."

Gwynna fought against the fear that threatened to overwhelm her. If only this were one of her dreams—but she knew it was not. She also knew what would happen next. Still, she struggled.

"I will always fight you!" she cried, wriggling fiercely against his ironclad embrace. "To the death, if need be!"

"I do hope that will not be necessary," drawled a familiar voice, "for I have not brought my mourning cloak."

Startled, Evans whirled. Gwynna fell back against the bed. The duke, she saw, was propped idly against the door frame, his arms crossed over his forest-green kerseymere coat as he watched them with casual curiosity. Gwynna was surprised to realize that he was almost as tall as Evans, although his build was nowhere near as massive. His graceful pose reminded her of a sleek cat whose careful languor disarms his prey before the strike. The image surprised her, for she was quite sure that the Duke of Claremont would run the other way at the first sign of trouble. Still, something about him now seemed supremely dangerous. Even as she formed that thought, his lips curled into a smile, and he bowed slightly in their direction. Then he lifted his quizzing glass and studied them with a condescending eye. She grimaced at his posturing. He was ever preoccupied with matters of appearance, it seemed.

"My dear Miss Owen," he began, his eyes flicking over her and returning quickly to the man at her side. "Perhaps your visitor will hasten to assure me that talk of your premature demise is all in jest. Funerals are so dreadfully inconvenient."

He looked at them expectantly, his expression bland but oddly unwavering. Gwynna rose to her feet, mesmerized by those hazel dyes, wondering if she had not been right after all. For the Duke of Claremont *did* look like a cat—a lynx perhaps—benignly eyeing his prey. She felt a silly urge to smile. No, that was not right; it was difficult to imagine him with tufted ears. A tiger, then. Or a lion. God. She was losing her mind. If Claremont was a lion, Christmas Evans was a raging bull elephant and more than a match for any challenger.

She said nothing. Evans cleared his throat. "I am the Reverend Mr. Christmas Evans," he rasped. "Miss Owen and I were having a discussion. I do not believe I know you, sir." His words were polite enough, but Gwynna saw the thick cords of his neck pulsing furiously.

"Gideon Traherne, at your service." The duke bowed politely before adding, "Lately afflicted with the rather cumbersome title of Duke of Claremont."

Evans's eyes widened in shock. His brows came together like thunderclouds. "*Claremont?* Then you are related to Miss Owen? To that animal who seduced her mother?"

"I am Miss Owen's guardian, at least for the moment." His voice was elaborately casual, his features impassive. "I take it you knew my cousin, the previous duke?"

Evans glared at him indignantly. "That corruptor of young women? That base and licentious knave who ruined a young girl's life?" His voice rose in outrage. "I should say—"

"Cut line, Evans," Gwynna interrupted angrily. "You

never met my father. Or my mother, for that matter. All you know is the poisonous gossip you and your followers have been spreading about us since you arrived here."

He turned on her, his face florid with rage. "It is thou, Daughter of Sin, who poisons the air with thy blasphemy and lies!" He waved a finger before her face. "Conceived in iniquity, thou art destined for the fires of hell," he rasped, his face inches from hers. "Repent, or I cannot answer for thy soul, Gwynna Owen. You will listen to the voice of thy salvation!"

"I should think Miss Owen rather prefers not to listen for the time being," the duke drawled. "Perhaps you would be so good as to leave the care of her soul for another occasion." The words were spoken calmly enough, but for the first time Gwynna heard an edge in the rich baritone.

Evans seemed to recall himself. He turned toward the duke, who now stood poised gracefully on the balls of his feet, his long arms limber at his sides. There was an air of waiting and readiness about him, although he looked as calm and relaxed as before. Definitely a tiger, Gwynna thought in reluctant admiration. Evans eyed him warily for a moment. Then his face filled with suspicion.

"I am a man of God. I have known Gwynna since she was a child. Her spiritual salvation is my dearest goal. I am forced to wonder, however, about your presence here." He paused to allow the statement to sink in. "This house belonged to Gwynna's grandfather, an honorable man," he continued reverently. "Owing to the circumstances of her birth, Gwynna's reputation is already damaged beyond repair. But I would not see this place tarnished by sordidness. There are those who would assume the worst about your presence here alone with such a woman."

The duke did not move. "Those people would be insulting my ward," he said quietly, "a young lady under my protection. That would be unwise."

The two men locked gazes. The duke's hazel eyes were unwaveringly cool in the face of Evans's fierce glower. The coal-black eyes were the first to look away.

"I will not answer for the thoughts of others," Evans said gruffly, "but I will pray that the tongues of gossips will be stilled." He turned to go, then paused. "As Miss Owen's guardian, *if* you are legally her guardian"—his lips curled in a sneer—"you will wish to do what is best for her. I should like to discuss that matter with you upon another occasion if I may. You see, it was her grandfather's wish that her future be joined with mine. Therein lies her salvation."

The duke's brows rose. "How interesting," he murmured.

Evans looked from the duke to Gwynna, then abruptly stalked from the house. Gwynna breathed a sigh of relief.

"I never thought to see Evans faced down. No one here challenges him. He is like a king on this island, ruling with that iron fist of his and that wretched prosing." She grinned.

But the duke returned no answering smile. Instead he studied her gravely. "I take it this is the man who plagues your dreams. I am neither deaf nor blind, Miss Owen. You are in real danger here. The man will return."

Gwynna averted her gaze. "Evans was my grandfather's friend. He will not hurt me."

"That is a lie. In point of fact, he has already done so, has he not?"

She looked up in surprise. "Why do you say so?" she asked, flushing.

His sharp gaze held hers. "I have never before seen fear in your eyes, Miss Owen. You faced down those rogues on the moor, though it meant almost certain death. You do not hesitate to wave that dagger about like a bloodthirsty Welsh warrior. Foolishly or no, you do not fear death's unknown horrors. But there was fear in your eyes just now, fear born of experience, of some horror you have already known."

Gwynna tried to look away, but he touched her chin with his fingertips so that she was forced to look directly into that steady gaze. Amazingly, it was kind. "I saw his eyes, Miss Owen," he said somberly. "They were the eyes of a man who lusts desperately for a woman. A woman he has had a thousand times in his dreams." He paused for a heartbeat. "And not nearly enough in his waking moments."

Gwynna closed her eyes as her face burned in shame. "I did not give myself willingly to him," she whispered fiercely.

A gentle touch caressed her eyelids, then feather-light fingers brushed a lock of her hair. It was more than she could bear. As a great sob escaped her lips, he pulled her to his chest. She buried herself in the comforting warmth of his arms as tears streamed down her face.

"No," he murmured, "I cannot imagine that you did. But he does not look to be a man who would concern himself with such niceties." He fell silent, and his hands gently stroked her hair. Gwynna inhaled the comforting scents of sandalwood and spice. "Do you wish to tell me what happened?" he said at last. "I could call him out, if that would help."

She did not know whether to laugh or cry. Her head shot up in disbelief. "*You!* Why, you would never best Evans. He is a mountain of a man, and ruthless as well. He would more than dirty that expensive linen of yours. He would rip it to shreds!"

He was silent for so long that Gwynna thought she must have offended him. Finally she saw a smile play about the corners of his mouth. "You are correct, of course," he said. "For a moment I forgot myself. I would be loath to risk Weston's best, even for my only ward."

His tone was light, but the copper lights glinted with something unreadable. "He is not worth the effort," she said bitterly.

He led her over to the bed, sat her gently down, and pulled up a chair for himself. "I do think you had best tell me, after all," he said quietly. "For now, at least, we are bound together in this venture."

Gwynna stared at the tips of her toes, wondering how to begin.

"It is difficult to explain," she said at last. "You see, the Druids believed that the human soul is immortal. I suppose that is how they sanctioned human sacrifices. Death merely transforms the body. It does not change the spirit."

He frowned, clearly uncertain as to where she was leading. "Do you not see?" she asked impatiently. "I have no fear of death. If I die, I join the ancients. Owen. My mother. I have spoken with them. They are waiting." She looked to see how he had taken her words.

At least he did not scoff. Nor did he smile. Instead he cleared his throat. "I see. It is the living who give you difficulty, then?"

She smiled bitterly. "Yes. Evans in particular has always been intolerable. He led a band of nonconformists here ten years ago, and since then he has brought many of the islanders under his sway. The last respectable Anglican priest fled the island over five years ago. Evans has taken over the churches. He is a tyrant. No one will challenge him."

"Except you. Is that how it started?"

She nodded. "I tried to persuade some of the wealthier islanders to donate food to those who have suffered because of the high prices and food shortages. Evans objected. His church already had a relief effort. But it is a joke because most of the food never makes it to the needy."

"Why?"

"Evans must needs keep his people dependent on him. If they were well fed, they would not look to him for their salvation. I cannot prove it, but I believe he somehow manages to manipulate the food supply, thereby ensuring that they will always need him. When I tried to solicit donations, Evans told the donors that they risked their souls if they did business with a woman like me—a whore who was the daughter of a whore." Her eyes hardened. "That is when he first raised the issue of my birth. Many people had forgotten about it until then."

She took a deep breath. "I also tried to organize the harbor workers, to persuade them not to allow the oat crop off the island. Evans fought that, too. You see, I threaten his primacy. The only way his kind can survive is to be against something. For a long time it was the Church of England, but there is no real Anglican presence here now. So I became his target."

"But that is not what torments your dreams, is it?" His penetrating eyes held hers. "We have already agreed that you do not fear battle."

She averted her gaze. "It was after my grandfather became sick. He had befriended Evans when he first came to the island. When Grandfather grew ill, it was only natural that, notwithstanding our hostilities, Evans was often here. Only he did not leave when Grandfather fell asleep, as he did often during those days. Evans followed me around, speaking about how I should earn redemption for the 'sin' of my birth. When he offered marriage, I laughed in his face."

"Most undiplomatic."

"I was raised not to suffer fools."

His mouth quirked upward. "As you have said."

Gwynna blushed, then rose. "I do not wish to dwell on this matter," she said briskly. "Suffice it to say that Evans forced his attentions on me one afternoon when my grandfather was too ill to hear or care if I cried out. Which I did not." Her mouth was grim. "Evans fell asleep afterward. That is when I got a chance for revenge."

His brows rose. "The dagger?"

She nodded. "He bears the scars still. But he beat me horribly. That was on the day before my grandfather died."

"And then you left the island. But now you return. Why?"

"I had hoped to persuade my father to recognize my claim and to give me what monies were due me. I wish I could say I had only the welfare of Anglesey at heart, but I also wanted revenge. With the money I could mount my own relief effort, blunt Evans's power, and eventually destroy him."

"But you discovered that your father was dead. And so it is I who hold your fate in my hands."

She eyed him contemptuously. "No, Your Grace. My fate lies in my own hands, not that of some man. With or without your help, I will fight."

"But you need me, do you not, Miss Owen? For if your claim to legitimacy is not proven, you will never silence Evans. You may see yourself as some avenging angel, but the people will not follow a woman whom a man of the cloth has branded as a harlot, bred to sin from the moment of her conception."

She met his gaze evenly. "I am an Owen. I think the people will follow me. But, yes. I need you."

His eyes narrowed. "And you would do anything to get my cooperation, would you not, Miss Owen? Including lying about all of this to win my earnest and undying sympathies."

How foolish she had been to think that he might believe her. For a moment he had seemed gentle and kind and understanding. But she could see that he did not trust her and never would. He could not conceive of putting an ounce of faith in someone like her, whom he must view as the veriest riffraff.

"Yes. You are right," she said in a voice dull with disappointment. "I would lie, cheat, and steal to win your assistance. It is likely that I have already done so. So why do you not simply leave me and Anglesey and return to your own world?"

He stretched out his legs and put his hands behind his neck in a pose of careless leisure.

"Because," he drawled. "I saw the man's eyes. His desperate, damning eyes."

CHAPTER 6

"'TIS THE PLAGUE. THERE IS NO HOPE."

Gideon sat up abruptly, his senses alert and tingling. The words were as clear as if someone had spoken them here in his darkened room. But even as he looked quickly around, he knew that there was not a soul in his chamber, not a single noise in the Bull's Head Inn at this ungodly hour. The only sound came from outside, where the wind's fierce whine signaled a brewing storm.

"No hope."

He sighed heavily. Gwynna Owen was not the only one tormented by dreams. Those words had haunted his sleep since he had heard them a year ago in Vienna. They had sent Elizabeth into a paroxysm of grief and left Gideon staring furiously at the dour doctor who had seen fit to consign Elizabeth's parents to their fate in such a stark fashion. His betrothed had not been able to accept such blunt news; her constitution, like her delicate beauty, was more fragile than robust. By the time death carried off the Earl of Throck-morton and his countess, Elizabeth was gravely ill herself. Gideon refused to have the unfeeling quack come near her. And so, even as the carefree ebullience of Vienna dissolved in confusion following Napoleon's escape from Elba, the betrothal trip that was to have accompanied an international diplomatic triumph dissolved in the despair of death, illness, and endless nights attending the woman he was pledged to marry. He knew, as he mopped her feverish brow, that death was lurking over her like some grinning dark angel from hell.

Gideon lay back on his bed and stared at the ceiling. Elizabeth Throckmorton had entered his life many summers ago when her spendthrift father had first leased the property that marched with the Traherne land. As children they had hidden in the shadows, watching as the earl and his lady opened their alfresco balls. Elizabeth had stared in rapturous awe at the elegant dancers as they moved in the light of the glowing lanterns and twinkling stars. Even Gideon, lonely and bearing the weight of a title that had passed to him at far too early an age, was touched by the magic. In their fine clothes and elegant manners, the lords and ladies looked like cavorting dolls. There was no unpleasantness, no tears or grief, no hint of the lesson he had already learned—that life was fragile and could be ripped away by something as swift and faceless as death. No hint that war flirted at the edges of their sheltered existence, that men would die and lives would be lost in the desperate effort to contain a tyrant. In their proper clothes and their pasted smiles, the elegant lords and ladies were impervious to such things. Their fancy armor kept their world relentlessly safe and secure.

He had learned much from those summers; Elizabeth had not. Coddled and protected by doting parents, she saw only the gaiety of that life. When, years later, she accepted his properly eloquent proposal, it was with a giddy laugh that told him she had no inkling of his true feelings or of the peculiar circumstances that had forced him to offer for her. She could never have withstood the news that her father had lost every shilling on an ill-advised venture in the East, that she was left without hope of a dowry or even a shilling to her name. She never knew that Lord Throckmorton, in an effort to secure his daughter's fragile future, had begged her childhood friend to spare her the penury and disgrace of the spinsterhood that would probably be her lot. Gideon, mortified by the spectacle of Lord Throckmorton pleading for a husband for his daughter, had been unable to refuse him.

And so, when the dour doctor had pronounced those words in Vienna, it was the first crack in the sanctuary of Elizabeth's sheltered existence, the first time she had known such pain and hopelessness. Hours later she was orphaned and on her deathbed.

Gideon closed his eyes against the image of his bride on her wedding day, her lashes barely fluttering against deathly white skin, her once-glorious blond hair splayed out against the pillow like a dull and lifeless halo. She had not even been able to speak her vows.

Gideon had paid the priest, or whoever he was, to ignore such details. The man had not looked askance at the dying bride, not questioned whether she had pronounced the words that would bind her to Gideon for eternity.

Eternity.

Gideon rubbed his tired eyes. Gwynna Owen had some peculiar notions about that particular state. If Elizabeth had died, he supposed that she would be floating around like one of Miss Owen's spirits. Perhaps then he could finally explain to her why, on the tenth day of her illness, with the shadow of death on her face, he had suddenly needed to defeat that dark angel. Why he had scoured Vienna for a priest who would ask no questions. Why he had felt it his sudden and compelling duty to keep his promise to her father before death could make a mockery of it. Why he had married Elizabeth Throckmorton and thumbed his nose at the dark forces that threatened them all.

She had not died, of course. On her first morning as a married woman, she had rallied, and he had felt a cautious surge of triumph. On the next day she was strong enough to feel mortified at the knowledge that he had had the intimate care of her person during the days of her illness. On the third day, he had told her about their marriage. She had held his hand, smiling through the tears that streamed down her face. She was eternally grateful for his devotion.

He could not stand it.

Gideon pulled the covers over his head. His wife thought him a saint. He supposed that even now she was resting on some down featherbed in that elegant convalescent home, thankful for a husband so loving and devoted that he had married her on her deathbed. She understood nothing. His act had been one of obligation, a promise he had made to her father, but it had also been an act of defiance. He had spit in death's face, refusing to let Elizabeth go without taking his name. He had done battle with death and won. Even now the knowledge filled him with satisfaction. He had not seen that dark angel again.

Until now.

Gideon's eyes flew open. *Fool.* How could he have been so stupid?

He jumped out of bed and threw on his clothes, for once not bothering with a cravat. With a haste born of dawning certainty, he flew into the night.

SHE WOULD NOT BE AFRAID. Here in the darkened house she had known all of her life, the house filled with her grandfather's spirit, there could be no fear. The raging storm outside had simply heightened her senses, made the familiar seem strange. There was nothing evil out there, not really. It was only her fertile imagination turning the dancing shadows into ghostly villains.

Gwynna fingered the dagger under her pillow as the wind whistled eerily through the trees outside. It was an unearthly sound, like the wailing of all souls. Trees dipped and swayed, their silhouettes flickering wildly on the wall and their branches rattling the windowpane like some ghastly spectral creatures demanding entry.

She pulled the coverlet up to her chin. She had never feared storms; she used to close her eyes and imagine that the tumult outside was Owen himself rallying his men for an assault. The men would echo his battle cry and, mounting their horses, thunder off into the fray, their swords clanging and clashing as they met the enemy in glorious battle.

No real-life villain would be afoot on such a night. Only a fool would think of braving this storm. Or a demented man out for revenge, out to satisfy his blood lust. She swallowed hard as the image of two coal-black eyes came suddenly to mind.

Gwynna heard it then, a scratching noise almost masked by the wind's howl. There was nothing more for a moment, then a tiny squeak. A door moving on its hinges.

Someone was in the house.

She might have known he would come. He could never let her be. She had seen the furious promise in those demonic eyes this afternoon. She knew he would return; she had not known it would be so soon, and on a night like this. She had been foolish not to go with Claremont to the inn. But it had somehow seemed important to stay here. She would meet Evans on her own turf.

Gwynna eased out from under the covers, her bare feet landing silently on the floor. Once before he had made her little room the place of her violation. She had vowed that he would never do so again. She unsheathed her dagger and waited silently in the dark.

Suddenly the window shattered behind her. She whirled with a shriek. Shards of glass rained onto the floor. It was a tree limb, nothing more. But her heart was pounding. Then another noise came from the doorway. Gwynna turned toward it, wincing as her feet trod on broken glass.

A large shadow hurled toward her.

Gwynna gripped her dagger. As the dark figure grabbed her, she plunged her knife home.

He twisted away, but Gwynna knew she had found her mark. Even as he parried her thrust, she felt the initial resistance, then the sickening sensation of the blade penetrating human flesh.

Oddly, he did not cry out.

Instead he silently pulled the dagger out of his body and, in one fluid motion, wrenched her arms behind her. She felt a terrible shooting pain. Then, as if she were a bag of feathers, he tossed her onto the bed and forced her arms above her head. As he pinned her with his crushing weight, she knew that she was done for. She screamed in desperation. Perhaps someone, somewhere, would hear her cry. It was her last weapon in this mortal struggle in the dark.

A hand instantly covered her mouth.

"Do you mean to wake the dead, woman?"

Gwynna's eyes widened at the familiar baritone. A sudden flash of lightning illuminated the golden highlights of his sandy hair.

"*You!*" she gasped.

He sighed. "Your servant, Miss Owen."

"But what are you doing here?"

"Rescuing you, I thought," he said in a strained voice. "Contrary to my expectation, however, there appears to be no one in danger here except myself." He released her and sat up, only to slump forward. Gwynna eyed him in alarm.

"The dagger! I felt it go in. You must be in dreadful distress!"

"Distress?" He put his hand to his side. It was covered

with blood. His brows rose. "I rather doubt you can imagine the whole of it, Miss Owen."

Gwynna gasped. "But you must let me tend you! At once!"

"I think not," he said through gritted teeth. "At the moment it seems most unwise to allow you anywhere near me." Quickly he removed his jacket and shirt and began to rip the shirt into strips. "A rather excellent bit of lawn," he muttered, eyeing the cloth mournfully. "On second thought, perhaps you might fetch a candle and some water."

Gwynna rushed to comply. She watched silently as he proceeded to wash the wound. As he sat bare-chested on her bed, his elegant lawn shirt in tatters and a gaping hole in his side, the Duke of Claremont appeared utterly collected and composed. He might have been sitting in a London drawing room carefully adjusting his cravat. She stared at him in amazement. "Does nothing perturb you, Englishman?"

He was silent, but as his eyes met hers in the candlelight, she saw that they were anything but calm. Angry copper fire blazed from their depths.

"As a matter of fact, Miss Owen," he said evenly, "I am finding that quite a bit perturbs me as far as you are concerned. It perturbs me that you disregarded the matter of your safety and insisted on staying here tonight. It perturbs me more that I was so foolish as to allow you to do so, when anyone could see that that madman was only waiting for the right time to return and deal privately with you. It perturbs me that I awakened in the middle of the night with a conviction that the devil himself was bound for this cottage."

Gwynna's eyes widened. "I felt it, too. How odd. Perhaps Evans did intend to come here tonight, but was put off by the storm." She looked at him assessingly. "You were not deterred by the weather, were you? You came to rescue me anyway."

"A rather dubious venture, as it turned out," he replied dryly. He fixed her with a stern gaze. "You are my responsibility for the nonce, Miss Owen. As such, your safety is my concern. We will have no more nonsense about your staying alone in this dilapidated cottage. Do not delude yourself that that dagger of yours will serve against a man such as Evans." He winced. "Although it might, perhaps, slow him down."

A crash of thunder shook the rafters as he lifted the candle to get a better look at his wound. The angry gash had stopped bleeding. Gwynna said a silent prayer of thanks that he had had the agility to dodge the worst of her thrust. "Here is some basilicum powder," she said.

She watched as he dabbed the wound with the powder, wincing at what must have been searing pain. Her eyes wandered inadvertently to his bare chest, quite unable to keep from admiring the smoothly sculptured muscles brought into tantalizing relief by the flickering candlelight. Her eyes widened in shock as she saw the great white scar that ran from the tip of his right shoulder diagonally down the center of his chest. It descended to his waist and then was hidden by the fabric of his trousers. Her eyes flew to his face. He was watching her.

"Did you expect that your dagger was the first to mar my person, Miss Owen?" he drawled sardonically. "I regret to disappoint you." His gaze slid away from hers, and he returned to the task of fashioning a bandage from his shirt.

"I did not mean to be rude," she began, her face flushed. "That must have been a grave injury."

"And you are dying to hear about it, I suppose. Very well, Miss Owen." He tied the bandage firmly around his wound. "I was eleven at the time. A pair of highwaymen held up the carriage in which my parents and I were riding. I threw myself in front of a knife meant for my father and accomplished nothing save the sustaining of a nearly mortal injury. The bandits were still laughing at my pitiful attempt at valor when they finished off my parents."

Gwynna gasped. "How horrible!"

"Quite."

His voice sounded suddenly weak. He closed his eyes and gingerly eased his body down on the bed. The gnarled oak limb that had crashed through the window shifted, and more broken glass rained onto the floor.

"Not the best of accommodations," he observed in a faint voice. "Entirely too much rain dripping in the window for my taste, and those glass shards are doubtless quite trying on the feet. Nevertheless, I trust you will not object if I lie here for a bit. I do not feel up to leaving just yet."

Gwynna gave him an assessing gaze. "I believe you are in rather more pain than you let on, Englishman. In fact, I am beginning to suspect that there is much about you that is not at all what it seems."

He crossed his hands over his chest.

"You must never breathe that to a soul, Miss Owen. It would utterly shock my tailor."

Soon his breathing lapsed into the even rhythm of sleep.

GIDEON OPENED HIS EYES to find himself in a bed that was much too small for his frame. His shoulders and legs were cramped from trying to fit the mattress, but that discomfort paled in comparison to the fact that his side ached like the very devil. His brain was so fogged that it took him a second or two to recall what had happened. When he did, it was with an oath that expressed perfectly his opinion of his ill-advised behavior.

What had he been about, charging in here like some

knight-errant, simply because that gloomy Evans creature had invaded his nightmares? For that matter, had he actually offered earlier to call the man out? Who knew if Gwynna Owen had told the truth about any of it? She had every reason to lie to him, to present herself as a wounded innocent trying to clear her mother's name, fight a tyrant, and save the poor downtrodden islanders. She had played the noble avenging angel to perfection. And he had fallen for her Banbury tale, even believed that Evans had assaulted her. Most likely, she and that madman had been lovers for years. If she had driven the man crazy, well, he could well believe that. Gwynna Owen was the most provocative, maddening woman he had known.

But what if she were telling the truth? What if Evans *had* forced himself on her as her grandfather lay dying? The man was capable of it, of that he had no doubt. It was that thought—and the thought of her alone in this house with only an ancient dagger between her and a madman—that had made him leave his bed at the inn so precipitately and rush out into the teeth of the storm.

Some protector. Laid up in a doll-sized bed with a hole in his side and not a decent shirt on his back. His old friends at the foreign office would have laughed unmercifully at such a sight. Fortunately none of them were here. There was only this fierce young woman and her trusty dagger, and even she was not around at the moment. Probably out sacrificing cows on some ancient Druid altar. He lifted his body and groaned. Bloodthirsty wench.

"I brought you this. It was one of Grandfather's and not up to your usual quality, I am sure. But it is all there is."

Gideon's head spun as he tried to focus on the figure in the doorway. Gradually the unruly red hair and sapphire eyes came into clear view. She was holding a garment that appeared to be a shirt. Of stout sacking, if he did not miss his guess. He groaned again.

She hastened toward him with an expression of concern. "Is the pain so very horrible?"

He frowned. "The only thing that is horrible, Miss Owen, is the thought of my wearing that coarse garment. I have a delicate constitution, you know."

She stood back and crossed her arms. "You will not gammon me, Englishman," she said, eyeing him consideringly. "Your constitution is anything but delicate, much as you would like to hide that fact. You forget I did battle with you last night—and lost to your superior strength and skill, which for some reason you are at pains to hide from the world."

His brows rose. "You wound me, Miss Owen." He paused before adding wryly, "Again."

She laughed, and Gideon found himself staring at those dancing eyes and soft, rosy lips. Had he actually kissed them once? Twice? That seemed ages ago. He cleared his throat.

"I will be dressed in a moment, Miss Owen. Then we will discuss the arrangements."

She frowned. "What arrangements?"

"Where you will sleep, of course. I have no intention of allowing you to stay alone in this cottage for another night. Do you have a friend or a relative, someone who can come to you? Better yet, another house you can go to?"

She bit her lip. He was prepared for an argument, but instead she surprised him. "My cousin Bridget lives several miles away, just off the Amlwich Road."

"Excellent. We will see her this morning. That is, after I return to the inn to get more suitable clothing."

"I am not certain you should exert yourself, sir."

Gideon's brows rose. "You flatter yourself, Miss Owen.

That dagger of yours did little real damage." He stood, forcing his expression into one of cool imperturbability.

She eyed him dubiously. He returned her a confident glare. Unfortunately he then swayed alarmingly. In an instant she was at his side, her arms around him, taking his weight on her shoulders. A thin sheen of perspiration rose on his skin as he balanced against her, wondering if he was about to disgrace himself by fainting at her feet. He shifted his body, his weight on the arm he had thrown over her shoulder to support himself. The tip of his finger accidentally brushed her breast. He cleared his throat and moved away awkwardly, trying to stand on his own.

"I am fine, Miss Owen," he said in a determined voice that he hoped did not betray the effort his independence had cost him. "There is no need to play the ministering angel."

She eyed him skeptically, and put her arms around him. "It is clear that you need help. You lost quite a bit of blood."

"That is vastly preferable to losing my head," he replied in a constricted tone. He stared at the wall ahead of him, trying to marshal his wayward thoughts.

"What are you talking about?" she asked in confusion.

He turned to her with a sigh. "Miss Owen, kindly remove your arms from around my person. I am but slightly wounded, not incapacitated. All of my masculine senses are still functioning. It is not necessary to test them with your feminine charms."

"Test them . . . !" she echoed, looking up at him in amazement. "What do you take me for, Englishman? Some vengeful temptress out to seduce you on your sickbed?"

"I am not sick . . ." he began wearily.

"No, I can see that you are not," she retorted. "Your skills at insulting me are still wonderfully intact." Angrily she pushed at his chest. "Furthermore," she began, only to break off as he swayed slightly and fell backward onto the bed.

"Oh!" she cried, reaching for him. "I am sorry. I did not mean . . ."

"Damnation." As her hands touched his, he abruptly pulled her down, ignoring the pain as she landed square on his chest. "I do not know what you are about, Miss Owen," he growled, "but it is time someone taught you a lesson."

He brought her head down to his and kissed her fiercely. Through her thin frock, he could feel her softly rounded breasts pressing against his bare chest.

He could have kept himself in check had it not been for the fact that she suddenly began kissing him back, moaning softly as he found one breast and, merciful heaven, even helping his hand to burrow under the fabric of her gown. As he kneaded the soft flesh, her hands moved over him. He was completely unprepared for her response, unprepared to find himself being kissed with such wild abandon. When, after an eternity of this sweet torture, she gently touched his face and looked at him from heavy-lidded sapphire eyes, Gideon knew that he was thoroughly lost. With a groan he reached under her skirt.

Those creamy thighs, the ones he had dreamed of as he once pondered her dagger's hiding place, were soft and unbelievably smooth. Entirely unsuitable for sporting weaponry. They were, however, perfectly positioned for the next stage of his exploration. He heard her moan as his fingers found the moist place between those wondrous thighs. In a moment her body began to move, instinctively helping him pleasure her. Gideon thought he would go mad watching the passion unfold over her delicate features. There was no artifice, no self-consciousness about her as she gave herself up to his touch. She was completely uninhibited, different from any other woman he had known. He was enthralled by the awe-filled manner in which she embraced her own sensuality. She was both temptress and innocent, a thoroughly fascinating woman.

He lost all sense of time. When at last she cried out in ecstasy, Gideon felt a moment of pure awe. She was unutterably beautiful.

He enveloped her in his arms as she collapsed onto his chest. She lay still for a moment, then her hands began to move over his body. Gideon bore her silent ministrations in hushed wonder.

Suddenly she stilled. She held out her hand. It was covered with blood. Quite a lot of blood, actually.

"You have reopened your wound," she cried.

Gideon stared in amazement. Now he felt the searing pain in his side. Had he been so lost in her that he was completely removed from any sensation save that of desire?

Evidently he had. Good God.

He smiled weakly up at her. "I rather think it is I, Miss Owen, who have learned the lesson this morning."

And as his blood seeped silently onto the sheets, Gideon closed his eyes, muttering a wan prayer that the other wound, the small one he had just this moment noticed in his heart, was not mortal. He had heard that Cupid's arrows could be lethal.

CHAPTER 7

GWYNNA STOOD FACING THE STONES, EACH TWELVE FEET HIGH AND eight feet in breadth. Twelve in number, they stood in horseshoe formation, silent and still as judges. She lifted her face to the chill rain, letting it cleanse her. Then, fingering the red glass ring that hung on a chain around her neck, she faced her majestic, motionless audience.

"Before Teuth, I ask forgiveness," she whispered, her voice hoarse with emotion. The stones stood stiffly erect, keeping their mystical silence. But Gwynna knew that here, in this ancient place of assembly, the spirits were listening. "I have faltered," she continued, her head bowed. "I humbly ask for strength."

But even as she spoke the words, she wondered if they would be taken up to the high place beyond the clouds where wishes and prayers were heard. She was beginning to suspect that the ancients were not entirely sympathetic to her plans. They had always taken in outcasts, so perhaps they did not support her mission to get rid of a miscreant like Evans. Moreover, they had been notoriously loose in the matter of intimate relations; perhaps they did not even view her indiscretion with the duke as a great sin.

Gwynna closed her eyes in mortification. Never had she been so overcome in the presence of a man. He had confounded all of her expectations with his display of courage last night. This dandy, this overdressed man of leisure, had raced through a storm to her rescue, then calmly pulled a dagger out of his side, fought her into submission, and ministered to his own wounds with the air of one for whom such an exercise is routine. In his way he was just as baffling as these old stones. Gwynna was filled with curiosity about his past, about the man underneath those fine clothes.

She blushed furiously. Another moment with him this morning and that aspect of her curiosity, at least, would have been satisfied. Until she discovered the new blood from his wound, she had been within an inch of ripping away his clothes in her desperate need to join their bodies. She had been like a wild woman, swept away by uncontrollable passion. She did not understand it. Evans's violent invasion had left her feeling sick and unclean, but she felt no revulsion with the duke, only a burning need that shocked her with its ferocity.

Was that how it had been with her mother? Had Megan Owen felt that consuming need for William Traherne? For the first time, Gwynna felt a seed of doubt about her mother. Perhaps she *had* given herself to William Traherne as a young maiden, without benefit of marriage. Had Gwynna herself not done the very same thing this morning? Not as a maiden, precisely—Evans had seen to that. But she had indeed been an innocent in the ways of passion. When Gideon Traherne had suddenly pulled her down to him and kissed her, she felt a burst of desire so strong that nothing would have prevented her from satisfying it.

Her weakness had jeopardized her entire mission. She must always remember that the Duke of Claremont regarded her as a fraud and an opportunist, a woman capable of offering her body in exchange for his money and acceptance of her legitimacy. He would think her capable of anything to achieve those goals.

Well, and she was determined, was she not? She would not let this misstep deter her. She would endure his contempt, the leering, knowing looks that would no doubt be her lot when she saw him next. Truly, men were all alike.

Liar. The small voice inside was mocking. He was nothing like Evans. Evans had not made her weak with passion; nor had he had been concerned with her pleasure, only his own.

She shook her head. She did not understand the duke, or that odd confession of his at the end. But she did know that she was truly afraid; her principles, her inhibitions, her very sanity seemed to flee in his presence.

At least the ancients could help banish her fear, for they feared nothing. Gwynna reached for her dagger and ran its blade along one of the stones, sharpening it until it gleamed. She tested it with her finger. It was perfect.

Holding it aloft, she offered a silent tribute to the heavens. Then she faced the stones.

"This sacrifice, O Teuth, I humbly make in the name of Megan Glendowr Owen."

She pulled her gown off her shoulder, exposing her left breast. Slowly she brought the dagger to her mouth and kissed the blade. Finally, holding the weapon with both hands, she turned the point toward her. In one swift movement, she pricked the skin over her heart.

"What in God's name are you doing?"

Gwynna whirled toward the voice. The duke, now dressed in his own elegant finery, was sitting astride his horse at the edge of the stone horseshoe. "What are you doing here?" she demanded.

He did not answer but jumped off his mount and strode to her side in two long steps. With a fierce growl, he snatched the dagger from her hand. His face was suffused with rage as he stared at the drops of blood that trickled from her wound.

"I never took you for a coward, Miss Owen," he rasped. There was an intensity to his voice that Gwynna had never heard.

Gwynna had never imagined that he could display such emotion. "What are you talking about?" she asked in confusion.

"Suicide, of course," he replied in a clipped voice. He was watching her intently.

"What?" Gwynna was incredulous. Now, for the first time, she saw a flicker of uncertainty in his hazel eyes. Then his expression suddenly became unreadable.

"It is not in the least flattering to think that my lovemaking has driven a woman to such an end," he complained lightly, although his eyes burned into hers. "It is puzzling, however, in view of the fact that you seemed to be enjoying yourself this morning."

Gwynna flushed in embarrassment. "Why, you conceited man! I would no more kill myself over you than I would fly to the moon! As usual, you have misunderstood the situation entirely."

The intense look in his eyes vanished, and his face assumed that familiar bland expression. "Then what, if I may be so bold as to ask, are you doing, Miss Owen, standing in this circle of stones, one breast exposed, bloodying your person with the tip of this cursed dagger?"

Hastily Gwynna covered herself. She raised her chin defiantly. "I am certain that my ways must seem strange to you, Englishman. But I assure you, to the ancients this is perfectly understandable."

"No doubt," he retorted dryly. "And if I were an eagle, I could understand flight. But as I am neither a bird nor a spirit nor one of your Druids, Miss Owen, perhaps you would be so good as to explain."

She bristled. "I was performing a small sacrifice, as one does when asking Teuth for something."

"Does one?" His brows shot skyward. "I see. And who is this Teuth?"

"The supreme being. *Duw*." She waved her hand in exasperation at his incomprehension. *"God."*

His forehead cleared. "Do you mean that you were *praying*, Miss Owen?"

"In a manner of speaking, yes. I was asking Teuth for strength to overcome my weakness. To continue with the tasks at hand."

He eyed her consideringly. "What weakness would that be, Miss Owen?"

Gwynna flushed. "My weakness of this morning. With you. I fear I quite lost my head. It is not like me at all. Let us not speak of it. It is most awkward."

He was silent for a moment, and Gwynna squirmed under his assessing gaze. "I see," he said at last. "And do these prayers require the spilling of blood?"

"Of course. I usually prick my finger. But this morning's weakness was so excessive that it was necessary to offer Teuth the blood of my heart."

He arched one brow. "Miss Owen," he said after a moment, "you are an utter barbarian."

GIDEON SAT GLUMLY ON A ROCK and watched her out of the corner of his eye as she calmly completed the ritual. It had not been difficult to find her. He might have known that she would not stay in her cottage waiting patiently until he returned from the inn attired in something more respectable than flour sacking.

The rain had left the roads muddy, and it was a simple

task, despite the lingering drizzle, to pick out the small prints of Gwynna Owen's boots. He was not entirely surprised to find that the tracks led to one of those dreadful Druid places, but when he saw her standing in the midst of those stones pointing the knife at her breast, his heart had leapt to his throat.

He had had plenty of time for recriminations on his way to the inn and back. Plenty of time to rehearse the apology and little speech he would give her. Plenty of time to think about Elizabeth, and to ponder how it was he had temporarily lost his mind since meeting Gwynna Owen.

But all those words fled like so many dust clouds swept away by the rain when he saw her standing there, the dagger to her breast. The full import of his crime struck him anew in that heart-stopping moment. She might not be an innocent, but she was under his protection, his ward, if only for a few days. A woman who deserved more than being seduced by the man who held her fate in his hands, a married man at that. The other thing that struck him, even as he jumped down from his horse and raced to pull that deadly dagger away from its fragile target, was how very much he wanted Gwynna Owen to remain in this world.

"Small sacrifice" indeed. He might have known.

It did nothing for his humor to be made out the fool, to come racing to the rescue yet again, when all she was doing was pricking her skin to satisfy those blood-lusting gods of hers. The woman was a menace. Let her carve herself up like a turkey at Michaelmass. It was nothing to him.

He eyed her dourly. She was chanting something in Welsh as she wiped her blood on a large, flat stone, her face a picture of concentration. It was the first time he had scrutinized her delicate features without her knowledge since, well, since he had watched waves of passion wash over them this morning. He tried not to dwell on the memory, but as he watched those full lips chant the incomprehensible words, he could not banish the recollection of how they had felt against his.

At last she was finished. He glowered as she came toward him, and the familiar sapphire eyes met his uncertainly. There was an oddly vulnerable look in them that brought a lump to his throat. It struck him that she did not know how to proceed, either. Well, *someone* had to rise to the occasion. There was no need to speak of this morning after all. They both knew the experience must never be repeated. He would begin as he meant to go on. The same as usual.

"Come, Miss Owen, let us be off," he drawled. "Your dallying here has cost us the afternoon, not to mention allowing this infernal drizzle to positively wilt my attire. I am bound to get you to your cousin's today."

As he had expected, she bristled. "I was not 'dallying,' sir. It is too bad you understand nothing but your own narrow ways. It has always been the same with you English."

"I am always willing to learn, Miss Owen," he said with a mock bow. She had readjusted her clothing so that the senseless, barbaric wound to that beautiful skin was not apparent, thank God. An odd little ring dangled around her neck. Some talisman, no doubt.

Now there was a harmless topic.

"For instance," he continued idly, "perhaps you care to tell me about that ring you have worn today. Glass, is it not?"

She nodded. "'Tis the *Glain Nider*," she explained. "Few people have them now, but they were made by the ancients in various colors. Mine is red, as you can see."

"And its purpose?"

She hesitated. "It is meant to prevent or cure disease."

He absorbed this information in silence. "I suppose I must

ask," he said at last, a pained expression on his face. "Against what disease are you seeking protection, Miss Owen?"

"Against you, of course, Englishman." She eyed him defiantly.

Gideon arched one brow and gave her a look of wounded innocence. When she emitted a small, melodic laugh, he knew he was undone. He smiled and was fascinated to see the answering twinkle in her eyes. He sighed and brought himself back to reality.

"Miss Owen," he said earnestly, his voice now devoid of artifice, "you do not need an ancient amulet to protect yourself. It is my job to do so, at least for the nonce. I realize that may give you no great confidence, particularly in light of this morning's, er, activities, but I swear you shall have no more cause for concern in the future. I must deeply apologize for taking advantage of a woman—lady—under my protection."

Her pixie face was somber as she looked up at him, her cheeks flushed. She nodded solemnly, but all she said was, "How is your wound?"

"Healing," he said shortly, and strode off toward his horse.

It did nothing for his mood to realize that, as she had come on foot, he would have to take her up behind him, to feel that soft form nestle against his back and her arms hug his middle all the way to her cousin's house.

BRIDGET GRIFFYTH SHOOK HER HEAD, setting a profusion of reddish curls in motion around her face. "'Tis bad, very bad, Gwynna," she said. "With this wet summer, the corn harvest will be late. The oat crop is already well down. Bread prices are so high that few can afford it. There is talk of starvation this winter. I suppose you have seen the roads. Filled with beggars."

Gwynna nodded. Vagrants had lined the Amlwich Road yesterday when the duke brought her to Bridget's home near Red Wharf Bay. "'Tis a good thing the vagrancy laws are not strictly applied," Gwynna replied grimly. "The Beaumaris jail and castle together would not hold them all."

The two women walked in silence down to the harbor, where Bridget's husband, Daniel, was loading horses with the coarse sand used as manure throughout the island. It was the best of any on Anglesey, full of shells dug when the tide was out and carried in heaps to beyond the high water mark.

Gwynna squinted against the horizon. Several ships bobbed offshore, waiting to take cargoes of limestone and marble to markets abroad. Later today she and the duke would begin searching the records of all the churches on Anglesey. Perhaps together they would find something she had overlooked, but she had already searched many of them.

It had done her no good to inform the duke of that. He was an extremely stubborn man.

"Have you been up to Amlwich? Trouble is brewing there for certain." Bridget's words intruded into her thoughts. "So many of the men are out of work—nearly a hundred, I hear. Ryan still has his job in the mine, but he says the agents pay only when they feel like it."

At the mention of Bridget's brother, Gwynna smiled. "How is my ragamuffin cousin?"

Bridget grinned. "Not a ragamuffin anymore, but a grown man. And courting a girl from Llanelian. Never thought I'd see Ryan settle down. You will be amazed when you see him. I take it you plan to go there as well?"

Gwynna nodded. "We have to check all the churches, although it is a wasted effort, I am afraid. But perhaps I can use the trip to talk to some of the employers. If we can raise a few hundred pounds to purchase corn for the winter, trouble might be avoided."

Bridget eyed her warily. "Mr. Evans might have a thing or two to say about that."

"Evans does not worry me," Gwynna replied evenly.

"When are you going to be sensible, Gwynna? Evans is too powerful to take on. Half the people on the island fear him. The other half give him a wide berth."

"They will listen to me." Gwynna's mouth was grim.

Bridget shook her head. "Evans has poisoned them against you."

Gwynna's chin rose defiantly. "No Welshman will turn his back on an Owen, no matter what lies Evans has fed them. You will see."

Bridget hesitated. "The presence of the duke certainly helps. If he were to acknowledge you as a Traherne . . ."

"Which he will never do without proof," Gwynna put in. "But it does not matter, Bridget." She scanned the horizon. The ships were beginning to head out. Soon they would be no more than little dots in the distance. "I shall best Evans on my own. I do not need the duke."

But hours later she was forced to admit that his presence did have a way of galvanizing people to action. He was playing the aristocrat to the hilt; his manner was stiffly formal, as if nothing intimate had occurred between them. The rector of the first church had eyed her nervously, but after a look from the duke, he pulled out the dusty records for their perusal. As she had expected, there was nothing concerning her mother's marriage. It was nearly dusk before they arrived at the second church, near Beaumaris. The man who met them at the door was positively quaking in fear, and when the duke pulled out his quizzing glass and inspected him with a frown, the man blanched and ran away.

"We must be frightfully covered with road dust," the duke

observed blandly. "I cannot think of another explanation for the man's odd behavior."

Gwynna rolled her eyes heavenward. "As usual, Englishman, you are so wrapped up in the matter of appearances that you have missed the true circumstances. This is Evans's own church. That is why the man was so frightened."

His brows rose. "Then by all means let us beard the lion in his den." He opened the carriage door, descended, and held out his hand to help her out. "You are not afraid, are you, Miss Owen?" he asked as he took her hand.

"I am not afraid of anything, Englishman," she retorted fiercely.

"Modesty was never Gwynna's strong suit," rasped a harsh voice. Christmas Evans stood on the steps of his church, his bushy brows together like a thundercloud, watching them like a dark, brooding angel.

"Ah, the lion has sharp teeth," the duke observed lightly. "Shall we, Miss Owen? I promise to protect you from his claws."

This last was said so offhandedly that Gwynna assumed it was another of his sardonic comments. But he held her hand for an extra moment, and when she met his gaze, his eyes were full of warmth. "I promise," he added softly and squeezed her hand.

Gwynna's heart tumbled in her chest. "I do not need your protection," she said angrily, tearing her hand away. He merely arched a brow.

"Then perhaps it is I who need yours," he drawled. "I should hate to muss my cravat in a dustup with Evans. You have that little dagger of yours, I trust. Effective, if used properly. I am counting on you to save us, Miss Owen."

Gwynna glared at him. He merely smiled and brushed a speck from his lapel. His face was a mask of polite hauteur as he took her elbow and escorted her to the church steps.

CHAPTER 8

"WE METHODISTS MUST SEEM STRANGE TO YOU," CHRISTMAS Evans said, his smile barely masking the sneer in his voice. "After all, a duke is steeped in Anglican ways from the moment he leaves his wet nurse. It has always puzzled me, incidentally, that you English prefer to use surrogates for such intimate tasks. You hire women to suckle your children, clean your homes, and service your base desires." His eyes were challenging as he handed Gideon a cup of tea. "Such ways are foreign to us Welsh."

Gideon merely smiled benignly. "Quite true. We like to avoid messy tasks altogether. How astute of you to have divined that aspect of the English character. But then, I have always heard that the Welsh are excellent judges of human nature." He took a sip of tea. "Your Druids not only judged human nature, they burned it upon their altars. Alas, we have the Romans to thank for the passing of those gentle priests into oblivion. But the Romans always did have their own ways of silencing dissenters. A talent passed on to your warmongering princes, I might add."

He arched a brow consideringly. "That is what you are, is it not, Mr. Evans? A dissenter? I suppose you are fortunate, then, that we English have never adopted Welsh ways. Else you would surely have had your throat slit and your life's blood spilled upon a slab of granite ere this." He smiled again, the picture of bland civility.

Evans's face, however, was positively florid. Gwynna looked from one man to the other. "Perhaps we should get to the point," she began.

"It is not surprising that Claremont does not understand our ways," Evans interjected harshly. "Anglicans care nothing for Welsh customs and heritage. Their priests made no pretense of trying to educate our children. Their bishops could scarcely bother to visit Anglesey above once a year. An islander had to travel to Bangor to lay eyes on a genuine bishop."

He rose to his considerable height and spread his arms wide. "We Methodists, on the other hand, have established schools that teach children in their own language. Welsh customs and language are respected here, not banished." His fist rose to the ceiling. "Our people are proud once again, thanks to us," he said in a soaring voice. He paused before adding, "And to God, of course."

"Of course," Gideon murmured, thinking that it was easy to see how this madman commanded his flock. Besides his imposing stature, he was clearly a master of theatrics.

"He congratulates himself on restoring Welsh pride, while dozens of our people line the roads, reduced to begging for handouts," Gwynna said contemptuously.

Evans's brows came together again. "It is regrettable that the poor are always with us," he intoned, "but we have an excellent relief effort. People know they can come to us for food."

Gwynna set down her teacup. "You are a fraud, Evans. You give the people only enough to keep them from starving. You manipulate them through their stomachs, so that they always have to return to you for sustenance. You care only for yourself and your power. If you truly wanted to help, you would help the poor help themselves. Give them jobs. Encourage the wealthy to set aside funds so that all can eat and grow strong enough to work again. Let the landowners hire the poor to work the farms in exchange for food. There are many things that could be done, but no one will lift a finger because they are afraid of incurring your wrath."

"Fraud?" Evans's face was suffused with rage. "How dare you talk to me of fraud when you try to pass yourself off as the legitimate daughter of a duke. When you allow people to believe that there is a shred of truth in your claim. When all the world knows the real truth. That your mother was a harlot and you a base-born—"

"Unfortunately," Gideon drawled, rising fluidly from his chair despite a protest from his injured side, "we English do have one or two bloodthirsty customs, such as calling out those who have insulted ladies under our protection. I am afraid I must do so, Mr. Evans, should you not reconsider your words. It would be a dreadful inconvenience," he added with a mournful air, "since I have not brought my valet or my excellent dueling pistols. I am terribly afraid there is no choice, however."

Evans blinked, as if unable to decide whether Gideon was in earnest. Although he did not doubt that he could quickly put an end to this haughty nobleman, it took him no time to decide that a fight was not in his interests.

"Merciful heaven! A minister of God fighting a duel? I should think not. You will forgive my too hasty words. The fact that Gwynna and I are old acquaintances leads me to speak so freely to her." Evans rubbed his hands together briskly as he eyed Gwynna, a glint in his eyes. "I have long maintained that marriage would tame that wild spirit. As her guardian, you can only agree, I am sure." He reached for the teapot. "How does it happen, by-the-by, that you are traveling together without a chaperon? You will forgive me, but it is the kind of thing that Gwynna does without thinking, and it could give rise to more slurs upon her reputation."

"My relationship with the duke is none of your business, Evans," Gwynna retorted. "He agreed to escort me to Anglesey to look for records of my mother's marriage. It was my wish that no one else come along to intrude upon such a private matter."

Gideon arched a brow. "I do hope, Mr. Evans, that you are not suggesting anything improper about our relationship," he said mildly. "As Miss Owen's guardian, I would—"

"Yes, yes, I know. You would have to call me out," Evans interjected irritably. "Well, I do not have time for such matters, Claremont. The two of you are welcome to search whatever records you may find here. I am delighted that your relationship is entirely proper. If I should discover that it is not, of course, I should have to take appropriate action. Now, if you will excuse me, I have to prepare a sermon."

Gideon inclined his head politely and, as Gwynna opened her mouth to fling Evans yet another biting retort, gently put his hand at her elbow and escorted her from the room. The minute they were out of earshot, she whirled on him.

"Why do you cater to him?" she demanded fiercely. "Another moment and you would have been offering to black his boots."

"Oh, surely not!" Gideon recoiled in mock horror.

Gwynna sighed in disgust. "I should have known you would never stand up to him. It would be too much of an inconvenience."

"Not to mention the strain upon my wardrobe," he murmured in agreement. She stared at him indignantly. "My dear Miss Owen," he drawled, "I regret I do not have your courage. I am sure that if I had, I should have pulled out a sword and joined you in knifing the man to bits. Then he would have become a martyr, revered throughout the island, and you and I would find ourselves clapped in irons for murder. But at least we would have taken care of Mr. Evans in time-honored Welsh tradition."

She glared at him for a moment, then stalked off. With a pained sigh, he followed her out the door.

It took over a week to search the churches on the island. For Gideon it was a trip through a land of mystical beauty. He had never imagined that such a small place could hold such wonder. From the flat sandy beaches of the coast to the black soil of the low grounds and the reddish clay of the midlands, Anglesey was a captivating island.

And Gwynna Owen was a thoroughly captivating guide. It was necessary for him to pretend, of course, that they had not shared the sort of intimacies that would normally have drastically altered the tenor of their relationship. It was necessary to pretend that there had not been that morning in her cottage, that he had not explored the most sensitive aspects of her body or seen her face awash in passion, and that he was nothing more than temporary guardian to this eccentric young woman.

He had long been adept at protective plumage, but maintaining the stiff formality that enabled him to keep her at arm's length was trying. Especially since everything about Anglesey and his guide was thoroughly engaging.

She led him over her island of mysteries, past ancient tombs and odd-shaped stones, one reputed to return to its site if carried away. Near Beaumaris they took in monastery ruins and the grave of Joane, wife of a Welsh prince and daughter of King John. Gwynna pointed out the land that William Traherne had purchased years ago, and Gideon found himself imagining a magnificent house built upon one of its hills overlooking the sea. They traveled past quarries of limestone and harbors plentiful in oysters, past residents busily employed in cutting and drying kelp for glassmaking. Others were making tallow or carrying millstones, sand, and lime over the island. But they also passed many others along the roads who were unable to find work.

Gideon noticed that Gwynna seemed to know many of these people; she often had the carriage stopped so that she could speak with them. It became her habit to take along extra provisions to give away.

"You cannot feed the entire island," he said to her on one such occasion. She shot him a contemptuous look.

"That is true, Englishman, but what is that to anything? You would have me look the other way, as you and your town friends are no doubt accustomed to doing?"

"The situation in London is different," he replied impatiently. "Most of the riffraff on the street consists of thugs and criminals."

She eyed him incredulously. "You truly do not see with those eyes of yours, do you, Englishman? 'Tis no different here than in all of England and Wales. People are starving because the government bans imports, forcing the price of corn and bread to rise, yet insists on exporting crops abroad. Meanwhile, the men who returned from war as heroes find only unemployment as their reward. You are like all of those rich lords who sit in Parliament passing laws that do nothing but worsen conditions for those not born to wealth and good fortune. Because of you, we must starve."

Gideon sat back against the squabs and closed his eyes. "It continues to amaze me, Miss Owen, that you have so many opinions on matters about which you know nothing."

She glared at him. "I know more about matters of hunger and poverty than you will know in ten lifetimes."

His eyes narrow slits, he studied her surreptitiously. He could not imagine why he enjoyed baiting her. Perhaps it was because it kept his mind from other thoughts, such as how well her figure was filling out now that she was eating regularly, and how wildly that reddish hair of hers was beginning to grow around her face. Then there were those other, ravishing images that came to mind. Gideon closed his eyes tightly, but the images did not vanish.

Damnation. It was torture having to spend hours alone with her trooping all over the island, seeing her skin flush with passion about one cause or another, watching that hopeful look spring into her disconcertingly familiar eyes when they entered a church, turning his head as she bit her lip in disappointment each time the search for records of her mother's marriage proved fruitless.

It would all be over soon, although there were still the next few days to endure. So far they had managed each leg of the search in day trips, returning at nightfall to her cousin's house, from which Gideon would travel on to Beaumaris for the night. But Holyhead was at the other end of the island, and they planned to spend the night at one of the stone inns that served travelers who took the packets to and from Ireland. Then they would travel to Amlwich, their last stop. Gideon sighed. He did not think he could look at another church.

"I suppose Holyhead gets its name from the great number of churches here," he observed irritably as they left the third such establishment, this one overlooking the sea in the shadow of Holyhead Mountain.

"A typical English view," she retorted. "Holyhead is only an English name. Long ago it was called Llan-y Gwyddyl— Irishman's Beach—after the rovers who built rude fortifications to protect their shipping." She eyed him impatiently. "To find the truth, you must go back to the Welsh. Do you not see?"

Gideon did not, but it was not worth discussing. He was

far more concerned about the dispirited look on her face. They had been at this for days and had found nothing. She must have expected this, but her disappointment was still evident.

"I suppose your earlier search included records on Holyhead?"

She nodded wearily. "Most of them. I had not examined all of the Holyhead churches. I suppose I had hoped that our search would end here."

"I wonder if your Mr. Evans happened upon them," Gideon replied as they walked toward the carriage, not sure why he was trying to persuade himself that the records even existed. "Although I doubt he would have destroyed them. It would be in his interest to show that his prospective bride is the legitimate daughter of a duke. Think of the consequence to him."

She grimaced. "Not everyone views a noble connection as an asset, Englishman. But you may be right. Evans is a reformer, but in his heart perhaps he secretly covets ties to the nobility he so publicly disdains."

"What about you?"

She looked at him in confusion. "What do you mean?"

"You disdain titles, the *ton*, and all that stands for. Yet if you can prove that your mother was married, it would mean that you are one of us. Lady Gwynna Traherne, daughter of the eighth Duke of Claremont and distant cousin to the ninth. Is that revolutionary mind of yours cringing at the thought?" He handed her into the carriage. "You would belong to us, my dear," he added in a silky voice. "Could there be a fate worse than death?"

She smiled, then, an impish, unexpected grin that made Gideon inhale sharply. Suddenly he was tired of long hours poring over musty church records. He had a craving to see the sunset. Or at least a puffin or two.

"Come." He grabbed her hand and, before she could respond, pulled her from the carriage and over to the rocky cliffs that plunged to the sea. When they stood on the sharp expanse of stone and looked down, Gideon heard her gasp in delight.

"'Tis the South Stack lighthouse!" she cried. "My grandfather and I came here often. We would spend the day hiking at Holyhead and scramble down the rocks to picnic at the lighthouse."

"Then by all means let us pay homage to the memory." He loosened his cravat. "Are you game?"

"What?" She looked at him in amazement. "But it is a hundred or more feet down. You cannot climb on those rocks. Think of your clothing."

He eyed her in surprise. "My dear Miss Owen. I am delighted at your concern. And, I own, somewhat astonished. Nevertheless, I cannot bear to end yet another day with my eyes filled with images of faded, nearly illegible names entered in a registry twenty years ago by moonstruck lovers."

Gwynna could only stare in disbelief as the very properly dressed Duke of Claremont scrambled easily down a fifteen-foot drop of rough gray stone, pausing on a slender ledge to look up at her as if he engaged in such activities every day. The amazing thing was that he looked perfectly at home against the wide expanse of chiseled rock.

"What is the matter, Miss Owen? Those skirts of yours not quite the thing for climbing? Or have you thought better of this exercise?" He shot her a mournful look. "Shall I have to explore the wonders of the lighthouse alone?"

She threw back her head and laughed. "Not on your life, Englishman."

In an instant she had hitched up her skirts, found a toehold of her own, and joined him on the ledge. They stood together, the wind blowing around them, a hundred feet above the churning foam.

"This is insanity," Gwynna said, laughing.

"Quite," he replied, edging toward the next crevice.

The surfaces of the ancient rocks had been worn into deep, furrowed shadows that looked to have been slipped from the gray and charcoal face of Holyhead Mountain. Gwynna could only stare in helpless wonder as the duke's long, elegant fingers found in the cliff holds that had not seemed to be there moments before. The rock scuffed his highly polished boots, and the sleeve of his finely woven shirt snagged more than once, but he moved with such grace that Gwynna found it hard to imagine a more agile athlete.

By the time they reached the bottom, Gwynna was breathing hard, but he jumped to the ground with perfect grace, looking as if he had barely exerted himself. She shook her head. He was a man of contradictions, always confounding her with something unexpected.

He smiled, his hands fitting snugly around her waist as he helped her down from the rocks. As his hands lingered around her, all thoughts vanished from her head save those sparked by that warm, laughing gleam in his hazel eyes.

"I believe you enjoy surprising me, Englishman," she said teasingly.

Instantly his arms fell away from her. His expression grew somber. "I fear you are correct, Miss Owen," he said tersely, although an odd light glowed in his eyes.

He turned toward the sea, where the slate-gray waters sent whitecapped peaks crashing into the rocks. A pair of gulls squabbled over a fish, and ravens and jackdaws cawed in the distance. When he spoke again, his tone was lighter. "A rather noisy spit of rock, is it not? But perhaps now that we have made the effort to get here, you would care to show me this lighthouse of yours."

Gwynna nodded, her tongue silenced by the copper fire she had seen in his eyes in the instant before he turned away. She had wanted more than anything to discover what lay behind that burning gaze. He had been so stiffly formal on this journey, as if they scarcely knew each other, as if they had not shared such earth-shattering intimacies on that morning in the cottage. She wondered whether the same erotic images that had preoccupied her brain had also intruded on his thoughts. Did he feel as she did—that for the moment they were alone on their private island, sheltered against these cliffs, safe from prying eyes? That on this quiet sea ledge the differences between their worlds faded like the distant cries of the gulls?

Gwynna swallowed hard. And wondered whether she had fallen in love with the Duke of Claremont.

He walked over to the little bridge to the lighthouse, which sat upon a large rock outcropping. The descending sun had painted the sky gold and bathed the rocks in shades of amber. His face was shadowed as he turned toward her, but she felt that copper spark as surely as she felt the glow of the sun's fading radiance.

His demeanor, however, was stiff. "Come, Miss Owen," he said with studied politeness. "I would see your lighthouse."

"My name is Gwynna. Can you not say it?" She blushed at her boldness, hoping her face did not betray how dearly she wanted to hear her name on his tongue. "It is not as though we are strangers," she added quickly, wanting to call back the words instantly as she realized that they were a blunt reminder of the morning in the cottage. She closed her eyes in mortification, then opened them again when she sensed movement in front of her.

How had he managed to cross the distance between them

so swiftly and silently? "Gwynna," he repeated softly. "It is a beautiful name."

He stared at her from hooded eyes, then extended his hand; wordlessly she took it. He led her across the small bridge and over the smooth, moss-covered rocks to the lighthouse. They gazed at the gray-and-white structure for a few silent moments, then walked to the seaward side of the rock. For a long while they stared at the orange horizon and listened to the roar of the surf. Finally he spread his jacket on the ground and gestured for her to sit. She looked at him in surprise.

"Your clothes . . ."

He shook his head, and she lapsed into silence. "Sit," he commanded quietly.

She lowered herself onto the fine fabric. He joined her, but she continued to stare straight ahead at the horizon. She felt his eyes on her, but she was afraid to meet his gaze, afraid she would not be able to look away. After a moment, she ventured a quick, sidelong look. Now he, too, was staring off to sea. How long could they continue to pretend there was not this powerful current between them? Her senses were overwhelmed by his presence, yet she did not know what to make of her feelings or even know how to begin.

"I have always loved this place," she said hesitantly.

"It is lovely," he agreed.

"It juts out into the water like the farthest point in the world," she said with a nervous laugh. "There are only the birds for company."

There was a brief pause. "Yes," he said stiffly.

The awkward silence stretched between them.

"I suppose it has been like this here for thousands of years," Gwynna said after a while. "It is almost as if we are the first people to sit in this spot."

He turned to her, his face grave. "Miss Owen— Gwynna. I am afraid this was a mistake. We should not have come here."

Now she had to look at him. His eyes were troubled. "You feel it, too," she said in an awed whisper.

Abruptly he turned back toward the sea. "I have a wife," he said tersely.

"Yes," she agreed quietly. "And you and I are very different."

"I have an obligation to Elizabeth." The tension in his voice was almost palpable.

She studied his profile. "You are wealthy and mannered. My grandfather would never have approved of you."

His mouth was set in a grim line. "My marriage is not like other marriages, perhaps, but it is a marriage nevertheless."

She eyed him speculatively. "You care only for the cut of your clothes and not a whit about the things I care about."

He turned to her in exasperation. "You see what you choose to, Miss Owen."

She pursed her lips stubbornly. "I believe that is *your* crime, Englishman."

A wave crashed against the rocks, the roar making further speech impossible for the moment. His gaze lingered on her mouth before once again meeting hers. She read the hunger in his eyes and knew at last that it matched her own. Impulsively she leaned over and softly kissed his cheek.

"What are you doing?" he demanded, startled.

"In the cottage you gave pleasure to me," she whispered, feeling unaccountably bold as her arms stole around his neck. "'Twould give me joy to repay you."

"What?" He looked thunderstruck.

Gwynna wanted him to understand. "It is not as though I am an innocent," she said gently, her lips nibbling at his.

His eyes filled with fury as he brushed her away. "I

care nothing for your twisted Welsh sense of duty, Miss Owen," he snapped. "You incurred no obligation toward me by gifting me with your pleasure. But you are playing a foolish game now. Perhaps you do not realize how foolish."

Gwynna stared at him in horror. He had it all wrong. She had intended no mercenary payment of debt, but only to assuage his hunger, to give him the pleasure that he had given her. It was the only thing she could give him, after all. Obviously she had been clumsy about it, but he need not have been insulting. Her face burned in embarrassment and chagrin. "'Tis true I know nothing of the games that occupy your set," she said heatedly. "But there is also much that you do not know, Englishman."

"I feel certain you will enlighten me," he retorted dourly.

Gwynna's own anger evaporated as she stared at him in dismay. How had the magic of that spark between them gone up in smoke? She was frantic to make him understand. Desperately, before he could say another word, she brought her lips to his.

Gwynna Owen was a determined woman, Gideon thought fleetingly before his senses propelled him out of the realm of reason altogether. Her mouth was sweet and soft as it rained kisses over him, her hands gently insistent as they fumbled with his shirt. When he felt her fingers on his chest making small circles on his skin, he groaned.

"Gwynna," he rasped against her lips in a last desperate effort to save himself. "I know you are discouraged that we have not found the records. But you will get nothing from me by playing the temptress. I cannot verify your claim without proof, no matter how enticingly you offer your charming body as incentive."

She stilled. "Is that what you think I am about, Englishman?" she demanded furiously. "Bribery and chicanery?

Then I was right: there is much you do not know." She jerked away from him.

They stared at each other in the waning light. "We had best leave," she said in a dead voice. "It will be dark soon."

A dull pounding filled his head as he forced his attention to the cliffs they had scrambled down in such harmony earlier. The sun was already too low to think about climbing them safely. "We should have started back earlier. It will be impossible to see on those rocks."

"Then we shall simply have to take the road," she snapped.

"Road?" he echoed in confusion.

She pointed to the bridge. Beyond it was a small dirt lane that wound in perfectly civilized fashion up to the top of the cliffs from which they had so precariously descended. He could not imagine how he had missed seeing it earlier.

He eyed her in astonishment. "Why, if you knew there was a road down the cliffs to the lighthouse, did you not say so?"

"Because," she said, sweeping to her feet and adjusting her clothing, "I wished to see you exert yourself, Englishman. For once."

His brows rose. "And did you enjoy the experience, Miss Owen?" he asked coolly.

"Oh, yes, Your Grace," she replied with a mock curtsy. "Yes, indeed."

CHAPTER 9

GWYNNA'S SPIRITS BRIGHTENED WHEN THEY ARRIVED AT AMLWICH Harbor the next day. The Liverpool pilot boats were at their usual moorings, waiting to guide ships whose captains were not familiar with the coast. Sloops dotted the harbor, and several men stood with fishing lines on a long piece of rock at the cove's edge. In an effort to break the strained silence in the carriage, Gwynna commented that the men were deep-sea fishing. The duke arched a brow, the first sign of interest he had displayed all day.

"They are only a few feet from the dock," he observed skeptically.

"Yes, but the water is very deep," she explained. "The harbor is formed by an excavation of large rock. When the tide is in, you can stand on the brim and fish for deep-water fish that come right up to your toes."

"I see," he said and yawned.

The man's arrogance was infuriating. "It is no good to play the bored dandy with me, Englishman," Gwynna snapped. "I can see that you put on the role as it suits you, like one of those floral waistcoats you wear so easily."

He cast her an offended look. "I do not wear floral, Miss Owen," he said haughtily. "Horizontal stripes are much more fashionable."

Gwynna sighed. They were at "Miss Owen" again, and had been since last night, when they shared an awkward meal at a Holyhead inn and exchanged fewer than a dozen words. Now she was determined to shake that air of bored complacency that he had worn since leaving the lighthouse.

"Does your wife share your appreciation of fashion?" she asked mischievously. "I suppose her gowns are all the crack."

His eyes narrowed. "You are being provocative, Miss Owen."

"And you are being obstinate and rude, Englishman."

He made no response, which further dampened the atmosphere in the carriage. Gwynna could bear his biting sarcasm, but his silent condemnation drove her to distraction. Not that she blamed him, precisely. After yesterday, he undoubtedly thought that everything Evans had said about her was true and that she had brazenly offered her body as payment for that morning in the cottage. He had no inkling of the burning need that had consumed her.

A burning need? For this stuffy, conceited, overdressed, self-important Englishman? A man who was everything she abhorred? She must be losing her mind. At all events, she would sooner die than let him know.

Gwynna swallowed hard. It was easy enough to retreat into her anger, but she knew that things were much more complicated than that. More and more, she had come to feel that the image he gave to the world was a contrivance. Yesterday, when she had seen the copper fire in those troubled eyes, a part of her had understood that Gideon Traherne, dandy par excellence, was a fraud. She might have realized it earlier, had it not been for the fact that she seemed to have lost the ability to reason in his presence.

Yesterday on the rocks she realized that the man under that elegant facade was someone she yearned to know better, someone she might love. She had ruined it, of course, by promptly throwing herself at him in a way that engendered his complete disgust.

The man was married, for heaven's sake, to some hothouse flower who doubtless moved gracefully through London ballrooms with nary a hair out of place. Even if he were not married, the Duke of Claremont belonged to a different world. She might fight for a man who was of her milieu, who believed in her causes and understood her ways, a man who would himself fight for what he believed in. For such a man, she would brave the wrath of the gods.

But the duke, even in those rare moments when he slipped free of that sophisticated facade, was not that man. He had undoubtedly chosen a woman who fit precisely his notion of a placid wife. Just why they were not together was somewhat confusing, but perhaps that was the way of the English. Gwynna wrinkled her nose in disgust. *She* would never live apart from a man she loved.

"Here is the village," she said with forced brightness. "It looks to be market day. Perhaps we shall see my cousin Ryan. The mines on Parys Mountain run only a half day on market day."

"I should enjoy meeting him, of course," the duke drawled with impeccable politeness.

Gwynna shot him an exasperated look. "Oh, do shut up, Englishman," she muttered.

He arched a brow at her rudeness, and she lifted her chin defiantly. "I am truly sick of your manners and your utter *reasonableness*. Do you never let down your guard?"

The hazel eyes held her for a moment, then he turned his gaze to the busy village street just coming into view. "Not without a fight, Miss Owen," he replied stiffly.

RYAN JONES EYED the well-dressed man whom his cousin had introduced as the Duke of Claremont, leaving everyone in the room who knew the circumstances of Gwynna's birth utterly stunned. Then, in her typically infuriating way,

Gwynna had promptly walked off to join the group of miners who met every market day at Ryan's house.

The duke, he noticed, followed Gwynna's movements with his eyes, all the while maintaining an expression of utter boredom on that noble face of his. Ryan was not fooled. He had seen enough of the world at twenty-one to recognize love when he saw it. Or lust. It was not so easy to tell the difference, especially since he himself vacillated between the two every time he thought of his Druscilla, which was almost constantly.

It was not easy being the head of the family, or at least this branch of it. He was lucky to have employment in the mines, when so many men were out of work. He could take care of his mother and the younger brothers and sisters. He supposed that Gwynna was one of his responsibilities, too, although that thought made him uneasy. Of all his relatives, she was the hardest to figure. She was fierce and independent and did not act silly and womanish like his sisters. It was nothing for her to sit in on the miners' meetings, which were usually spent grousing and cursing at their employers; the other women tactfully withdrew from such sessions, which tended to degenerate with the quantity of spirits consumed. The men seemed to enjoy having Gwynna around. She never hesitated to add her voice to the discussion, and they solicited her opinion as though she were one of them. Gwynna was not like any female Ryan had ever known. But then she was an Owen, and everyone knew that an Owen was not like anyone else.

This duke, though, was a potential problem. The man was clearly besotted, a well-heeled seducer like that relative of his who had ruined Gwynna's mother. Gwynna could be headed for the same fate.

Ryan cleared his throat. He had no experience in such matters, but he supposed that it was up to him to speak to the man, duke or no. There would never be a better time. The duke held back from the crowd, seemingly content to lean against the door frame surveying the room with an air of supreme self-possession. Ryan had never felt so ill at ease as he felt when he approached the man. He prayed that his voice would not falter like some bare-chinned youth.

"I would speak to you about my cousin," he said, relieved that the words had come out steady and even.

The duke arched his brows and fixed him with the sort of reproving look one might bestow on a wayward puppy. "Are you speaking about Miss Owen?" he said, his rich baritone filled with authority.

Ryan swallowed again. Damn the man. Well, he would not be intimidated. "Gwynna is my responsibility," he said, glowering.

This seemed to amuse the duke. One brow arched wryly. "Is she? I rather thought Miss Owen considered herself no one's responsibility except her own."

Ryan blinked. The man seemed to know Gwynna exceptionally well. *That* thought did nothing for his mood. "Yes, well, that is so. But it is my obligation to look after her interests, even if she does not agree."

The duke's face assumed an expression of pity. "Then you have my sympathies, dear lad. Such a task must be exceedingly difficult."

Ryan did not like being called "dear lad," but the man had spoken the truth, after all. Gwynna was a most difficult relative. He met the duke's benign gaze.

"That is neither here nor there, sir," he said with renewed determination. "The fact of the matter is, I must ask your intentions toward my cousin. The whole village can see you are traveling together with no more company than a coachman. Gwynna has made no secret of the fact that she passed the night at an inn in Holyhead. A man such as you must know what kind of interpretation may be placed on those events. What you must also know is that Gwynna's reputation, by virtue of her birth, has always been under a cloud. Lately certain persons have taken steps to assure that no one on Anglesey forgets that. I would not see my cousin the subject of more rumors."

"You refer to Mr. Evans's golden tongue, I take it," the duke replied, and Ryan noticed an angry glint in his eyes.

"Mr. Evans is not my concern at the moment, sir," he insisted heatedly. "It is you to whom I apply for reason. That is, *if* you are a reasonable and honorable man."

The duke's expression darkened. "I will grant you the benefit of your youth, Mr. Jones, and assume that you are not suggesting otherwise."

Ryan swallowed hard. "I mean no offense, but I cannot allow the injustices done to my cousin to go unaddressed."

The duke scowled. "Any injustice done to Miss Owen can be laid at Mr. Evans's door. Where were you when the good minister was spreading his lies? When your cousin had to face him alone?" he asked sternly. "It is to him you should apply for redress. He has wronged your cousin profoundly, and his treacherous gossip is the least of his crimes."

Ryan was confused. "The man is a nuisance and loves gossip in a way that I abhor in a man of God. But I am not aware of any physical harm he has done to Gwynna. What are you suggesting, sir?"

The duke appeared to hesitate. Then he smiled grimly. "Perhaps it is only my imagination, Mr. Jones. But I warn you: Evans is an evil man."

"That is not to the point, sir," Ryan said. "I must ask you to satisfy my concerns about your intentions toward my cousin."

The duke uncrossed his arms and looked down at him from his considerable height. Ryan had never felt so young as he did facing this polished, sophisticated nobleman. But when he met the duke's gaze, he saw something that made him feel better. There was something honest in his eyes and—Ryan could scarcely believe it—vulnerable.

"I have the deepest respect for Gwynna Owen," the duke said softly. "She is a strong and determined woman. It is not my intention to take advantage of her innocence."

Ryan was not certain he would have described Gwynna as innocent, even though he did not really believe the rumors about her. "With all respect, Your Grace, your very presence here risks compromising her."

The duke frowned. "Miss Owen is my temporary ward, as I have troubled to tell any and all who are interested. If records are found to prove her legitimacy, she would become my permanent ward, a woman whose position would command the highest respect. Do you think that I would wish to foster the slightest slur on her name, Mr. Jones?"

Ryan looked down at his toes. "No, sir. But what if no records are found? What if Gwynna is simply proven to be the base-born daughter of your late relative?" He forced himself to meet the duke's challenging gaze. "Wherefore your scruples then, Your Grace?" he demanded. For a fleeting moment, he thought he saw pain in the man's eyes. Then, as if a curtain had descended, the duke's expression suddenly became unreadable.

"It is my devout intention to maintain my scruples under all circumstances, Mr. Jones," he replied evenly. "Beyond that, I am afraid I cannot discuss my personal situation. Now, if you will excuse me, I believe I will look in on my ward. She seems to be waxing eloquent about something or other, judging from the rapt look in the eyes of your friends."

With that, the duke slipped over to the group of miners, a look of polite interest on his face.

Ryan shrugged. He knew when he was bested. If Gwynna followed down the road her mother had taken, that was her own business. He had done what he could.

"And so we must demand that the proprietors provide funds to purchase corn for all the people," Gwynna was saying, her voice filled with passion.

"But a thousand pounds, Gwynna," protested one man. "They will never agree to that."

There were murmurs of agreement. Gwynna shook her head. "Starving the workers does not help the mines," she insisted. "Your employers are not stupid. They know that."

There was more grumbling. A man in the back spoke up. "There are so many out of work, what do the owners care if the miners go hungry? There's always some poor beggar they can get to take our places."

This brought general agreement, and Gwynna shook her head in frustration. "But if we ask for the money as a loan, perhaps they will agree."

"And who's to pay it back, lass, tell me that?" asked one man. "No one here can afford to. The owners already pay us but a pittance. They will use a loan as an excuse to hold back even more from our wages. Some of us have been working for months without pay as it is."

"Even if we raise the sum," put in another, "I would lay odds that we'll get only the worst of the corn. They'll still ship the best of it abroad."

This observation set off a vigorous denunciation of export policies. It was some time before any voice could be heard above the fray. Finally Gwynna spoke.

"Why do we sit here grumbling?" she demanded. "Why do we not take matters into our own hands? Corn and oats from our shores go to Liverpool from this very harbor. There is nothing to say we cannot stop it."

A man in the back of the group rose. "Take matters into

our own hands? That is easy for you to say, Gwynna Owen. You have no hungry brats at home waiting for food, no family depending on what livelihood we can squeeze from the mines. If we stopped a ship in the harbor, we'd all be out of work before the next day. The mine owners would never stand for such as that. They'd be fearing we'd march on them next."

"But if everyone participated, they would have no choice," Gwynna insisted. "The mines cannot work themselves."

There was much debate for the next hour over whether such a strategy would work. Several of the men left shaking their heads; but others stayed on to hear Gwynna's tale of the men in Cheshire who marched about on the moors at night, drilling for just such an event as she was urging them to bring about.

"Riot is what yer talking, my girl," said one wizened man. "They won't stand for it, not at all."

"*If* they know it is coming," she replied. "You must take them by surprise."

"And where will you be, Gwynna, lass?" demanded another man. "You get everyone all worked up about storming ships and the like, then take yerself off on some fool's errand."

Gwynna flushed, and some of the men looked away. Everyone in the room knew what her "fool's errand" was, her quest to prove her legitimacy. And, although no one had mentioned it, everyone was keenly aware of the tall, well-dressed nobleman standing silently in the back of the room. Gwynna eyed her challenger defiantly.

"Are you accusing me of cowardice, Duncan?" she demanded.

He eyed her for a moment, then laughed. "Nay, lass, for every man here knows ye be an Owen. But I am saying that ye do not have our burdens. With this wet summer, the crops are bad. We're facing a winter of possible starvation. Ye cannot change that."

"We can try," she said fiercely.

Duncan shook his head. "Yer fiery words move us all, lass. But we've got more than the owners to contend with, or even the wealthy farmers. There's Evans. He takes his cut from every shipment that leaves the island. He'll not want to give that up."

Gwynna blanched. "Evans gets money from the shipments? But how?"

"After he rooted out the old priests, some of the wealthier farmers and mine owners got a bit nervous about his power. They were afraid his talk of reform would disrupt the shipping. They thought to buy him off before he could come after them with those reforms of his. And they did. They keep it quiet, but we know what goes on."

"The beast!" Gwynna cried.

Duncan shook his head. "Ye are young, lass," he said, rising to leave. The others rose also, and in a few minutes the room was cleared. Ryan saw the men out. Only Gwynna and Gideon remained behind.

Gwynna sat on a hard wooden bench, her eyes closed in frustration. The gentle hand on her shoulder caught her by surprise.

"It is difficult to fight a battle without any soldiers, is it not?" said a familiar voice.

She eyed him warily. "And where are *your* sympathies, Englishman? With your wealthy brethren who wish to preserve the old ways and keep their money, or with these men, trying to feed their families against enormous odds?"

"With you," he replied with a sigh. "I can make no pretense to objectivity."

She was startled. "I do not understand you, Englishman."

"That is because you are too much of a firebrand to think clearly, Miss Owen. Do not let my faint praise go to your head. I admire your courage, but your ideas are woefully misguided."

"Misguided!" She straightened indignantly. "That is just like you, is it not? You do not think it can be done. You would never dream of taking on an unjust system."

He arched a brow, then reached down and pulled her to her feet. His eyes glinted angrily. "Miss Owen, despite our rather intimate personal contact of the past, you do not know me at all, so any conclusion you might have in that regard is unwarranted."

She flushed. His eyes narrowed to slits. "As for taking on injustice, I can only say that, much as I admire your spirit, I cannot think you are in possession of all your faculties to imagine that you can single-handedly reverse England's export policy, feed the entire island of Anglesey, and rid the place of that idiot Evans to boot. Not even an Owen can manage such a feat."

She glared at him. "That is why you are a fool, Englishman."

"Undoubtedly," he muttered, and suddenly crushed her to his chest. She gasped but did not pull away.

A throat was cleared loudly, and they jumped quickly apart. Ryan stood at the doorway, a look of consternation on his face.

"His Grace," Gwynna said awkwardly, "was just leaving."

The duke arched a brow, but inclined his head in polite assent. Then, with a rueful look at Gwynna's furious cousin, he slipped quietly out into the night.

CHAPTER 10

THE RECTORY WAS AS DARK AND SILENT AS A TOMB. GWYNNA knew the house by heart, having often visited the kindly rector as a child. The man who now occupied the stone cottage was nothing like his predecessor, although she had not known the extent of his greed until two nights ago, when Duncan had explained about Evans's extortion scheme.

She adjusted the breeches she had donned for tonight's mission. This time, she was ready. Her dagger was snug at her waist. She had already performed the ritual ablution of battle. The interfering Duke of Claremont was tucked safely in his bed at the Bull's Head Inn; she had even checked with the innkeeper to make certain. Bridget's nag had been a bit skittish, probably because she sensed the approaching storm. But the mare had gotten her here, just the same.

Gwynna smiled grimly in anticipation. Christmas Evans would trouble no one after tonight.

GIDEON OPENED ONE GROGGY EYE. It was pitch black outside his window. He must have dozed off after dinner. His joints felt stiff, and his clothing was rumpled from his unexpected nap. He had not even troubled to take off his boots. The strain of traveling with Gwynna Owen had taken its toll on his meticulous habits.

He struggled to his feet and eyed his boots ruefully. They had not had a proper blacking since suffering the ravages of that climb down the cliffs at Holyhead. Tomorrow he would leave the Bull's Head Inn and Anglesey behind him; he was damned if he would return to civilization with scuffed boots. Might as well see if that innkeeper was still about.

It would be a relief to put distance between him and Gwynna Owen. There was no reason for him to remain, since nothing had been found to prove her legitimacy. He no longer doubted, however, that she was William Traherne's daughter. He had finally realized why her sapphire eyes were so familiar—they were the same shade as those in the lifeless, loveless face that had been William Traherne's. When he got back to London, he would arrange to send her a small allowance on behalf of her dastardly father. It was not her fault that she had arrived on the wrong side of the blanket. He had also been forced to acquit her of the worst of his suspicions. She was after his money, all right, but not for herself. The little fool would undoubtedly take her allowance and give it to the poor.

The stairs were dark, but there were a few candles lit in the taproom, and he heard dishes rattling. With any luck, the innkeeper could send a boy for his boots first thing in the morning.

Gideon sighed. Gwynna was an extraordinary woman, growing more beautiful by the day. In the three weeks since they had left Cheshire, she had filled out and lost that pinched look about her face. Her eyes had become even more luminous, like the sea that surrounded her fair island. It was increasingly hard to keep his guard up when he was in her presence. Had he not embarrassed himself before that young cousin of hers just the other night—after blithely assuring the lad he would keep his hands off her?

As for the incident at the lighthouse, he had tried to put it out of his mind altogether. He had clambered down those rocks like a silly schoolboy. Then, sitting at the edge of the sea pondering the horizon with her mere inches away, he had felt on the verge of some cataclysmic revelation, something he did not truly wish to know. That great expanse of sea and sky had suddenly closed in on him, like tentacles from some deep-water monster. He had to keep it at bay, had to keep Gwynna Owen from melting his resolve with her kisses. He did not really believe those accusations he had hurled at her so mercilessly. He only knew that she threw his well-ordered world into turmoil, and that something dreadful would happen if he did not regain control.

He did not know why she destroyed his sense of reason, why he was drawn to her in such a way that he forgot about Elizabeth, forgot about the differences between their worlds—in short, forgot himself entirely. He had never been so relieved as when he set her down at her cousin Bridget's house yesterday afternoon. He had not seen her since, having spent the day preparing for his departure and pondering how to make certain that Evans left her alone after he was gone.

He was frowning as he stepped into the taproom. The innkeeper peered at him from behind a pile of dirty dishes. "Ah, Yer Grace," the man said, shaking his head. "My wife's took sick, and my Mary has made herself scarce. No one to do the work but me."

"I will not keep you from your duties," Gideon said quickly. "I shall be leaving in the morning. Could you send a boy for my boots?"

The innkeeper shook his head mournfully. "If I can find young Davey, but who's to say? As I told Gwynna, there's no one to do the work around here when people take it into their heads to go off—"

"Gwynna?" Gideon interrupted sharply. "Miss Owen was here today?"

The innkeeper mopped his brow on his apron. "Tonight it

was, asking about you. Told her you were all tucked up for the night." He paused as he noticed Gideon's face. "I hope it was not important. I just assumed—"

But Gideon had already vanished. With a shrug the innkeeper returned to his work.

EVIDENTLY EVANS LIKED DRAFTS. Even on such a chilly and threatening night, there were enough windows open for any number of intruders to crawl through. Gwynna rubbed her arms to get warm. The man's blood ran cold, so why should he not prefer the chill to warmth? She lifted herself lightly over the windowsill and in the next moment stood in the darkened parlor.

She paused, listening.

There were no signs of activity. He must be asleep. She rubbed her hands together. It would not be long now. The smell of battle exhilarated her. She crept noiselessly toward the bedroom, her heart racing in anticipation. A clap of thunder rumbled somewhere, an ominous herald of Christmas Evens's fate. She smiled, savoring the thought.

Snores emanated from the large form in the bed. The man slept the sleep of the righteous, no matter that he was far from entitled to it, Gwynna thought bitterly, remembering how that bulky body had assaulted her, invaded her. It was only afterward, when he dozed, that she had been able to extract her small revenge. But it was not complete. Not yet.

Her palms were damp as she clutched the knife. This time she would finish him. This time Evans would pay.

HE HAD HOPED TO FIND HER safely ensconced for the night, but he was not surprised to find her bed empty. And although Captain was a fast goer, precious minutes had been squandered racing to Red Wharf. Her cousin Bridget, awakened from a sound slumber, proved to be thoroughly shocked at

Gwynna's absence and utterly devoid of ideas as to where the little hellion might have gone.

It did not take a genius to figure it out, however.

Gwynna Owen had nothing to lose. Now that she could not prove herself anything more than a duke's by-blow, any hope of salvaging her mother's name or her own reputation must be forever abandoned. Gideon had seen her face in Amlwich when she learned of Evans's extortion scheme. She meant to have her pound of flesh, and she would not tarry about it.

Damned bloodthirsty Welsh.

To the west, the sky was beginning to flicker fatefully, heralding a fast-moving storm. With a sinking feeling, Gideon spurred Captain onward.

GWYNNA TRACED A DELICATE LINE across Evans's throat with the point of her dagger. He gave a momentary snort, but still he slept, his mouth a great, gaping cave of snores. His lips were moist and fleshy, his hands thrown over his head and clutched into fat fists.

She never would have guessed that Evans slept naked. Her eyes roved over him dispassionately. His body was massive, its shapeless bulk built for physical domination, not for the sensitive exploration of the female form. Not like the duke, whose sensual mouth and finely tapered fingers were perfectly made for the art of love.

Her mind was wandering, she realized with an inward sigh. Somehow the duke had accomplished what she had once thought impossible after Evans's brutal attack. He had made her yearn for physical intimacy with a man. Not just any man, but for one man—Gideon Traherne.

Gwynna took a deep breath. It was amazing to think of how far she had fallen. From utter disgust at Evans's crude sexual urges, she had tumbled into a state of breathless longing, her brain completely occupied at any given moment with thoughts of the Duke of Claremont. Today had been an agony of thinking about him, knowing that he was making plans to leave her life forever.

Well, she was no lovestruck miss. She had a mission to accomplish. This time there would be no distractions. Christmas Evans would learn what an Owen could do. Again she tickled his neck with the tip of her blade. The sight of the sharp edge as it caressed his lumpy flesh made her smile.

"Do you plan to mount his head on the dining room wall," a voice drawled, "or simply set it on a spear at Beaumaris castle?"

Gwynna jumped.

"I believe I prefer the latter," he continued consideringly. "I should not think it pleasant to endure those eyes looking down at me at dinner."

In the darkness she could see only his silhouette, but she did not need the light to identify the tall, languid figure propped in the doorway.

"What are you doing here?" she demanded.

"Endeavoring to protect that sleeping oaf from whatever bloodthirsty revenge you have planned. A rather unexpected duty, I must confess."

"I shall not tolerate your interference," she said with a hiss. "Neither of us are your concern any longer."

He sighed. "Would that it were so, Miss Owen. Unfortunately you are very much my concern at the moment."

Just then Evans stirred. Gideon took a step forward. "A sound sleeper," he observed, peering at his form, and Gwynna thought she detected a note of tension in his voice. "Tell me, did he sleep like a babe in your grandfather's house—afterward?"

Gwynna eyed him uncertainly. "You believe me, then? About that day, I mean."

He closed the distance between them. Now she could see a strange gleam in his eyes. "I expect that you would not go to such extremes, Miss Owens," he said softly, "did you not feel yourself terribly wronged."

"'Tis not only I, but others whom he has wronged with his greed and perfidy," she insisted fiercely. "The man deserves to die."

"In due course, my dear," he agreed. "But not, perhaps, tonight."

"What is going on here?" rumbled a groggy voice. Evans rubbed his eyes and stared at them in confusion.

"I believe you were about to find your head separated from your body," Gideon replied easily. "Not precisely the English way of retribution, but then this is Wales, is it not?"

Evans's eyes widened in shock. He sat up and fumbled with the sheets to cover himself.

"I was not going to kill him," Gwynna protested.

Gideon arched a brow. "I suppose," he drawled, "that you were merely giving him an exceptionally close shave with the point of that dagger."

"What are you doing in my room?" Evans roared, finally in possession of his senses. He rose from his bed, his body draped in the bedsheets like some cumbersome giant. He groped for a taper and lit the candle at his bedside.

Gwynna eyed him derisively. "Now you look more like the fool you are, Evans. Regardless of Claremont's assertion, it is not my intention to kill sleeping people, no matter how villainous they may be. I only intended to give you the pleasure of waking with a dagger in your throat. Fear, I find, does wondrous things for the hearts of men."

Evans looked from her to Gideon. "You are mad, Gwynna.

I believe you are both mad. State your business and be gone."

"It is quite simple," Gwynna said in a matter-of-fact tone. "I have failed to find the papers legitimizing my birth. My reputation is thus unsalvageable. My grandfather is dead, so he cannot be harmed by the disclosure that his trusted friend molested me. I shall therefore dearly enjoy witnessing the shock and disgust of your devoted followers, not to mention countless others in your sway, when word of your crime against me gets around. I should think it will mean the end of your tyranny on Anglesey."

Evans's eyes grew bulbous, and he took a step forward, his expression murderous. "You dare not, Gwynna. I will denounce you as a whore."

Gwynna glared at him. "As you have already done as much, I cannot think that will affect me. You forget that I am an Owen. People will believe me, bastard or no, when I tell them of how you attacked me in my own home as my grandfather lay on his deathbed, when I tell them how you forced yourself upon me, you who are three times my size. And when I tell them how I revenged myself on you with my dagger. Go ahead, Evans," she taunted, "show the duke your scars—the scars that would have been so much more interesting had you not awakened just as I began."

"I do think I shall forgo that particular attraction, if you do not mind," Gideon said quickly.

Gwynna eyed him contemptuously. "I see you have a weak stomach, Englishman," she observed. "Very well, I shall happily describe it. The scar begins at his midsection and runs in a very neat fashion down to the area of his private parts. As I say, Evans awakened prematurely."

With an angry growl, Evans lunged for her. But Gwynna quickly evaded his grasp, and the sheets tumbled to the floor, exposing his body.

She smiled. "Behold, the evidence."

Evans grabbed for the sheets, but not before the candlelight had illuminated the neat, white scar on his abdomen. "I will kill you for this, woman!" Evans roared.

"You will burn in hell first," Gwynna retorted, waving her dagger menacingly.

"I should think this an excellent time to take our leave," Gideon interjected. In one fluid movement he caught Gwynna about the waist and propelled her toward the doorway.

"I am not done yet," she insisted. Turning to Evans, she smiled sweetly. "It is forgiveness that you preach, is it not, Evans? Very well, I shall try to forget—if not forgive—your transgression. Provided that you set this island free from your nefarious deeds. You must stop extorting money in exchange for allowing the ships to take food from the mouths of our people. You must stop opposing my efforts to set up a fund to feed the poor and create jobs for the unemployed. That is just the beginning. Perhaps I shall think of more."

Evans moved toward her, but Gideon stepped neatly between them and swept her from the room. "You have given him quite a bit to think about for the nonce," he said quickly. "Good night, Evans," he called over his shoulder. "No doubt Miss Owen can expect your swift and speedy reply."

His face as dark as a thundercloud, Christmas Evans clutched his sheets and watched them go, his coal-black eyes burning like the fires of hell.

Outside, Gideon untied Captain just as a crash of thunder sounded overhead. The horse sidestepped uneasily. Gideon looked around. "Where is your horse?" he demanded.

Gwynna's eyes widened in alarm. Bridget's nag was

nowhere to be seen. "The storm must have frightened her," she said. "I am afraid she has run off."

Gideon cursed. "We shall never find her in this storm." Lightning flashed around them just as large drops of rain began to fall. He jumped on Captain and pulled Gwynna up behind him. Another crash of thunder sounded, and the horse reared back as she clung to him for dear life.

"We will never make Beaumaris before the storm hits, never mind your cousin's house!" Gideon shouted. "Is there shelter nearby?"

Another thunderous boom nearly drowned out her reply.

"Only the tomb!" she shouted. "I am certain the ancients would not mind."

Gideon rolled his eyes heavenward. "It wanted only this," he muttered. "Kindly point the way, Miss Owen."

CHAPTER 11

THOSE INFERNAL ANCIENTS, WHOEVER THEY WERE, HAD CON-
structed an especially eerie place for their dead. A dirt path
lined with flat stones chiseled into uncanny uniformity
descended into the bowels of the tomb. Mounds of stone and
dirt heaped over the chamber gave it the appearance above-
ground of a gently sloping hill. Below ground, the earthen
walkway led inexorably into the subterranean blackness like
a road to nowhere.

Gideon had scarcely registered these gloomy observations before the storm broke over them in full force.
Whatever its other characteristics, he reflected as he dashed
after Gwynna into the darkened cave, the tomb did offer
excellent shelter.

Still, he nearly chose to take his chances with the storm
when he heard the incomprehensible chanting. The words
echoed around the cavern like some ghastly sepulchral spirit
set loose after thousands of years of silence.

"What in God's name are you jabbering?" he demanded,
his customary aplomb evaporating in the impenetrable
darkness.

"A Welsh prayer. It is proper to pay respects to the spirits
of those interred here," she said with quiet dignity from
somewhere on the other side of the chamber. "After all, we
are disturbing their resting place."

"I thought those spirits of yours rested elsewhere," he

grumbled. "Did you not tell me they wafted up to the clouds like so much smoke?" He pulled out what he hoped was his handkerchief and wiped the rain from his face. The darkness was oppressive, relieved only by the occasional flash of lightning outside the entryway. He might as well have been in his own grave. That notion did nothing for his mood.

"The Druids believed that, of course," she conceded. "But these tombs may have been made by an even more ancient race. We simply do not know. Therefore, it is prudent to acknowledge all possibilities—unless, like the rest of the English, you believe there is only one true religion."

He could not see her face, but he did not need the light to discern the contempt in her voice. Even in this ridiculous situation she was still taunting him for a fatuous fool. He had done everything to encourage the image, of course, but he wondered whether his vanity would ever recover from the battering.

He had more immediate concerns, however. Except for his shirt, which had been protected by his coat, he was soaked to the skin; he knew she was, too. Those breeches of hers would cling most uncomfortably. Soon they would both be shivering in the dark and damp. It would serve no purpose to catch their deaths in this infernal place. He hesitated before broaching his plan, then realized that he could scarcely sink lower in her estimation.

"Do not take offense at my suggestion, Miss Owen, but I suggest we remove our wettest garments. They will not dry completely, but they can at least be wrung out. The storm shows no sign of stopping. I should not think it wise to sit in soggy trousers for the duration."

Silence greeted his words. At last her voice came from the opposite side of the chamber. "I suppose it is not as though we would actually *see* each other."

"In this darkness I cannot see my own hands, much less any part of your charming person."

More silence. Then sounds of movement. "Very well," she replied matter-of-factly. "I have removed my breeches. They were excessively uncomfortable anyway. 'Tis the only time that I have found myself wishing for a frock. At least this old shirt is long enough for some semblance of propriety. I wonder how long the storm will last."

Too long, Gideon thought as he peeled off his boots and trousers and contemplated spending the next few hours alone with the half-naked Gwynna Owen in a burial vault. He put his hand on the wall and groped a few inches toward the tomb's entryway, where he had set Captain's saddle. The chamber was too small to stable a horse, so he had left Captain to find his own shelter in a nearby copse of trees.

He shook out the saddle blanket. It was damp, but not drenched. "I have a blanket, Miss Owen, if you will but direct me to you with your voice."

"Very well," came the reluctant response. "What should we talk about? Evans, I suppose. I wish I had the power of the ancients to know whether he will do my bidding."

He groped around the wall toward the sound of her voice. "I suppose that among their other talents they could see into the future?" he asked dryly.

"Oh, yes," came the disembodied reply. "They had marvelous powers. They could also produce insanity."

"That I can well believe," he murmured, his hand recoiling from something wet and slimy on the wall. It was a good thing he did not believe in ghosts. "There is sufficient madness on this island to make even a sane man doubt himself."

"Madness to one man is wisdom to another," she declared.

"One of your Welsh sayings, I suppose," he observed darkly.

"Not at all," she said indignantly. "'Tis my own thought entirely. You know, I believe I shall tell you a story. Will that help?"

"The sound of your voice will help me avoid breaking my neck, Miss Owen. Otherwise, I shall refrain from committing myself."

"And I shall ignore your insolence, Englishman. Very well. Once upon a time there was a great hero, Cuchulinn, who was enticed to the land of the fairies by a fairy named Fand. He fell madly in love with her, and when his heroic adventures were over, he returned home, only to find that he could not forget her. This would not do, you see, for he could not be a proper hero and go about his work if he mooned over fairies the day long. Is this at all interesting to you?"

Gideon moved steadily along the wall. "I have always enjoyed fairy tales," he replied politely. There was a momentary silence, during which he was certain she was pondering whether he was making sport of her. The woman seemed to take offense at everything. His foot slipped on a rock, and he stumbled briefly. "Keep talking, Miss Owen," he commanded.

"The Druids gave him a potion, which banished all memory of his adventures with the fairies, and most especially of Fand. This was a very good thing, for you see Cuchulinn's wife, Emer, had been consumed with jealousy, and she—" She broke off. "Perhaps this is not a very good story after all. I keep forgetting that you have a wife."

Her timing, as always, was impeccable. Gideon's groping hand came in contact with her shoulder in the instant she pronounced the word "wife." He felt the fabric of her rough-woven shirt over what he knew to be wondrously smooth skin. He recoiled in guilt at the lascivious turn of his thoughts. They stood in awkward silence as Gideon fought to control his suddenly uneven breathing.

"I know," she said brightly. "I shall tell you another story. About Etain, wife of the high king of Ireland. They were very happy together. But in a former existence, she was the beloved of the god Mider, who decided he wanted her back, and so he returned to carry her off. The king was distraught and consulted his Druid. Druids are very useful at finding things, you see. They use wands of yew."

"Of course," Gideon muttered. He leaned against the stone wall. Did the woman have any idea how maddening it was to stand so close to her, to inhale her scent mixed with the damp of her clothes?

"Dalan—that was the Druid—finally discovered Mider and the queen. A great cloud led him to her. The Druids have the power to speak to the heavens, you know. That is how they stir up the clouds."

"With their wands of yew, no doubt."

She eyed him suspiciously. "You are making sport of me again, sir. It is too bad you choose to be so ignorant about so many things."

Gideon sighed. "I suppose you are going to enlighten me once again, Miss Owen. Very well. How does one stir up the heavens?"

"You simply raise your eyes heavenward and cast spells against the elements," she replied. "Of course, it is preferable to have a group. When everyone does it, their combined power causes strife among the heavens and gives rise to clouds of fire. This is the source of the magic."

"The wealth of information you possess amazes me, Miss Owen," he observed, his breathing now under control. He gestured to the entryway. "Judging from the fury outside, it seems that someone has stirred up clouds of fire tonight. I might suspect you of such a deed, had I not known the manner in which you have been occupied this evening." He arched a brow in reproof. "It was exceedingly unwise, incidentally, for you to have gone to that madman."

"Evans?" she scoffed. "I know how to handle him. I should have done so earlier, but I had hopes that we would find the records." She paused. "I suppose there is no hope now."

Gideon was moved by the forlorn note in her voice. He patted her shoulder. "We looked everywhere, Gwynna."

She lifted her face to his. Even in the darkness he could see that her eyes were wide and luminous. "I like the way you say my given name," she said simply. "It is ever so much nicer than 'Miss Owen.'"

Gideon swallowed hard. No matter that it was pitch dark in this gloomy hole in the ground, he had never been more aware of their state of undress than at this very moment. He felt the saddle blanket in his hand and was suddenly reminded of his original task. Quickly he bent down and spread it over the tomb's earthen floor. "Here," he said. "There is not much blanket, but perhaps it is enough to wrap around you."

"Thank you." She eased herself down onto the rough wool. He hesitated, then tossed his wet jacket on the ground beside her. Gingerly he deposited himself on the soggy superfine, adjusting his wrinkled but largely dry shirt so that it covered him properly.

"I daresay my valet shall not forgive me," he said lightly, wondering whether he had lost his mind. Lightning flashed again, and Gideon was almost undone as it illuminated the steady, intent look in those sapphire eyes.

She smiled, and he had to catch his breath. "You are a fraud, Englishman," she said. "You have handled all of our adventures with perfect aplomb. This despite your oft-stated obligations to your tailor, valet, and anyone else who is pleased to help you create the image of a man of careless conscience obsessed with matters of appearance. I suspect you have had years to perfect this masquerade. My only question is why you began it."

Gideon shifted uncomfortably on the balled-up fabric of his jacket. Women were such interfering creatures. "You will pardon me, Miss Owen," he said stiffly, "if I prefer to keep my thoughts to myself."

She moved closer to peer into his face. "You think to fob me off with such an answer, Englishman," she retorted, "but I know you are not what you seem."

He inclined his head, willing himself to ignore the heady effect of her nearness. "I yield to your superior judgment and insight," he replied sardonically. "Are we to spend the evening engaged in inquisition? It is hardly fair, since I cannot remove myself from the premises."

"You can do whatever you want to do, Englishman," she replied heatedly. "That is the difference between us, between our stations and between our sexes. You can go anywhere with that supercilious demeanor of yours. No one questions you. You cloak yourself in the image of a man whose arrogance, wealth, and position demand that he be admired—from afar, of course. Nothing ever touches you. You move in and out of lives like a flimsy shadow that slips through the fingers the moment one tries to catch it."

He drank in the angry intelligence of those wondrous eyes. Their gazes held. Then another flash of lightning gave him the excuse to look away. "I commend you on your perceptiveness, Miss Owen," he said curtly. "Now you have no need to ask any further questions."

Gwynna stared at him, thunderstruck at the sudden realization that what she had said in anger was no less than the truth. But why had he adopted such a masquerade? She was burning with curiosity as she studied his profile. With his hair damp and mussed, he still appeared perfectly poised, even with his knees exposed from under that wrinkled lawn shirt. She blushed at the knowledge that he, too, had doffed his breeches. Quickly she pulled the blanket more tightly around her.

"What did you do in the war?"

He arched a brow in surprise. "A man of my indolent inclinations? You must be jesting."

"I do not believe that. Tell me."

He crossed his arms, leaned back against the chamber wall, and closed his eyes, managing to look infinitely bored by the topic. "I was a diplomat at Vienna. Earlier I was engaged in more clandestine activities."

"You were a *spy?*" Gwÿnna stared at him in amazement. *"You?"*

A wry smile flitted over his features. "Your word, not mine, Miss Owen. Besides, you have already branded me as a deceiver. Perhaps I have a faculty for the work."

"Do not play games with me, Englishman. I simply cannot see you dashing about, doing some murky, messy clandestine business. Think of the effect on your cravat."

His quick, engaging smile in response to her sally made Gwynna's heart turn somersaults. She drew closer, compelled by that heady magnetism and suddenly aware of a powerful current that owed nothing to the storm flashing outside.

"Don't."

The sharpness of his voice took her aback. Gwynna halted, instantly mortified. He must have thought she was about to throw herself at him again. He was still resting against the wall, but his eyes had narrowed, and he was watching her like a cat.

"Miss Owen," he said finally, his voice tense, "it seems

very likely that we shall have to spend the night in this godforsaken place. It is unfortunate, but neither of us is in a position to do otherwise. I do think it would be advisable, however, were you not to lean so close. It does strange things to my resolve."

Her back stiffened, and she moved a few inches away. "You need not fear that I shall compromise you, sir," she said rigidly. "I have no use for men, you see. Not in *that* way. The idea of intimate contact with a man revolts me."

As the lightning flashed, she could see his brows shoot skyward. "You will pardon me if I take leave to observe that your words are somewhat at odds with your past behavior in my presence."

Gwynna was thankful that he could not see her blush. "I cannot account for it," she acknowledged, looking down at the ground. "After Evans, I used to have nightmares about his hands on me. I swore that no man would ever touch me again." She hesitated, then met his penetrating gaze. "I do not know how to explain my behavior with you. For some reason you do not revolt me."

"That, of course, is most flattering," he said dryly. But his voice had softened. He took her hand. "What Evans did to you was criminal," he said quietly. "But you must not think that all men are thus. Relations between men and women can be magical. One day, perhaps, you will marry. I am certain that your husband will be nothing like Evans."

"Is that how it is between you and your wife?" she asked, feeling suddenly small. "Magical?"

He dropped her hand as if he had been burned. "Elizabeth and I were childhood friends."

"And friends do not experience that magic?"

He eyed her in consternation. "I did not say that, imp. Let us speak of something else."

Gwynna sighed in frustration. Part of her yearned to learn

about his marriage. The other part wanted to block it from her mind. "Very well. Tell me about your parents."

He seemed surprised. "I told you about them."

"You told me how they died, but not how it was growing up. I have always wondered what it was like living with one's parents."

He eyed her consideringly. "I had more of a childhood than you, I suppose, although it ended when I was forced to take up the title at the tender age of eleven." He looked away. "Like you, I was my parents' only child. I was always in their company. Even though I was a boy, I was admitted to the dinner table and to the weekly salons in my mother's drawing room. At night I used to stay up so I could admire them in their splendor as they left for the parties."

"And when they died, your world was shattered," Gwynna said slowly. Much about him had suddenly become clearer. "That is why you immersed yourself in the social whirl. You must have thought to recapture the pleasant world of your boyhood. And yet it did not bring back your parents." She nodded in sympathy. "The pain must have been unbearable."

He eyed her coldly. "Spare me your facile observations, Miss Owen. You understand nothing of my life."

"The emptiness of your refuge must have deepened your despair," she continued thoughtfully, ignoring his comment. "That is why you adopted that elegant, aloof facade. To protect yourself. I begin to understand why you are so untouchable, Englishman."

Instantly his hands were on her shoulders. "Cease your infernal chattering, woman," he commanded, giving her a shake. "You know nothing about me. Nothing. Do you understand?" His voice was filled with fury.

"I know enough to see that I have finally shaken you out of that elegant shell of yours, Englishman," she retorted defiantly. "Do you now mean to shake me until my teeth rattle? Pray, what would the *ton* say about such a murderously untidy passion?"

A crack of thunder sounded overhead, and Gideon stared at her in shock and fury. She was right. He *had* completely forgotten himself. He wanted nothing so much as to wring her neck. No, that was a moment earlier. Now he wanted something entirely different.

God help him.

He crushed her violently to his chest, wrapping his arms tightly around that pliant, delicious form. He needed to feel her warmth and the passion that made her so infuriating and compelling at the same time. She was so womanly and soft, yet so strong and fierce. He heard himself murmuring incoherent words against that unruly red hair. He would just hold her for a moment, one moment to breathe in that passion and let it fill his senses for all eternity. One fleeting, intoxicating moment, and then he would be himself again. Controlled. Calm.

Married.

But as he ran his hands feverishly over her shoulders, down her arms, around her rib cage, the unthinkable happened. Gwynna Owen threw her arms about his neck. Her lips parted, and those beautiful sapphire eyes gave him a look of pleading desire. He was lost, utterly lost.

With a low growl Gideon covered her mouth with his, relishing the taste of her tongue as it drove him beyond the far reaches of sanity. Her responsiveness was beyond anything he had imagined. She returned his kisses with wild abandon, writhing feverishly in his arms, pressing her body to his.

"Gwynna," he murmured, drinking in the wonder of her passion. She placed a fingertip against his mouth.

"No more talking, Englishman," she whispered.

Slowly her swollen lips met his again, gently at first, then more urgently until he was mad with desire. His hands roved over her, exploring her, claiming her. They slipped under her shirt and caressed her breasts, teasing the nipples into hard points. Her moans urged him on. He began to knead the smooth skin of her buttocks.

No.

The word pounded in his head like cannon fire, but then her hands unabashedly crept under his shirt, toying with the hairs on his chest. When her hand trailed lower, Gideon closed his eyes against the force of the heat that swept over him. With a groan, he pulled her into his lap, settling her against the swollen evidence of his desire.

Their eyes met. Hers were wide with—what? Fear? What a brute he was! He forced himself to speak.

"I am sorry," he rasped unsteadily. "I do not wish to be the cause of your nightmares."

She looked at him in confusion. "What?"

"You said you had nightmares after Evans . . ."

"What must I do, Englishman," she whispered fiercely, "to silence you?"

Before he could respond, she pushed him gently back on his elbows. Her eyes were luminous and pleading, her breathing uneven as she brought their lips together and nestled her body against his. Gideon tried to summon the last vestiges of his resolve, but when she gently eased him into her tantalizing warmth, he gave up the fight.

She was magnificent, blindly guiding the rhythm of their bodies, enslaving him with her passion. As she drew him deeper into the magic of their harmony, the force of her desire silenced his doubts. Here, in this eerie and dank cave, their joining transcended all else. He did not feel the damp earth under his back, or any of the discomforts of conscience. Her spirit commanded his, snared it back from that endless void it traveled and propelled it into a land of clarity and light. He had no choice but to follow. He knew he would die rather than do otherwise.

When at last the momentum changed, he was instantly aware of it. Suddenly she was the helpless one, her soft pleading cries awakening his senses to the fact that her movements had become increasingly more urgent. Gideon eased his hand between their bodies and stroked her gently. She gasped and then was lost on a wave of passion as he matched her rhythm with his own. When at last she collapsed onto him, shaking, he cried his own release, wondering whether he had truly floated up into those heavens of hers. He clasped her tightly, helpless with wonder and awe.

They lay in silence, alone in the dark cavern as the sounds of thunder rumbled outside. Gideon pulled the blanket around them, rubbing her back in gentle circles, feeling the glow of passion receding as the black abyss of despair rushed up at him.

What in God's name had he done? What was she thinking? Did she feel the same reverent wonder that had swept over him? Or only the loathing and revulsion she had felt with Evans? No, he thought, there had been no reluctance in her. A sudden suspicion dawned. He took a deep breath. He had to know.

"Was that, perchance, in payment for that morning in your cottage?" he asked softly, dreading to hear the answer.

Her eyes were filled with confusion, then sudden understanding and indignation. He knew she was thinking of those crass accusations he had hurled at her at the lighthouse. But then her anger vanished. "No," she said softly.

He sighed in relief, unsure why the question had been so important.

Fool. He should not be thinking such thoughts, nor

should he be lying here with Gwynna Owen after the most extraordinary lovemaking of his life.

"You ought to have worn the ring," he observed, trying to keep his tone light. "The one that wards off dire diseases and the unwelcome attentions of toplofty dukes."

She cocked her head and eyed him solemnly. "Your attentions were not unwelcome, Englishman."

"Gwynna," he began, wondering how he could say what must be said. She stopped his words with her finger against his mouth.

"Not now." She kissed him lightly, then sat back to study him. "You know," she began, "the ancients believed that whatever grew on the oak tree was a gift from heaven. Mistletoe was their special prize. They used a golden knife to cut it off the tree and then sacrificed two white bulls." She nestled against his chest. "So you see, Englishman, some things are simply a gift from heaven. Later, perhaps, the sacrifice."

He wrapped his arms around her, his heart shattering into a thousand pieces at her wisdom. "Gwynna Owen," he whispered in his agony, "you are a remarkable woman."

IT WAS A DIFFERENT DREAM THIS TIME, one filled with the rumbling of cannons, like the raging of some faraway battle. Perhaps it was the Romans, advancing on the group of ancients arrayed like sacrificial lambs along the shore, their arms imploring the heavens to cast out the invaders. Her bed was hard, like stone. He was a shadow watching her as she slept. Then she felt his hands caressing her, roving over her flesh, invading her most secret places.

But these hands were not clumsy or brutal. Warmth suffused her body as they moved over her, awakening her to fierce desire. This was not a nightmare, or even a dream.

All around her was bathed in black, but she could see the

gleam of passion in his eyes. As his face descended to hers, she stared—not into Evans's forbidding dark gaze, but into the Duke of Claremont's brilliant copper fire. A lazy smile stole over her lips as he pulled her into his arms and began to smother her with sleepy kisses. Now she remembered. The thunder, the lightning, the lovemaking that she would pay for a thousand times over. Still, she smiled.

"You are insatiable, Englishman," she murmured.

He pulled her tightly against him. The rough blanket chafed her skin. The earth was hard and unwelcoming, the chamber dank and dark. But these discomforts faded as his hands caressed her, forever marking her as his. Years from now, when it came time for her spirit to join the others, she knew she would remember this time and this man who had invaded her soul.

Was that how it had been with her mother, perhaps in this very spot? Had Megan Owen given herself to her lover, freely and eagerly, without a care for marriage vows? Gwynna was filled with wonder. In the eyes of the world, this was wrong. But somehow she knew that the spirits were smiling.

CHAPTER 12

GIDEON TENSED. EVEN HALF ASLEEP HE HAD HEARD THE FOOTFALL outside. They had a visitor.

"Quick," he whispered, the urgency of his tone jolting Gwynna awake. "Your clothes."

Dawn had cast the cavern into shades of gray, but it was still difficult to see as he donned his damp trousers. There was no sound of rain outside. The storm, he realized with a sense of foreboding, had probably stopped hours ago.

"Who is it?" Gwynna whispered.

Gideon's face was grim. "Someone who undoubtedly guessed that we would be forced to seek shelter last night. Who seized the first light to find us in this deliciously compromising situation."

Gwynna's eyes widened. "Evans!"

"I would bet my matched bays on it."

She scrambled for her dagger, her breeches all but forgotten. "We will fight him. To the death, if need be!"

He eyed her in amusement. "I am quite certain it is not the man's intention to engage us in battle. He is undoubtedly after revenge, since that is all you Welsh seem to think about, but I daresay he is not after blood."

"What, then?"

Gideon hesitated. She was so fierce, yet in her own way so vulnerable. He wanted to wrap her in his arms and protect her from the villainy of a man like Evans for all time. But that was impossible. Even now, even after what they had shared last night, he would have to leave her to fight her battles alone. His obligations lay elsewhere, with Elizabeth. In his inability to resist Gwynna's captivating spirit, he had wronged both women.

There was no honorable recompense within his power, and yet he owed Gwynna something. A handsome yearly allowance, perhaps. The thought made him cringe, for it would denigrate everything they had shared. Gwynna Owen was not too proud to demand her due as William Traherne's daughter, but she would never accept anything that looked like a reward for her favors. She would most likely fling his money in his face and come after him with that dagger.

He straightened his jacket. It still looked slept on. He had certainly made a royal muddle of things. And now the devil was at the door.

The crunch of rocks on the path outside heralded their visitor's arrival. "I think we are about to discover precisely what Mr. Evans has in mind," Gideon said wryly, even as he eyed her with dismay. Her rough-woven shirt scarcely reached to her knees, and her rumpled appearance invited all manner of speculation about her recent activities.

He forced a smile to his lips. "Your toilette, my dear," he reminded her.

Gwynna reached for her breeches just as a shadow filled the entryway. "Ah," said the voice of Christmas Evans, "they are found at last."

The pious, conniving bastard was fairly rubbing his hands together in glee, Gideon noted. He was followed into the cave by several of his followers. The men eyed Gwynna and her bare legs in stunned amazement. Evans could barely mask his delight at the spectacle.

Gwynna's face was flaming as she realized the direction of their thoughts. "Vultures," she muttered.

"Diplomacy, my dear," Gideon cautioned quietly. She bristled, but just then Evans's voice boomed through the chamber.

"It is wondrous, is it not, how history repeats itself?" He smiled a toothy grin. "First the mother, then the daughter. Both brought low by dukes of Claremont at this tomb, of all places. The devil moves in mysterious ways."

Gwynna eyed him with scorn. "You are a vile snake, Evans. It is you who are the devil's tool. Why do you not tell your friends about how you raped me in my grandfather's house?"

There was a collective gasp at this accusation, but Evans merely smiled. "My dear Gwynna," he said, his voice taking on the sonorous tones of a sermon, "I regret that thy sordid mind has led thee to create such falsehoods to distract our attention from these sinful circumstances." He shook his head pityingly. "You passed the night here with this man. Perhaps you simply sought shelter from the storm, but it is clear from the state of your clothing that a different sort of activity held sway."

"No one will believe you, Evans," Gwynna declared hotly. She eyed Gideon, who returned her a benign look that gave no evidence of concern at their predicament.

"On the contrary," Evans thundered. "This episode provides ample evidence of your lack of morals. Now no one on the island will support your rebellious plans. No one will believe your falsehoods."

He shook his finger in the air. "Daughter of iniquity," he intoned, "you have betrayed all that is honorable. You have made a bargain with the devil. You have lain with a man out of wedlock as did your mother before you. Any issue of such a union can only be the devil's spawn."

"Heir to a dukedom, actually," Gideon corrected in a languid drawl. "You see, Miss Owen is my betrothed."

The eyes of everyone in the tomb turned toward him. Gwynna stared at him in shock, but Gideon ignored her and returned Evans's astonished gaze with a bland look of his own.

"Unfortunately you have insulted my intended," he said mournfully. "I do detest violence, as I am certain you do, Mr. Evans. But you have chosen to remark unfavorably and in a rather public fashion on circumstances that should remain entirely between Miss Owen and myself. That is regrettable." He shook his head. "Thoroughly regrettable."

Christmas Evans, his mouth gaping, stood like a statue, his brows drawn together fiercely. Even by the dim light of the tomb, his face looked florid. His coal-black gaze moved from Gideon to Gwynna and back again. "What is going on here?" he demanded. "This must be some sort of trick."

Gwynna stepped forward. "The duke is pleased to intervene in our squabble, Evans, but this is between you and me. I have no plans to marry—"

"Before autumn," Gideon quickly finished. "That is another reason that Mr. Evans's slanderous accusations are so inconvenient." He placed a warning hand on Gwynna's shoulders, ignoring her outraged expression. "I should not care to have our reputations bandied about in such a brazen manner in the meantime. That is why I am afraid I must insist on satisfaction."

He smiled pleasantly, but Evans felt a chill at the steel in that gaze. His own eyes narrowed. There was something afoot here. Most likely the duke was bluffing. For whatever reason, it did not suit Claremont to have Gwynna disgraced before the whole island. Evans's lips curled into a toothy smile. Claremont would soon learn the consequences of trying to outfox Christmas Evans.

"I meant no insult," Evans replied smoothly. "Why, I had no idea that Gwynna was keeping such happy news from us.

That she is your betrothed makes the situation less . . . difficult." He cleared his throat. "But you must agree that the fact that you passed the night in such circumstances makes the exchange of vows more urgent, if only to protect Gwynna's reputation."

"Since when have you cared for my reputation?" Gwynna demanded, but her words went unnoticed as Evans and Gideon stared at each other like two dogs before the fight. The air in the cave was thick with tension.

Gideon arched a brow, giving the man one of his haughtiest looks. It was not too difficult to see where the villain was heading. *Well*, he thought in resignation, *in for a penny, in for a pound.*

"I am certain we shall do so at the earliest opportunity," he drawled.

"Wonderful," Evans said, rubbing his hands together. "Of course, you will not wish to risk word getting out about your, uh, night together. That is why I have decided to help you make the best of these rather unfortunate circumstances. I shall perform the ceremony myself, this very moment!"

"What?" Gwynna's shriek echoed off the walls.

"There is no need to rouse the dead, my dear," Gideon remonstrated. He turned to Evans with a pleasant smile. "I do not think a moldy burial chamber is precisely what we had in mind for the wedding ceremony."

"Oh, but this is just the place," Evans enthused, gesturing around him. "Surely Gwynna has told you that her mother claimed to have exchanged vows with the previous duke at the entrance to this very cave. No one believed her, of course. But it *is* quite the spot for lovers."

"This is ridiculous," Gwynna cried. "I have no intentions of marrying Claremont. Let us have an end to this charade."

Evans eyed them both. "Charade?" he repeated with a perplexed look on his face. He turned to Gideon. "Perhaps there is some misunderstanding? You do not plan to be wed after all?"

Gideon's brows rose. "Miss Owen refers to the fact that we have no special license. Nor have the banns been called." He ignored Gwynna's furious gaze.

"Ah. But that is no problem. We dissenters do not recognize Anglican ways. Here on the island our weddings are uncomplicated affairs, a simple pledge between a man and woman. It can be done here and now. I would be happy to oblige. That is, unless there is something you have not told me?"

Only that I already have a wife. Gideon's expression was veiled as a tumult roiled his brain. Then again, what difference did it make? A wedding performed by a deranged Methodist without a license or banns would not be legal under English law. Even a sham wedding would complicate his plans, however. He would be expected to take Gwynna home with him. Very well. He would take her to London and find her a wealthy husband as soon as possible. She would be safely settled, some other man's responsibility. She could return here as Lady Bountiful, bestowing the man's money on whatever cause suited her. She could tell her friends that she had remarried after her duke became impotent or died, or whatever she cared to say. No one on this remote island would know otherwise. The main thing was that she would not be in disgrace. He owed her that, at least.

"Not at all," he responded easily. "Except that we are not moles. I daresay it is more pleasant outside in the sunlight. Now that I think on it, the notion is quite appealing." He stroked his chin. "Yes, I believe we shall accept your offer."

This pronouncement seemed to turn Evans to stone. "Perhaps," Gideon added pleasantly, "you would be so kind as to allow my wife-to-be some privacy to repair her attire." He arched his brows expectantly.

Evans stared at them, his mouth gaping at the duke's capitulation. He could have sworn that the man was bluffing. No man of his stature and wealth married a penniless island bastard. "Of course," he murmured at last. "We shall await you outside."

The moment he and the others left, Gwynna turned on Gideon furiously. "Are you insane?" she demanded.

"I do not think so, but the matter is open for debate," he replied. "My dear, please put on those breeches. If I must marry a woman who is dressed like a man, she should at least be thoroughly turned out."

She stared at him in exasperation. "But you are already married!"

Gideon's brows shot skyward. "Do not shout, my dear, or the man will surely hear you. This is only a charade, you know, not legally binding. But do not sign any papers, or we shall be liable for transportation for participating in such a ceremony. I should not worry overmuch, however. There are benefits to a dukedom, and one of them is the ability to avoid the consequences of such trivialities."

"You are a hypocrite," she declared.

Gideon began to brush his wrinkled jacket, although it was clear the task was hopeless. "I am certain a bride has offered her groom more tender endearments on her wedding day," he drawled, "but I suppose I shall have to be satisfied with that."

Gwynna crossed her arms. "I will not do this, Englishman." She began to pace the chamber.

He looked up from his task and fixed her with a sharp look. "It is your wish to be disgraced as your mother was, then?"

"My reputation is already in shambles. I have nothing to lose."

"Then think of the child."

She halted, startled. "What child?"

He applied himself anew to his jacket, studiously avoiding her eyes. "There might well be a child as a result of what has passed between us," he said lightly. "I cannot think you would wish it to be called bastard."

She blanched. "I would kill anyone who did."

His mouth thinned. "That would be very satisfying, I am sure. But it would not help the child. You cannot kill everyone who jeers at your offspring. You know better than anyone that such remarks will come, even from other children, and that they will take their toll."

Gwynna took a deep breath. "What you say is true. But I do not see how participating in a sham ceremony will solve the difficulty. You would still not be my lawful husband."

He waved a hand of dismissal. "Another triviality. We will simply find you one posthaste, my dear. That way any child you have will be born in wedlock."

She stared at him in amazement. "Just like that? You talk as if it is so easy."

He smiled. "When the size of the dowry I intend to give you becomes known, there will be no shortages of suitors willing to overlook the fact that you may be carrying another man's child."

She scowled. "You would buy me a husband, then."

"That is why it is known as the Marriage Mart, my dear. I did not invent the system."

"It is abhorrent," she said, appalled. "So typically English."

Gideon sighed. "We may discuss its merits or lack of them at another time. At the moment, your Mr. Evans is waiting to marry us."

"Why can we not simply wait until I know whether I am breeding?"

"Because by then the entire island will know about last

night. You—and any child of our union—will be thoroughly disgraced." He eyed her impatiently. "Come, let us go."

"No." Her chin was set in a stubborn line, but he could see a trembling about her lips.

"Gwynna," he said softly, "it is my weakness that brought us here. Let me do what I can to make amends. Let me protect you. After today, that man will not dare to bother you again."

"Weakness?" she echoed in surprise. "What do you mean, Englishman?"

He touched her chin with his fingertip, then bent down and brushed her lips with his. "This," he whispered, drawing her close.

Gwynna's body trembled as she felt his warmth through the softness of his shirt, felt his heart beat against hers. His lips brushed her earlobe. All the memories of the night returned.

"Please," he whispered, his hot breath sending shock waves through her.

The copper fire in his eyes made her heart hammer mercilessly. There was an odd thundering in her ears. It would mean nothing, he had said. A simple charade to protect the child. Slowly, scarcely daring to breathe, Gwynna allowed him to take her trembling hand and lead her out of the darkness.

"I DO NOT WANT YOUR MONEY. You are trying to ease your conscience for what happened in the tomb and for that farce of a wedding." She eyed him indignantly. "Your newfound concern for my financial security is touching, Englishman. But I shall not be paid off like some common whore."

Gideon looked away from the pleasant scene he had been contemplating out the carriage window. "We have been over this," he said wearily. "This money is not intended as payment for anything. It is money that is yours. As William Traherne's daughter and now as my ward."

She eyed him disdainfully. "I shall not take one farthing for a dowry. I have no wish to curtsy and scrape before fawning fribbles who care for nothing but the cut of their clothes and the size of my bank account."

"You will take what I give you," he said sharply. "I shall have the papers making you my permanent ward drawn up forthwith."

"I do not wish to be your ward. I want only what is due me as William Traherne's daughter."

He sighed. "That you shall have. I have told you that repeatedly. The papers will acknowledge your legitimacy."

"You do not know the truth of that," she said defiantly. "We found nothing on Anglesey to substantiate my parents' marriage."

"Let us just say that it is most convenient now to assume that they wed. The marriage prospects of the legitimate daughter of a duke are vastly superior to those of a by-blow."

She crossed her arms and glared at him, but the jostling of the carriage forced her to abandon her defiant pose in order to hold onto the seat. "You are an utter hypocrite," she retorted.

"So you have said." Gideon turned his head back toward the window.

"And a bigamist."

He raised a brow. "There was no crime committed, Gwynna. That ceremony was as insubstantial as one of those Druid spirits of yours."

"Oh!" She glared at him. "You know nothing, English-man."

Gideon closed his eyes and tried to retreat into sleep. Not

that he would rest easy in this carriage with a furious
Gwynna Owen. He wondered whether she had her dagger
strapped in its usual place, and whether she was at this
moment contemplating sticking it between his ribs. Oh,
well. Soon they would be in Cheshire, just long enough to
assemble a proper wardrobe for her. Then they would be on
to London. Soon, but not soon enough, she would be some
other man's headache.

Bigamist. The thought was laughable. There was nothing
remotely valid about that idiot Evans's rambling wedding
ceremony. The man had looked so ill with rage that Gideon
doubted he knew what he was saying. Gwynna herself had
been too dazed to do anything but mutter her vows
incoherently. Gideon was glad he had not given her time to
reconsider the ceremony. She would never have seen that it
was the only way to save her reputation and protect her from
that snake.

Now he was honor-bound to secure her future. It was the
price he had to pay for what had happened in the tombs.
And for what must never happen again.

Gideon opened one eye. She was sitting opposite him,
staring out the window as her beloved Wales rambled by.
She was still furious. He could tell by the set of her
shoulders and the high color that suffused her cheeks. Her
eyes were a deeper shade of blue than usual, and her fingers
were clenched tightly in her lap.

They had set out almost immediately after the ceremony,
pausing only to gather Gwynna's clothes at her cousin's
house and stop for his things at the Bull's Head Inn. All that
time Gwynna had barely said a word. It was only now, after
they had been on the road for hours, that her tongue had
begun to unleash an angry torrent of words.

She would calm down. Reason would prevail. She would
see that finding a husband was the only way. Of course, it

would take time, time they did not have if she were already breeding. Moreover, she would undoubtedly insist on approving of the man, and he had a sinking feeling that she would be hard to please.

And, to tell the truth, he would not see her wed to just anyone. No, her husband must be honorable and kind, not the sort to be blinded by lust for her dowry and her beauty. He must be the sort of man who would appreciate her finer qualities, her fierce independence and determination, her will to fight for what she believed in, her refusal to be cowed by the obstacles facing her. Her future husband would have to understand that Gwynna Owen, despite her small size, deceptively fragile build, and strange beliefs, was made of strong, noble stuff. Not just any man would do for such a woman. If not for Elizabeth . . .

Gideon swallowed the lump that came to his throat. There was no use going down that road. He stared at the petite woman across from him, trying to imagine a tiny babe with her eyes, her hair.

IT WAS A FULL QUARTER HOUR before Gideon heard the sounds of the chains indicating that Rowland was at last endeavoring to open the door. In the meantime, he and Gwynna stood stiffly on the crumbling steps in the same awkward silence that had prevailed during the trip here.

"Damnation," Gideon muttered. "I have been gone nearly a month. One would think the workmen would have gotten around to doing something about the door."

"Perhaps," Gwynna said with mock sweetness, "it is because there is so much else to occupy their attention." She gave him a speaking look as a large chunk of rock fell from a high stone carving, barely missing his head.

He glared at her. "One of these days, Miss Owen, that sharp tongue of yours will get you in trouble."

"I am sure it would be preferable to the present state of affairs, Englishman," she said in a chilly voice.

The door creaked open, and Gideon was forestalled from agreeing with her. When Rowland greeted them a moment later, however, Gideon began to understand that things indeed could get a great deal worse.

"Ah, Your Grace," the servant said. "I apologize for the delay. We have just been seeing to the comfort of your guest."

Gideon frowned. "My guest?"

"She arrived this morning."

"*She?*" A sense of foreboding began to creep over him.

"I am afraid that the bedchambers are still not what they should be," the servant rattled on, "but I believe we have managed to accommodate her."

"Rowland, just who is this guest of mine?"

Gideon's eyes shot to Gwynna, who was looking around in obvious boredom—that is, until a female voice trilled a greeting from somewhere behind Rowland's balding head.

"Gideon!"

He looked up in horror at the figure that appeared in the doorway. "Elizabeth!"

Gwynna's head shot up. Gideon felt her keen sapphire eyes on his face as he watched the elegantly dressed young woman tripping lightly down the steps toward him. He knew that it pleased Gwynna to see him so discomfited. The wretched imp.

An enigmatic smile flitted about Gwynna's lips as she stepped forward to greet the Duchess of Claremont.

"Your Grace," she said politely. "It is a pleasure to meet you. I believe that we have *much* in common."

Gideon uttered a low curse.

CHAPTER 13

IF ELIZABETH WAS SURPRISED TO SEE HIM RESIDING IN A MOLDY old castle, she did not show it. She was too much the lady to react with anything but aplomb at the shoddy surroundings. Still, the workmen had made some progress, and if the castle was in shambles, it was at least improving. What puzzled Gideon was the reason for her sudden visit. This he was to learn when she floated into his study an hour after his arrival. She looked lovely in pale lilac taffeta. Half-mourning suited her far better than those black silks in which she had draped herself until a few months ago. The lilac complemented her golden hair, which was swept back into a sleek coil at her neck. She smiled shyly.

"I did not tell your butler that I was your wife," she began nervously, "so I suppose he thought it odd that a young lady with only a maid in attendance would come all this way to visit an unattached gentleman."

Gideon tried to imagine Rowland even noticing such a detail. "I assure you," he said dryly, "he never gave it a thought."

Elizabeth sat somewhat tentatively in a worn leather chair and adjusted her skirts. "I did not know whether your staff knew about me," she said, twisting a lace handkerchief in her hand. "Since our marriage has remained secret for so long, I wondered whether you preferred to keep it so."

Gideon looked at her in astonishment. "I thought I had

made my wishes clear, Elizabeth. I have repeatedly asked you to agree to repeat our vows so there can be no question about our marriage. It is you who have insisted on secrecy." He rubbed his temples. "I assure you," he added in a strained voice, "that I have long wearied of this charade."

Elizabeth rose abruptly, her ivory skin even paler than usual. She brushed a wispy tendril away from her face. "You have been extraordinarily patient this year," she said, her voice betraying a slight tremor. "I am sorry it has taken me this long to come to my senses. After Mother and Father died, I simply could not face the notion of being married. It did not seem right, somehow, to try to claim my happiness in the midst of such sorrow."

Her limpid green eyes filled with tears, and she took a deep breath. "I wish to be married as soon as possible, in the proper way," she said in a firm voice. "I wish to be a proper wife."

Her bottom lip trembled, and her lashes fluttered against the tears. Gideon reached her side just as they streamed down her cheeks.

"Elizabeth," he murmured, taking her into his arms, "there is no reason to cry." He tilted her chin so that he could study her face. "Unless you are not sure, that is. A year is a long time. Perhaps your feelings have changed."

This suggestion precipitated a new burst of crying. Elizabeth blew her nose into the delicate snippet of lace. "No, Gideon," she said tearfully, the words barely audible through her handkerchief, "they have not changed. I wish to be married."

Gideon eyed her consideringly. Despite the strained look her crying had given her, she looked healthy and well. She had lost the gauntness that she had worn since her illness. Perhaps those doctors had known what they were about after all.

Now he would have a wife. There would be no more secrecy. He waited for the expected surge of joy but was not completely surprised that one did not come. It would take time—and patience—to get to know each other again.

He bent to kiss her. It still felt odd, thinking of Elizabeth as his wife. They had always been friends, but in a short time she would be much more than that—his helpmate and lover. As their lips met, he tried to ignore thoughts of another woman who at such a moment would have vigorously returned his kiss, challenged his thin control, and driven him mad with passion. Elizabeth merely stood still, waiting for him to finish. Her lips were dry and unresponsive.

With a sinking feeling, he abandoned the kiss, wondering if this marriage would be a different sort of purgatory, perhaps more painful than the year-long ordeal he had just endured.

He felt a rising sense of panic. And an enormous feeling of loss. It was all because of Gwynna, the little imp, that he could think of no other woman. She had her revenge. Damned, bloodthirsty Welsh.

THE DUCHESS OF CLAREMONT was actually quite nice, Gwynna thought grudgingly. She did not allow people to call her "Your Grace," preferring to be called Lady Elizabeth, presumably because she wished to keep her marriage a secret, for reasons best known to her. The servants did not even appear to know about it. Neither did the duchess hang on the duke's arm, or smile affectionately at him, or even visit his room at night. Of this last fact Gwynna was acutely aware, as she still occupied her old chamber next to his.

Marriage between members of the *ton* was evidently an odd sort of arrangement. Then again, these English were always arranging things without the least sensibility of the effect upon one's feelings. Witness the duke's misguided plan to fob her off on some witless English lord.

She propped her chin in her hands and stared glumly out the window of her room. There really was no choice. He was offering her the means to secure her own future, lift the cloud from her parentage, and gain enough money in the process to help the islanders. It was an honorable offer, more honorable than a woman in her position might expect. What did it matter if she had to put up with some offensive English dandy she had not yet even met, endure his oafish lovemaking, and bear his children? There was no future in staying here, watching Gideon and his wife together while jealousy ate away at her.

Gwynna sighed. The ancients must have had a remedy for the sick and unhappy feelings consuming her. They would have mixed a potion to make her forget the night in the tomb and all the other times she had shamelessly burned with desire for Gideon Traherne. She must try to remember that he had no need for her; he had a beautiful, elegant wife. Gwynna knew that she could never be part of the world that had produced so elegant a flower as Lady Elizabeth.

But try as she might, she could not see a future without Gideon Traherne in it. Glumly she stared into the sunset.

They ate dinner in the dining room, the workmen having restored the room to a semblance of its former glory. Gwynna commented on its changed appearance.

"Yes, it is much improved without the bats," Gideon observed sardonically.

Lady Elizabeth merely smiled in that blank way that she seemed to adopt with her husband. Gwynna thought it odd that the duchess showed surprisingly little curiosity about her. If the circumstances were reversed, Gwynna knew that *she* would never tolerate her husband traveling about the countryside with a young unmarried woman. But Lady Elizabeth did not seem the sort of woman to be subject to fits of jealousy.

Gwynna found she could not work up any anger toward the duchess, who was far too pleasant and remote to foster such extreme emotions. But the jealousy festered inside, and Gwynna thought she would soon go mad with the effort of maintaining the air of polite pretense that Gideon and his wife had adopted. Playacting must be what life in the *ton* was about, she thought morosely.

She turned to Gideon, who was eyeing the rather dry fricassee of rabbit with an air of resignation. He was dressed impeccably, his snowy white cravat tied in an especially intricate style that he must have devised himself. He looked perfectly comfortable in his exquisite attire, in the manner of one who is born to such elegance. Gwynna, on the other hand, had tripped repeatedly on the long skirt of her new watered-silk gown.

He had greeted her at dinner with an abstracted smile. In fact, in the two days since his wife's arrival, he had barely met Gwynna's gaze. When she did catch his eye, she found a look so shuttered and remote that it put him utterly beyond reach. Gwynna knew it was foolish to think to see some spark, some covert expression that at least acknowledged what they had shared. But his lack of warmth toward her still hurt. Evidently nothing they had shared meant anything to him.

Men of his power and wealth would not be affected by a night of lovemaking, however passionate, with a woman of tarnished name and virtue. They had women falling at their feet; even their mistresses moved in the first circles. A baseborn island nobody would mean nothing to him. He was probably mortified to have her as his ward. With his wife here, the entire situation was undoubtedly most uncomfortable for him. At least he was suffering, Gwynna thought grimly, although not half as much as she.

"When did you mean to go to London?" she asked in a flat voice.

He speared a stalk of asparagus. "As soon as the village seamstress can produce some suitable gowns for you for traveling," he replied. "When we get to London, we will see a proper modiste." He turned to Lady Elizabeth. "It is a relief to have a female to advise my ward on these things. She does not value my advice."

Lady Elizabeth gave Gwynna an unexpectedly warm smile. "Oh, my dear, Gideon's taste is impeccable. But I will be delighted to help. By the time you are ready for your come-out, you will be the most fashionable young lady in London."

"Thank you, Lady Elizabeth," Gwynna murmured. "I really know very little of such matters. But I would not want to take too much of your time."

"Nonsense. I must see the modiste at all events. I must have a wedding gown."

Gwynna stared at her in confusion. "Wedding gown?" she repeated blankly. Gideon, she noticed, had paused with his fork midway to his lips, a strange expression on his face.

Elizabeth colored. "Oh, that is— Oh, Gideon, Gwynna is your ward. Should she not be told?"

He put down his fork. He did not look pleased. "This is between us, Elizabeth."

But Gwynna was not to be put off so easily. "Do I understand that you mean to purchase a wedding gown, Lady Elizabeth? For *yourself*?"

Elizabeth bit her lip and looked an appeal at Gideon, who was eyeing Gwynna in irritation. "Leave it, imp," he ordered. "This does not concern you."

Gwynna's eyes darkened to deepest blue as she fixed him

with a steady gaze. "That is not precisely true, sir," she said evenly. "As your ward and the daughter of William Traherne, I find the matter of your marriage of great interest."

"We really should tell her," Lady Elizabeth interjected softly. "I thought you were weary of secrecy, Gideon."

He looked into the two pairs of eyes, one earnest and pleading, the other bordering on murderous. He sighed. "Very well, Elizabeth." He turned to Gwynna. "Elizabeth and I are getting married." At her stunned look, he quickly added, "Again."

Gwynna stared at him, dumbfounded.

"Oh, Gideon," Elizabeth remonstrated, "you cannot simply leave it at that. Gwynna, my dear, I quite understand that this must be confusing. The truth is that Gideon and I were wed in Vienna a year ago, but we kept it a secret. I was too ill to truly participate in the wedding service, and Gideon has always had some doubts about the man who performed it. I am not certain that the marriage would be recognized here. Gideon has been urging me to repeat our vows in the church to remove any question about the matter. It has taken me a long time to recover from my parents' death and my own illness, however."

She pursed her lips. "It was I who insisted on secrecy," she said, blinking rapidly, and Gwynna saw a glistening of tears in her eyes. But Lady Elizabeth smiled brightly. "Now we plan to have an official wedding, just as though it is the first and only one." She looked quickly at Gideon. "Gideon has been very patient."

Gwynna blinked in astonishment. "So you are not really . . . that is, you are not . . ."

"Elizabeth *is* my wife," Gideon said curtly. "The wedding will be but a formality."

Elizabeth played with her napkin. "Gideon and I were pledged to each other before my parents succumbed to the plague in Vienna. I was near death myself when he sent for that cleric. I have never understood why he did so, but——"

"That does not matter," Gideon interrupted in a strained voice.

"Gideon was wonderful," Elizabeth continued, a tremor in her voice. "And of course he has paid for my convalescence, all my doctors——"

"That is enough, Elizabeth," he commanded harshly.

Lady Elizabeth looked at him in surprise. "Why, Gideon," she said reproachfully. "I do not recall when I have ever heard you so out of temper."

Gwynna's eyes narrowed as she absorbed this information. It seemed possible that he was not married after all, not in the eyes of any English authority, anyway. He had lied to her—or at least not told her the whole truth. "Perhaps," she offered sweetly, "the duke is out of countenance because his past has just caught up with his present."

Abruptly he scraped back his chair and rose to his feet. Then he strode from the room, right into the hapless footman who was bringing in the pudding. There was a crashing sound, accompanied by a splatter.

"Oh, your boots, sir," the footman cried. "I am terribly sorry, Your Grace."

The women heard only a darkly uttered curse.

THE GENTLE TAPPING at her door stirred Gwynna from the murderous state in which she was contemplating her revenge on the Duke of Claremont. The man seemed inordinately fond of questionable weddings. She wondered what lay beyond the tale she had been told at dinner. There was something rather naive about Lady Elizabeth. Had he seduced her? And been forced, after she became ill, to scramble for some disreputable cleric for appearance's sake? Poor Lady

Elizabeth! Sick and orphaned in a foreign country, at the mercy of that insensitive, lust-filled coxcomb.

"May I come in?"

Lady Elizabeth stood on the threshold. She wore a pale pink dressing gown, and her hair had been plaited into a long, smooth braid.

Gwynna scrambled to her feet. "Why, yes," she replied, offering her a chair and taking one for herself. Lady Elizabeth accepted it with a smile. For a moment she played with a thread of her robe. Then she looked at Gwynna, her expression anxious.

"I am afraid you might have gotten the wrong impression of Gideon tonight," she said hesitantly. "It is all my fault, for it is so difficult for me to speak of that time."

"Please, Lady Elizabeth," Gwynna reassured her, "there is no need for you to do so."

Elizabeth smiled. "Oh, no, it is most important," she said. "James—my doctor—says that it is very important to talk about my feelings. He thinks it helps cleanse the body of poisons that produce ill health. I do not pretend to understand such things, but my health has been much better lately, so he must be correct."

Gwynna nodded uncertainly, and Elizabeth continued. "I have noticed that you and Gideon seem to have a rather strained relationship." Gwynna flushed, but Elizabeth merely smiled. "It does not surprise me in the least. Gideon can be very set in his ways. You seem like a most independent young woman. And brave. Gideon has told me of your difficulties."

"I see." But she did not, having no clue as to what yarn he had concocted. Lady Elizabeth soon enlightened her.

"I do so admire you," she said, "taking care of your ailing grandfather all those years until Gideon finally found you. Who would have guessed that the former duke was so eccentric that he told no one of his marriage, or that he had a child? Gideon tells me you were forced to live in poverty all those years until he learned of your existence. He was so surprised to come across the marriage documents among the duke's papers. It is just like him to drop everything to go rescue you from that dreadful island."

Gwynna's expression darkened at the web of half truths he had spun. "Yes," she muttered dourly, "just like him."

"That is what I have come to talk to you about," Lady Elizabeth said. "We are all members of the same family now—or soon will be. I do not know what is the trouble between you and Gideon, but I cannot let you think ill of him because of me."

"Lady Elizabeth," Gwynna began, "there is no need."

"Oh, but there is," Elizabeth insisted. She rose and began to pace the room nervously. "Gideon did not wish to discuss it, but you see, I owe him everything. I admire him more than I can say."

"I suppose that is because you are in love," Gwynna said lightly.

Elizabeth gave her a strange look. "Yes, I suppose," she said. Her face flushed, and she turned away. "My parents and I had joined him in Vienna for a holiday celebrating our betrothal. The town was so gay then, filled with diplomats and parties. It was very exciting. But then Napoleon escaped, and there was chaos everywhere. My parents fell ill, and I had no one to help me take care of them. Gideon took over. Later, when I became ill, he nursed me night and day." She blushed. "I have little recollection of that time. Gideon and I have always been the best of friends, but it is still mortifying for me to think of how intimately he cared for me."

That did not sound like something a wife would say about her husband. Gwynna eyed her curiously. Lady Elizabeth must have read her mind, for she turned to face her, an expression of intense embarrassment on her face.

"I still do not know why he sent for that cleric. Gideon's ways are sometimes mysterious to me. I think he thought to protect me by giving me his name. Perhaps he was afraid it would be discovered that he was staying in my room. But there was too much chaos for anyone to pay any attention to us. Later I worried that word would get out that we were married in havey-cavey circumstances. But even though one of Gideon's friends witnessed the ceremony, there had not been so much as a whisper about our scandalous wedding. Gideon has respected my wish for secrecy. He has played his part well." Elizabeth smiled. "The entire *ton* thinks him one of the most eligible bachelors in London."

She took a deep breath. "Gideon saved my life and safeguarded my reputation. I owe him everything. But I have repaid him miserably, I'm afraid. I forced him to endure a year of waiting while I was mired in despondency and indecision. He has had to live like a monk."

Gwynna nearly fell off her chair. "A *monk*?" she repeated numbly.

Lady Elizabeth flushed deep red. "I know that men have urgings," she said hesitantly. "It cannot have been easy for him to spend a year in a marriage in name only. I have urged him to take a mistress, but he will not hear of it. Gideon is such an honorable man. He is really quite different from the way he chooses to have the world see him. He is—"

"Do you mean to say," Gwynna interrupted, "that you and the duke have not—" She broke off, aghast at her own rudeness. "I am sorry, Lady Elizabeth. This is none of my business."

Elizabeth gave a shaky laugh. "I did not intend to give such a full accounting of our marriage," she acknowledged, blushing. "But it is true. Though Gideon and I have been friends for years, we have never been lovers."

Not lovers! Gwynna could hardly comprehend it. Then perhaps that night in the tomb had meant something to him after all. She frowned. Or perhaps he had simply been without a woman for so long that he could not resist what she had so freely offered. *That* seemed unlikely, however. Gideon Traherne was an extremely handsome and desirable man. There must have been dozens of women willing to help him, however unwittingly, over the temporary celibacy of his marriage.

Lady Elizabeth sniffed into her handkerchief, and Gwynna was instantly remorseful at such thoughts. "That will change," Gwynna said gently, "once you are married."

"Yes," Lady Elizabeth replied shakily.

She put her handkerchief to her face and, with a muffled "good night," left the room.

"I will have this letter sent off immediately, Your Grace." Aloysius Busby eyed the duke uncertainly. His Grace was as dapper a member of the quality as he had ever seen— keen eyes, a strong chin, an imposing physical specimen, not in the least enfeebled. But the man's mind had evidently been greatly altered since his trip to Wales. He had just dictated a letter to his London solicitors directing them to prepare papers allocating the princely sum of seven thousand pounds annum to Miss Gwynna Owen, the young woman with whom he was at drawn daggers only a month ago. It seemed perfectly aboveboard; the young woman was to be made the duke's permanent ward. There was the unsettling fact, however, that the duke could produce no documents providing Miss Owen's legitimacy.

"What shall I say about the marriage lines?" Mr. Busby asked after a moment's hesitation.

The duke looked at him from under a pair of arched brows. "It is not necessary to say anything other than that I have discovered that the late duke was married to Miss Owen's mother," he said testily.

"But— That is, the solicitors will want some proof," Mr. Busby ventured. "The revelation that His Grace was married may affect other aspects of the estate."

The duke tapped his fingers impatiently on his desk. "It is not convenient for me to provide the documents at the moment, Mr. Busby. At all events, my solicitors work for me, as do you. I assume they will be happy to take me at my word."

There was no mistaking the sharp gaze in the duke's eyes. Mr. Busby quickly nodded. "As you say, sir."

"Good. Now, Busby, you will direct the solicitors to draw up the settlement documents for my wife."

"Your *wife*?" Mr. Busby's mouth fell open. "I had no idea that you had married, Your Grace. May I offer my belated congratulations."

The duke rose in irritation. "No, Busby, you may not. I am afraid I misspoke. I should have said that the papers are for my *fiancée*, Lady Elizabeth Throckmorton."

Mr. Busby's forehead furrowed in confusion.

"Do not feel bad, Mr. Busby," came a voice from the doorway. "The entire matter is just as confusing to the duke."

Mr. Busby looked up to see Miss Owen, her appearance drastically altered since he had last seen her. She wore a sedate gown of robin's egg blue trimmed at the neck and sleeves in ivory lace. It was one of the village seamstress's better efforts, cut with understatement to show off her petite figure to great advantage. Miss Owen's hair was somewhat longer than it had been when he saw her last, and it fanned out like a reddish halo around the delicate features of her face. Those extraordinary blue eyes of hers were gleaming with intelligence and something else. Defiance? Mr. Busby wondered if the duke knew how challenging it would be to have this young woman as his permanent ward.

Evidently he did. Mr. Busby could almost see the lines of strain deepen on the duke's face. But His Grace merely arched his brows in that haughty way of his.

"You are interrupting, imp."

"I merely wanted to show you my new gown. And to tell you that I am going out on the moor. You asked me to inform you of such things, remember?"

The duke glowered. "I asked you to refrain from going out on the moor alone, if I recall. There is too much seditious activity in the area. I do not wish you to run into any unsavory types."

She lifted her chin. "I have a dagger. I shall be perfectly safe."

The duke rolled his eyes heavenward. "Take a footman, Gwynna. We have more than one now, you know."

"No."

"Very well. Then stay here."

"We are leaving in three days. There are prayers to be offered. The rock outcropping half a mile from here is just the right site."

The duke eyed her in consternation. "Prayers?"

She met his gaze with quiet dignity. "It is necessary to offer sacrifices before doing battle, Englishman. It is the way of the Owens."

"Gwynna, we are merely going to London," he said in exasperation. "There are no battles to be fought. It is a perfectly civilized place."

She simply eyed him steadily.

After a moment, the duke threw up his hands. "Very

well," he said with a sigh. "I will escort you after I finish my business here."

"Thank you." She turned and left the room. The duke's gaze lingered on the doorway for a long time afterward.

Aloysius Busby thought he had never seen such troubled eyes.

CHAPTER 14

HE WAS DOING THE RIGHT THING. IT WAS ABSOLUTELY NECESSARY to keep that thought uppermost in his mind. It was imperative that he go through the wedding ceremony with Elizabeth, imperative that he provide for Gwynna and find her a husband. There were two women in his life now. Two women whose futures rested in his hands.

He was going to lose his mind.

Gideon spurred Captain onward. He had elected to ride rather than travel with Gwynna and Elizabeth in the confines of a closed carriage. The wind felt good on his face, freeing somehow, though he knew that was but an illusion. Everywhere he turned there were responsibilities and obligations. It had been that way since his parents' deaths shattered his world and abruptly ended his childhood. It was then that he learned the necessity of pretending to be someone he was not.

During the war, his associates had been puzzled by the way the strain of clandestine activities had rolled off him like so much rainwater off a downspout. To them, he appeared unflappable, the carefree dandy who refused to take death seriously, who weathered danger with equanimity.

She knew, the infuriating wench, that it was all a facade. That the reason danger held no more meaning for him than a game of charades was that he had already endured far worse than Napoleon and his minions could have devised. There were no words to describe the pain that tore through him when his parents were ripped from his secure, cherished existence and he found himself bereft and in the charge of his father's cold, demanding, soulless cousin.

William Traherne.

A man as devoid of passion as he was of sensibility, who cared not a whit for his new charge, who saw the young viscount as an onerous claim upon his time. A man as heartless and calculating as anyone Gideon had ever met, who had not a shred of humanity in his shriveled soul.

Who never would have married Gwynna Owen's mother, not in a thousand years.

Gwynna did not know how fortunate she was to have escaped being reared by her father. Perhaps William Traherne had mellowed in his final years, but whatever the man had become, Gideon would forever hold the image of a scowling tyrant standing over him with a cane, beating him to within an inch of his life after his parents' funeral.

"A Traherne does not cry like a woman," the duke had decreed stonily, and Gideon had stood with his head bowed, shamed by the fact that tears ran down his face in rivulets.

Mercifully the duke had never come to visit. Once a year he traveled to London and summoned Gideon in order to deliver his acerbic judgments on the boy's performance at Eton, then Oxford. The rest of the time Gideon was left alone in his parents' town house or at their country estate with only a few servants for company. As an orphan shunned by his only living relative, he had carefully constructed his armor, the elegant veneer that allowed him to move through the glittering world his parents had inhabited without opening any new wounds. With his facade in place, the pain of their loss receded; none of the duke's harsh judgments could reach him. Upon attaining his majority, he simply pretended that William Traherne had never existed. The duke had apparently died alone and friendless; the man deserved whatever sorrow and evil fate dealt him.

But it seemed that Gideon's cousin had had the last laugh, saddling him with a woman who was so different from the passionless soul who sired her that Gideon sometimes doubted whether William Traherne's blood ran in her. Except for the eyes, those devastating sapphire jewels. On the father they had been judgmental, harsh, unforgiving. On the daughter they radiated the fires of life, passion, love.

Gwynna Owen was everything that her father was not. More than that, she was the most captivating and riveting woman he had ever known. She could make him feel things he had not dreamed he was capable of.

He sighed. There was no Druid potion to make him forget her. They were linked on some level that he had just begun to comprehend. She might even be carrying his child, although he tried not to think of that possibility. What he did think of, nearly every waking minute, was the fact that he was about to auction her off to the highest bidder.

With every mile that brought London nearer, Gideon steeled himself. No one played society's game so well as he, or so easily shrugged his shoulders at grim reality. But he would need all his skills and then some to see this little drama through. That was why he must always remember that he was doing the right thing.

If only his dreams were not filled with sapphire flames.

ELIZABETH THROCKMORTON TOOK A DEEP BREATH and opened her door. The only noises in the inn came from the tavern room below them. On this corridor all was silent. She stepped into the hall, pausing outside Gwynna's room. There was not a sound within; Gwynna had probably been asleep for ages.

Elizabeth grimaced, trying to remember when she had last enjoyed a peaceful night's sleep.

Tomorrow they would be in London. The chain of events would be set in motion, and they would be caught up in a whirlwind of activity. She would never get another opportunity like tonight. She smoothed her hair. It fell over her shoulders like spun gold. James had once told her that, although it was exceedingly improper of him. He had realized it the instant the words were out and had flushed beet red.

She straightened her flowing pink robe. James had liked this, too, although he had never said so. She could read it in his eyes. Doctors were not supposed to look at their patients in quite that way. James was very careful to have a nurse present during her examinations, but sometimes the nurse turned her head, and Elizabeth could see the yearning in his eyes. They were nice eyes; brown, and steady. Like him.

During her months at the convalescent home, they had become friends, like her and Gideon—only different somehow. James's face was very earnest and sincere, already showing the lines from the emotions that were reflected so easily there. There was no mystery about James's feelings.

He was in love with her.

Elizabeth slipped down the hall toward Gideon's room. Her pulse pounding. She had told James everything; he understood why she had to marry Gideon properly, although he had looked at her with such sad eyes at the time that her heart had nearly broken. He had held his tongue, not speaking the words that she knew he desperately wished to say. James was an exceedingly honorable man.

Just once, though, he had done something most improper. They had been alone in the garden, having taken a late-evening stroll to watch the fireflies. As he pulled her into his arms, Elizabeth's pulse had raced out of control. When he kissed her, she had felt the most amazing urges. Accordingly, she had kissed him back, something she had never done with Gideon. His response had both scared and thrilled her. Elizabeth remembered the feel of his hands as they moved over her, the hardness of his body as he pressed her to him. It was the most exciting experience she had ever had. Almost immediately, however, he tore himself away and delivered a halting, breathless apology that left her wishing that he were not such a proper young man after all. That realization had caught her by surprise. She had never before given such matters a thought.

She paused with her hand on Gideon's door. James would always live in her memory. But a passion like theirs was not the stuff that lasting relationships were built on. Respect, duty, position—these were the backbone of marriage.

When she left the home just two weeks ago, she had been at peace with her decision. She had been prepared to sacrifice love and passion for the marriage her parents had so wanted for her, the marriage she herself had wanted a year ago. But since arriving at Claremont Castle, her resolve had weakened. She had felt nothing with Gideon, not even when he had kissed her. He was most handsome, and it was pleasant being with him. But there was not that giddy sensation that erupted with James.

Surely it was possible to feel a spark of passion for a man she did not love. She must not let Gideon down again. She had to give his kisses a chance, had to know if they could be happy in *that* way. Tonight she would find out. She could not imagine why she had any doubts, really. The ladies fell all over him; she was sure his lovemaking would be expert. Not that she knew about such things, but she was determined to learn for herself. For she had begun to think that such matters were very important after all.

Taking a deep breath, she knocked lightly on his door.

"Gideon?" she said softly. "It is Elizabeth."

There was a momentary silence, then a muffled response. "Just a moment."

The door swung open. Gideon was wearing a dressing gown that appeared to have been hastily wrapped around him. He looked groggy with sleep.

"What is wrong?" he asked, his brows furrowed in concern.

She managed a smile, though inside she was quaking. She had never seen Gideon without his formal attire. In his nightclothes, he looked so . . . masculine. The edges of the dressing gown did not meet completely over his chest. She wondered how James would look similarly attired. Perhaps if she imagined that Gideon were James, she could manage this. "May I come in?" she asked tentatively.

He arched a brow but stepped back to allow her entry. He did not close the door. Instead he merely stood there, waiting for her to speak.

"I— Gideon, could you close the door, please?" she said, feeling terribly awkward.

He gave her a questioning look, but obliged and crossed the room to light a candle. He placed it on the table next to the bed, then turned to look at her. Even in his robe, Gideon cut an imperial figure. Elizabeth felt most awkward, not knowing whether to sit or stand or simply plant herself in front of him and demand that he kiss her. How did one go about seduction? Particularly with a man who was subjecting her to such unnerving scrutiny.

"What is this about, Elizabeth?" he asked when still she failed to speak. "Are you ill?"

"No," she replied quickly. "That is—I have never done this before, Gideon. You must excuse me."

His brow furrowed again. "Done *what*, Elizabeth?"

Blushing furiously, she looked down at her feet. She took

a deep breath. "We shared the most unthinkable intimacies in that hotel in Vienna, Gideon—even though I was not aware of it—but I still feel rather awkward standing here in your room."

"Of course you do," he said gently, moving toward her. "There is nothing to be afraid of, Elizabeth. Please tell me whatever it is that is bothering you. I will not take advantage of the situation. You do not have to worry that I will press my attentions on you."

Her head shot up in irritation. "Fiddlesticks, Gideon. That is just what I want you to do. You see, I am trying to seduce you. I just do not know how it is done."

His brows arched skyward, and he stared at her as if she had two heads. "Seduce me?" he repeated blankly.

Elizabeth pouted. "You need not gape at me as if I were a fly in your soup. You could make it easier. I am quite certain that you know much more about these things than I do."

He frowned, still trying to comprehend. "You wish me to make love to you?" he asked incredulously. "Why?"

She forced a smile to her lips. "Because we are married. Or about to be. It is the same thing, I suppose. Do not married people do such things?"

He placed his hand under her elbow and guided her gently toward a chair. His face was full of solicitous concern. "It is your illness, again, is it not? I will speak to that doctor personally. He should not have discharged you so soon . . ."

"My doctor has nothing to do with this," Elizabeth cried, then clapped her hands over her mouth in mortification.

He eyed her in consternation. "Elizabeth, will you stop shrieking? Sit down and tell me what this is all about."

Elizabeth perched gingerly on the edge of the chair, every

nerve and muscle tensed. He was angry. She had made a muddle of things.

"I suppose I am somewhat nervous about our marriage," she said at last. "After all this time, we are finally to be husband and wife. I thought to see what it was like. You know, to . . . to lie together." She looked up at him, her face awash in embarrassment.

He blinked in astonishment. "I hardly think this is the time," he began, then stopped suddenly to clear his throat.

"Nonsense," she said airily. "How can there be a better time? There is no one here but us." She patted her hair nervously and smoothed the edge of her robe. Then she looked into his face, her eyes imploring. "Please, Gideon."

He stared at her, his face unreadable. Elizabeth felt utterly humiliated. Apparently making love to her was the farthest thing from his mind. He probably thought she was insane for barging into his room and propositioning him so brazenly. He certainly did not want her. Her body sagged in despair. She felt like crawling under the chair.

But then he pulled her gently to her feet and, wrapping his arms around her, kissed the top of her head. It was comforting, but more brotherly than she had in mind. Tentatively she lifted her face to his. His penetrating eyes searched hers. Very slowly, his mouth descended. Elizabeth felt her lips tremble as he touched them.

His kiss was very expert. At least she supposed it was. His lips brushed hers gently, teasingly, with steadily increasing pressure until they settled nicely into place over the fullest part of her mouth. Dutifully returning the kiss, Elizabeth discovered that his tongue was flirting with her lips, demanding entry. She quickly obliged, and the kiss deepened into a most startling exercise. His hands stroked her hair, then moved down her back to press her into him.

She was conscious of his firm chest against her breasts as his hands began to wander over her. When they slipped inside the front of her robe and began to work the buttons of her gown, Elizabeth drew back in alarm. James had never taken quite so many liberties, and she was not certain that things should go this fast. But then, Gideon was her husband—or would be soon. It was all most confusing.

He was watching her face, his eyes carefully hooded. "Do you wish to stop?"

Elizabeth took a deep breath. "No," she said firmly. "Please continue."

Even as she spoke, he had already resumed his gentle exploration of her person. He made short work of her buttons, and soon his fingers were teasing her nipples, encircling them in a tantalizing motion that sent goose bumps down her spine. She wondered whether James would know such tricks. He must. He was a doctor, after all.

Elizabeth felt weak as she imagined James's strong, capable hands doing such delicious things to her. She wondered whether his body would move against hers in such a delightful rhythm, whether his fingers would trail in such a riveting fashion down to the tender part of her thighs, wandering upward until they touched that most private place, sending tremors through her body.

With an abrupt cry, Elizabeth broke free of Gideon's embrace. Fumbling with her gown, she managed to join most of the buttons before she looked up at him, tears streaming down her face.

"I am sorry, Gideon," she said unsteadily. "I suppose I am too nervous." With a quick, jittery smile, she ran to the door, threw it open, and darted back to her room.

From his doorway Gideon watched silently until she was safely inside. Then he closed his door and walked over to snuff out the candle. As he reached for it, he saw that his hands were trembling.

"Good God." The words caught in his throat.

GWYNNA PACED HER ROOM, filled with nervous energy, even though it was hours past midnight. She was mulling the same thought that had consumed her for three days, since that night Elizabeth had come to her room.

They had not lain together.

What did she care about the English law that made that hasty Vienna wedding so dubious? She had her own standards for such things. And by those standards he was not married: the vows had not been consummated. Gwynna was exultant.

Lady Elizabeth was a beautiful woman, cut from the same elegant fabric as Gideon. Perhaps he loved her. These English had some curious notions about love. But perhaps he merely felt honor-bound to marry her. The more she thought about it, the more her spirits soared. Not only had he once been betrothed to Elizabeth, he had also gallantly tended her in a manner the English would find most compromising. Yes, he would feel obliged to marry in such circumstances.

Gwynna understood about honor. It was part of her code, too. So why, she asked herself sternly, was she contemplating such an outlandish plan? A plan that, if successful, would send honor to the bottom of the sea? The answer was as plain as could be.

She was in love with Gideon Traherne.

That she had fallen for a man as different from her as night from day was something she would have to sort out anther time. For now, time was short. They would be in London tomorrow. Action was needed. An image of Elizabeth's beauty drew her up short. She would make a lovely bride, adorned in some fabulous London creation, on the arm of the most elegant man in England.

Gwynna threw up her hands. What was she supposed to do? Strew rose petals in their path? She was too much an Owen for that. No, every instinct she had commanded her to fight. Love was worth fighting for. The Englishman had invaded her soul; she had no choice. Fate had given her this chance. By the time they got to London, it would be too late. She had to act now.

Gwynna knelt before a solitary candle that had burned nearly to a stump. She raised her dagger to the light and allowed it to catch the golden fire as it glinted off the blade. Slowly she chanted:

> *"Eryr digrif afrifid*
> *Owain, helm gain, hael am ged . . ."*

Gideon awoke the instant his door creaked on its hinges. He must have forgotten to lock it. All this madness was making him careless. Slowly he edged his hand under the pillow and gripped his pistol. It fit neatly into his palm.

The door shut quietly, leaving the room in total darkness. But there was now a dark shadow near the door, and he could hear the intruder's soft, shallow breathing. He leveled the pistol at the dark form.

The shadow began moving toward the bed. Gideon frowned. A thief would have headed straight for his clothing or other valuables. This one was advancing on him. A nagging thought entered his brain.

Elizabeth. Could she have returned?

No. This figure was small and moving surely and unmistakably toward him. Elizabeth would probably have hesitated and broken into a fit of nervous crying. He followed the shadow's progress with his pistol. Whoever it was, the figure had a sense for stealth.

It was also whispering. In Welsh.

> "A'r gwiw rwyfg a'r gorefcyn
> A'r glod i'r marchog o'r Glyn."

He swore. It wanted only this to make the night complete. "What in God's name are you about, Gwynna?" he growled.

She halted inches from the bed. He could not see her face, but it was easy to discern the defiant lift of her chin.

"I am here to seduce you, Englishman."

Gideon cursed again.

He set the pistol down, swept the covers aside, snatched the candle from the table, and strode purposefully to the hearth. Fumbling with the punk, he struggled to control the chaos rampaging through his brain. By the time the candle gave off its amber glow, he was more composed. He was also thankful that he had kept his dressing gown on after Elizabeth's visit; it provided at least the illusion of decorum. He turned toward Gwynna, satisfied that he was in control of his faculties.

What he saw nearly made him drop the candlestick. Gwynna Owen was standing before him, clad only in a thin chemise.

"You walked from your room wearing *that*?" he demanded.

She eyed him defiantly. "I was prepared to defend myself, if necessary," she said, raising her dagger to the light. "But everyone is abed at this hour, Englishman. I had no fear of discovery."

Gideon rolled his eyes heavenward. "It is time you got it through your head, Gwynna, that your dagger would be about as useful as a child's toy should you be accosted by some ruffian."

"I had no fear. Owen was with me."

He stared at her. "I do believe you are a candidate for Bedlam." He sank wearily into a chair.

She cocked her head and smiled at him. "You are looking at the situation with English eyes," she said softly. "You should try a different way of seeing." Slowly she knelt on the floor before his chair. With the tip of her dagger, she pushed the straps of her chemise off her shoulders. The garment fell down around her waist. "You have never really looked at me, Englishman," she murmured in a husky voice.

Gideon's eyes were riveted on her. The candle's glow burnished her smooth skin to finest amber, and the shadows caught the sculptured beauty of her breasts. Her eyes radiated heat, their deep blue fire engaging him with stunning directness. He closed his eyes against their fierce invitation. "Go, Gwynna," he rasped. "Take one of my shirts to cover yourself. I will escort you to your room."

"No."

Sudden anger coursed through his veins. Did the little fool have any notion of what she was doing to him? He stared down at her. "I am not a violent man, Gwynna, but I want you gone. I cannot account for my actions if you do not leave this room instantly."

No sudden fear appeared on her face, no sudden shrinking from the possibility of his temper or unbridled passion. Instead a slow smile spread over her tantalizing mouth. Without another word, she began to massage his bare ankles. As he stared at her in appalled fascination, her hands smoothed the bony part of his knees before continuing their inexorable path upward to his thighs. The sudden heat in his groin told him there was not another moment to lose.

"Enough," he growled, struggling to his feet and pulling

her up. He meant to set her away from him, but her body brushed his throbbing hardness as he pulled her to her feet. He groaned and saw her mouth pull into a sensual smile of delight.

"You see, you cannot fight this, Englishman," she said. "It is our destiny."

"The only 'destiny' you and I have, Gwynna Owen," he said severely, "is to find you a husband so that you are no longer my concern." He took a deep breath. Gingerly he slipped the straps of her chemise back in place.

Now if he could just get her out the door. But the same strategy that had dispatched Elizabeth would never work with Gwynna. He had only to show Elizabeth that she did not want him, not yet, although perhaps she would in time, just as in time he would be able to kiss her without thinking of Gwynna's ripe, enticing lips. But tonight Elizabeth had not been ready, despite her stated intentions, and it had been easy to speed her on her way.

Gwynna was another matter altogether. She radiated passion from every pore. And she was determined to have him. God help any man who was Gwynna Owen's destiny.

His eyes narrowed. Was this some new trick? She had objected to his plan to find her a husband; perhaps she thought to distract him, to obscure his duty with her passion. He would not countenance her defiance.

He put his hands on her shoulders and turned her toward the door. "I hope that when we arrive in London," he said in his haughtiest voice, "you are able to keep your wanton impulses under control. None of my acquaintances would wish to take a slut for a wife."

She whirled to face him, and he felt a surge of relief at the fury on her face. That would cool her passion. But though her sapphire eyes glinted steel, there was no sudden tirade of words. Instead she pointed the tip of her dagger at him.

"Take off your robe, Englishman. Even so flimsily attired, you positively reek of sartorial splendor."

Gideon wanted to laugh. The little wench. To think she could threaten him with that piece of tin. She edged around the bed, a strange gleam in her eye.

"I know you do not think I will use this, Englishman," she said in a low, crooning voice. "Perhaps you will have second thoughts when I tell you that Owen has decreed that you shall die tonight unless you make love to me."

Gideon blinked. "I see," he said carefully. "Perhaps you would care to explain why the inestimable Owen has chosen to interfere in my affairs?"

"It is his duty," she replied defiantly. "You are my destiny. He is bound to fulfill the promise."

"What promise?"

"To take care of his own. I am his direct descendant, you recall."

Gideon shook his head. It was time to end this nonsense. "Gwynna," he began, but broke off the instant he saw her hand.

She had taken his pistol from the bed. It was pointed directly at his chest.

"Now, Englishman," she purred with a smile, "you may take off your clothes."

CHAPTER 15

GIDEON STARED AT THE BARREL OF HIS PISTOL BUT, OTHER THAN A mild arching of his brows, gave no sign that the loaded gun pointed at his chest provoked him in any way.

"I do not suppose you have given a single thought to the consequences, not to mention the inconvenience, of having my blood on your hands," he drawled.

The sapphire eyes gleamed wickedly. "Do not be silly, Englishman. To kill you would defeat the purpose." She lowered the pistol but did not put it down. "You half believed me, though, did you not?"

He merely returned her a bland gaze, trying to ignore the murderous anger rising in his own veins. "You flatter yourself, imp. I would never mistake mischief for madness."

"But you might mistake my intent, Englishman," she warned. "That would be a grave mistake. For while I would not put a bullet into your chest, I might well put one into the ceiling. I imagine even the lofty Claremont would be embarrassed if the entire inn was roused by pistol fire to find a naked woman in his bed. Not to mention the effect upon Lady Elizabeth."

His eyes narrowed. "I told you once before, Miss Owen," he said coldly. "I do not suffer extortionists."

She moved closer. "Not even when pleasure is the price demanded?" Her voice was low and husky; despite his anger, it set his pulse to hammering. She toyed with the strap of her chemise.

"Put down the pistol," he ordered, forcing himself to ignore the tightening in his groin.

"Not until you do as I have commanded," she said with sudden ferocity. "I want to see you, Englishman. All of you."

Their gazes locked. *I will kill her for his*, Gideon thought. But as her defiant eyes continued to hold his, he was suddenly arrested by the oddest notion that beneath that blue steel was uncertainty, even anguish. He wondered, then, whether this fierce warrior's role she played so convincingly was *her* armor, keeping her from exposing her need.

Gideon frowned at the thought. It was difficult to imagine Gwynna needing anyone, but perhaps anything was possible. Since their return from Anglesey he had tried to put their relationship firmly back into the realm of what was polite and correct, knowing that he could permit no other way between them. He had assumed that she understood it was because he was bound to Elizabeth. He should have realized that Gwynna was not one to be persuaded by anyone else's idea of what was correct behavior. She had probably been angered and hurt by his aloofness. He would have to explain.

"Gwynna," he began gently, but she cut him off.

"Silence, Englishman," she ordered. "I am waiting for you to obey me. Take off your clothes."

Bloody hell. Anger surged anew in his breast. The woman was as single-minded as a bull moose. Stubborn and unrepentant. Undeserving of sympathy or mercy. His eyes narrowed.

"Perhaps you will be pleased to remember that I do not respond to threats. You will have to take what you want. If you dare, that is."

Her eyes grew wide, and for a moment she looked uncertain. But she did not retreat, except to place the pistol carefully on a stool. He could have taken it then, but he was determined to face her down, the little witch. She stepped forward, this time with her dagger. In one swift movement, she cut the sash that held his dressing gown in place. She pushed the fabric aside with the tip of her blade. The garment fell to the floor in a heap.

Gideon had not counted on feeling so vulnerable as her eyes roamed over him, from the top of his head to the tip of his toes. He could not pretend to be aloof from the exercise, as his arousal was plainly evident.

But Gwynna was not interested in pretense. A low sound escaped her lips, and the dagger clattered to the floor. She smoothed her fingers over his chest as he stood motionless, willing his body not to respond. Her mouth rained soft kisses down the jagged path of his scar as her fingers caressed his flesh into heated pools of desire.

"You are beautiful," she murmured, "like a god."

It was too much. He grabbed her arms and shook her. "Gwynna," he rasped urgently, "I am not a god, or one of your Druids, or one of those fierce Welsh princes of yours. I am only a man, and not a very heroic one at that. I do not even have the strength to send you from this room, although I know that I must. We must stop this now."

She eyed him somberly but said nothing. Instead she pushed him gently backward toward the bed. When the back of his knees touched the mattress, he sat down and watched, spellbound, as she slipped the chemise from her body. Then, completely naked, she lifted her chin and looked at him from brilliant sapphire eyes glistening with unshed tears. He was stunned to see the slight trembling of her lips.

"Gwynna," he murmured helplessly.

She reached for him. Instantly he pulled her into the circle of his body. He ran his hands feverishly over her smooth flesh, exulting in the feel of her skin on his. With a low groan, he laid her gently on the bed. "God help me, Gwynna," he rasped as he covered her body with his. "I cannot help myself."

She put her finger against his lips. "Hush, Englishman," she said. Her voice was thick with desire. "I have already said that you are my destiny. For now, that is enough."

He shook his head in helpless wonder. Later, when he drove himself into her, her fierce cries of passion shook his very soul.

Gwynna stared at the young man sitting in the front parlor of the duke's town house. He did not look like a doctor. In fact, he looked more like a nervous suitor waiting for the appearance of his ladylove. She greeted him with a smile.

"Lady Elizabeth will be right down," she said, wondering what it was about the news that Dr. James Youngblood had come to call that had sent Elizabeth shrieking for her maid to redo her hair.

Elizabeth had been rather out of sorts since their arrival in London, but so had she. Gideon's cavalier treatment angered her. He had deposited them in his house and promptly taken himself off to some hotel, leaving them to the care of his servants and the fashionable shops on Bond Street. They were instructed to spare no expense in completing their wardrobes. A few days after their arrival, a genteel lady by the name of Mrs. Biddingham had appeared, bearing a letter informing them that the duke had hired her to be their companion and chaperon. Gideon himself had not been seen since. That was three weeks ago.

Gwynna was intensely bored by London. One shop was exactly like the next, and she cared not one whit whether the modiste chose the bishop's blue silk or the willow green for her morning dresses. An elegant London miss evidently was expected to wear a great many unnecessary items, from evening hoods for the opera, to crowned bonnets for shopping, to silly cutaway caps for simply sitting around one's house. Gwynna had shocked her chaperon and even Elizabeth by refusing to wear a corset.

Elizabeth had led them on round after round of morning calls, and although London was said to be rather empty of people, Gwynna found herself exhausted by the tedium of innumerable such visits. One was expected to take great delight in the gossip about this party or that, or the latest antics of the Regent's set, but to ignore anything of substance, like the newspaper accounts of disturbances among the iron workers in Staffordshire, the plight of the colliers, the crop failures, and the secret meetings demanding Parlimentary reform.

All the while, the leaders of the country did nothing to ease conditions for the poor and jobless. One sage advanced an absolutely ludicrous proposal to put prostitutes in asylums so that they could weave woolens to support the poor. Did not the fools see that that was no solution to anything? Once or twice during social calls Gwynna had tried to bring up such matters, but her effort was met with such horrified looks from everyone—including Elizabeth—that she quickly subsided into silence.

For all its mindlessness, however, life in London did manage to prevent her from mooning over Gideon. Elizabeth kept them so busy that Gwynna had no time to think. She was glad he was not living with them. It would have been torture to see him every day, to stare at his magnificent hazel eyes and remember the blinding copper fire that had blazed for her that night at the inn.

Evans had been right after all: she was a wanton. She had shamelessly and brazenly thrown herself at Gideon, staging that outlandish drama in his room that had finally stripped him of his defenses. She had disgraced herself utterly in her passion. A man used to refined ladies like Elizabeth would find her behavior repulsive in the extreme. Oh, he had wanted her, that was as clear as the fact that he had taken her against his better judgment. Even in that magical moment when their souls had met in the desperate fulfillment of desire, she had seen the anguish in his face. He did not want her in his life.

There was a new brittleness to her days. Gwynna felt constantly on edge, as if waiting for some disaster to happen. She had meant to fight his plan to marry her off, but to what end now? He still meant to marry Elizabeth. A night of wild passion had not changed that, although she had foolishly hoped that when he saw how perfectly they fit together, how ecstatically their souls met, he would recognize that their destinies were entwined.

She frowned. Perhaps she had misread her fate. Was something this difficult and tormenting truly meant to be? For the first time, Gwynna knew the bitter taste of doubt and defeat.

"James!" Elizabeth's voice was unnaturally high and her color unusually deep as she swept into the room and greeted the young man. Gwynna eyed her curiously. Perhaps Elizabeth had a fever.

"Lady Elizabeth," he replied, rising. "It is good to see you in such fine health."

They stood looking awkwardly at each other for a long moment. Since Gwynna was expected to remain in the room for propriety's sake, she did not think to avert her eyes from what was suddenly a very interesting spectacle.

Finally Elizabeth perched gingerly on a chair near the divan, where the young man then sat at rigid attention. "Dr. Youngblood saved my life, Gwynna," she said, fluttering her lashes.

"Oh? I thought it was the duke who deserved that honor," Gwynna said mischievously.

Elizabeth blushed. "Yes, of course. But Dr. Youngblood is a wonderful doctor. He is the reason I recovered."

The good doctor flushed.

"Tell me, Doctor," Gwynna asked, "what is it that brings you to London? I would have thought your presence in demand at the convalescent home."

Dr. Youngblood cleared his throat. "I came to town to purchase some supplies," he said. "Lady Elizabeth's letter said she was staying at the Claremont town house, so I thought to look in and see how she was doing."

Letter? Gwynna eyed Elizabeth with new interest, noting that she had the grace to blush at the revelation of such unusual correspondence.

Elizabeth's eyes darted quickly to Gwynna. "I felt obliged to inform the doctor about my progress," she said hastily.

"Of course," Gwynna murmured. It was plain to see that these two were besotted. Her mind whirled with this new information. If Elizabeth was in love with Dr. Youngblood, then why was she marrying Gideon? Gwynna knew she would never understand the ways of the *ton*. Perhaps it was unacceptable for a lady of good breeding to marry a lowly doctor. But perhaps, she mused, if given a bit of encouragement, love would take its course. After all, Gideon was not here to protect his interests. Gwynna smiled as the doctor rose after a few minutes to take his leave.

"If you are staying in town for a few days, perhaps you would honor us by coming to dinner," she said cordially. "We never go out at night, you know. The duke plans to launch me properly next month when the parties begin, and I have been properly schooled in the ways of society. But it is dreadfully dull around here at the moment."

The young man's face brightened, and he looked hesi-

tantly at Elizabeth. "I would not wish to impose," he said
carefully.

"Nonsense," Gwynna responded quickly. "We would be
profoundly grateful for the diversion. You must come this
very night."

"Gwynna," Elizabeth began, but Gwynna waved a hand
of dismissal.

"There is nothing amiss in inviting Dr. Youngblood to
dinner," she said. "You will not deprive me of his company.
I have been dreadfully bored of late." She turned the force
of her brilliant eyes on the doctor.

"Tonight," she said and had the intense satisfaction of
seeing him nod.

"GIDEON! I HAVE RUN YOU TO GROUND AT LAST. What in the
name of all that is holy are you doing in London? I expected
you to be enjoying the air in Brighton with the royal set. Or
rusticating in that castle of yours at the very least. But why
a hotel, of all places?" Drew Sinclair eyed him curiously.

Gideon studied the Earl of Westbrook over the rim of his
port. It was his fifth glass, or perhaps his sixth. He had
stopped counting. "You will forgive me if I do not rise to
greet you, Drew," he drawled morosely. "There are too
many wrinkles in these trousers already."

Drew smiled as he took the chair next to Gideon's in the
newly remodeled saloon. He poured himself a glass. "What
has you so blue-deviled, man? I have not seen you so out of
sorts since Vienna. Though there was ample cause then, to
be sure."

"Ah, Vienna. The crux of the problem," Gideon replied
lightly. "But tell me, how is Lady Westbrook?"

The earl shook his head. "Breeding again. And concoct-
ing the vilest potions for her morning sickness. The house
positively reeks of them. I decided to take myself off to

town. I need a new hunter, at all events. Why don't you come with me tomorrow to Tattersall's?"

Gideon arched a brow in an expression of utter boredom. "Horses do not interest me at the moment."

"I see. It is only the port at the Pulteney that consumes your attention, is that it?" The earl eyed him curiously. "Is presiding over a dukedom so wearying?"

Gideon downed the contents of his glass and set it on the table. "Not at all, my friend," he drawled. "It is merely that my solicitors have decided that I have committed not one but two illegal marriages and therefore face scandal and perhaps transportation for my ill-considered acts. It seems that I must marry one of my wives in earnest and persuade the other not to bring the matter before the courts. Meanwhile, the ladies themselves have taken over my house, while I am left to considerably less comfortable quarters here." His mouth quirked upward in an ironic grin. "So you see, there is nothing in the least trying about being a duke."

Drew blinked. "It appears that you are in quite a bumblebath. Would you care to tell me the whole?"

Gideon closed his eyes wearily. "Only if you are prepared to swear secrecy. And if you are not averse to hearing about Druids, Welsh warriors, immortal spirits, and the like. I have discovered that it is sometimes necessary to take such things seriously."

An hour later, the Earl of Westbrook was eyeing his friend in amazement. The cool, polished Gideon Traherne was the last person on earth he would have expected to find embroiled in the affairs of a little Welsh spitfire. He guessed, from the look on Gideon's face, that there had been some omissions in the story of Gwynna Owen. He had a pretty good notion of what those might be, but he made no comment about this. Instead he picked up another thread that had caught his attention.

"You did not need your solicitors to tell you that the ceremony in Vienna was invalid," he said. "I warned you at the time that that priest of yours was a fraud. He would have done anything for the amount of gold you promised him. I own that I was surprised you did not hasten to repeat the vows once you returned home, but I figured that was your business. When I heard that you had inherited the dukedom and were playing the gay bachelor about town, I assumed that you and Elizabeth had come to an understanding to forget the past."

Gideon eyed his friend over the rim of his glass. "I have never properly thanked you for keeping what happened in Vienna a secret. Elizabeth's recuperation was difficult. For many months she would not discuss the future. Now, though, she wishes a proper wedding. I suppose we will be married at St. George's, with all of London in attendance."

"And that is not what you wish?" the earl asked quietly.

Gideon sighed. "Elizabeth is a beautiful woman, an exceptional lady with excellent deportment. She will be an admirable duchess. I should never have to worry about her embroiling herself in scandal. Moreover, with her parents gone, she has no one. I never considered any course of action but marrying her."

"Until you met Miss Owen."

Gideon leveled a steely gaze at his friend. "Miss Owen is a most inappropriate choice for a bride, a fact I intend to keep hidden from whatever nodcock decides to offer for her. She has the ability to make one forget one's . . ." He paused, searching for the word.

"Self-control?" the earl supplied helpfully.

Gideon frowned but did not correct him. "I have certain . . . responsibilities toward Miss Owen now," he said, his expression so pained that it left no doubt in Drew's mind as to how far things had gone. "I intend to see her comfortably settled. But I am obliged to marry Elizabeth. And I shall."

Drew shook his head in sympathy. Gideon merely waved the subject away dismissively. He pulled out his quizzing glass and subjected the earl to mock inspection.

"You know," he drawled, "I have never told you how married life appears to agree with you."

That comment was all the inspiration the earl needed to launch into a recitation of the joys of his marriage. Gideon poured himself another glass of port and listened, an expression of polite interest frozen on his face.

CHAPTER 16

MUD OOZED AROUND GWYNNA'S BOOTS, BUT SHE WAS TOO EXCITED to notice. Around her was a mass of humanity. It was a rough sort of crowd, mostly laborers and craftsmen, restless and seething, with an air of anticipation. She kept to the edge of the field, wary of getting too close, for fear someone would see through her disguise. It had taken some doing to outwit Mrs. Biddingham, but in the end the harried chaperon was only too glad to leave Gwynna to her shopping expedition, as long as her maid was in attendance. Not that Mary was easy to get around, either. It had taken considerable pleading and not a few coins to get the maid to agree to accompany her to Merlin's Cave, a public house near Spafields, where Gwynna took a private parlor and changed into her boy's clothing. From there, it was a simple matter to make her way to the midday rally. But there was no cover of night to enhance her disguise, and Gwynna felt increasingly uneasy. She knew this group was a suspicious lot, always on the lookout for government spies.

Still, the excitement in the air outweighed her fears. Gwynna had been determined to come to this meeting since reading the handbill tacked onto a post in Drury Lane last week. The words of Mr. Henry Hunt had filled her with awe and admiration. Here, at last, was someone trying to do something about the deplorable conditions England had forced on its citizens. The man expressed her own sentiments, only much more eloquently.

And so her heart swelled as she stood on the edge of a muddy field to the east of town, a place she suspected ladies of the *ton* did not even know existed. The assembled crowd was a poor and largely powerless lot, but their courage gladdened her heart.

And there was nothing else to gladden her heart at present, other than the amusing antics of Lady Elizabeth and James Youngblood. The good doctor had somehow found a way to extend his London trip, and so he had become a regular visitor at Gideon's town house. So regular, in fact, that had Gideon ever bothered to appear, he would have surely run into the lovesick pair. It was as plain as punch that Elizabeth and James were meant for each other. And just as plain that they were consumed by guilt. Elizabeth was at sixes and sevens, preoccupied equally by her obligation to Gideon and her love for James. To help matters along, Gwynna had taken to inventing excuses to leave them alone when James came to call. She had also informed the duke's disapproving butler that Mrs. Biddingham's naps were not to be interrupted for such a silly reason as keeping Lady Elizabeth and her doctor company for appearance's sake.

"If a young lady is not allowed to speak privately with her *doctor,* Adams, I do not know what this world has come to," Gwynna admonished the servant.

Gwynna had made it her mission to engage Mrs. Biddingham in such avid conversation after dinner that the good lady quite forgot about the soulful looks and tender sighs that were occupying the couple in the corner of the drawing room. And if Elizabeth and James decided to take a turn in the garden, Gwynna was suddenly consumed by the desire to read aloud to Mrs. Biddingham from one of the chaperon's favorite Minerva novels.

All in all, things were going quite well, with both

Elizabeth and James fair to the breaking point. It would serve Gideon right to find—whenever he deigned to present himself—that Elizabeth was not precisely overjoyed to see him.

They had all benefited from Gideon's absence, in fact. Gwynna had managed to avoid thinking about the cursed man more than a dozen or so times a day, and she supposed she was as well on her way to forgetting about him as could be expected. Which was essential, since next week he was to come gather them all up and embark on the round of parties intended to secure her a husband.

Gwynna clutched the dagger that she had tucked in the waistband of her breeches. Here at the edge of this muddy field, she felt more alive than she had in weeks. She felt useful, as if she could somehow contribute to the change that was in the air, change that men like the Duke of Claremont did not want or understand.

How ironic that in another week she would, as his ward, join the cream of society, the elite that ruled society, dominated Parliament, even held the Regent's purse strings. With their wealth and power, they held sway in everything, whether they were at parties in town or retiring to their enormous estates in the country. Meanwhile, people who went hungry to feed their children stood shoulder to shoulder here, waiting for a savior.

But Mr. Hunt did not come. Instead, a stranger arrived in a hackney coach, driving right into the middle of the crowd, seemingly oblivious of the dirt and mud tossed at the vehicle by the mob. Gwynna gathered that this man was therefore not an emissary of Mr. Pitt's, but it was not clear whether he was a friend of Mr. Hunt's, either. He stood on the roof of the coach and addressed them, gradually winning the crowd's approval.

"Immorality has paved the way for corruption, and

corruption has taken its permanent seat in government," the man shouted. "It cannot be dislodged unless the people rally around and inform those who possess the seat that they had no right to sit there and that the populace has a right to dislodge them."

"Hear, hear," came the shouts.

The stranger lifted his finger in warning. "Be on your guard against enemies, for they are near."

"Hear, hear."

"They are in every quarter of the globe. But do not fear, for it is they who fear you. Their hearts tremble because they know that now is the time, the moment, when tyrants should be made to suffer!"

Gwynna was filled with awe. Here was another who shared her views. There must be many, many more. Her vision was not a false one. Change *was* possible, despite all those stubbornly resistant aristocrats.

With that, the man in the hackney drove off, leaving the crowd stirred to a frenzy of excitement. Then word came that Mr. Hunt would address them over at Merlin's Cave. There was much impatient rumbling over the news that he was not coming to the field, but finally hundreds of people marched to the alehouse.

Gwynna hurried to keep up with them. She had never seen so many people. Most were men, but here and there a few women joined in. She strained to catch their conversation.

"Who was that bloody cove?" asked one woman who clutched a babe to her breast.

"A Mr. Parkes, someone said his name was," said another. "Looked like a gentl'mun to me."

A man next to them began to laugh derisively. "You women will believe anything. How do you know he was not one of those spies sent to stir things up? Pitt is just waiting for some spark of violence to turn his soldiers on us."

One of the women eyed him saucily. "And how do we know that you ain't one, either?" At the man's scowl, she shook her head. "You see, Alice? You canna' trust the men, not any of them."

Gwynna was inclined to agree with those sentiments, but for different reasons. She hurried along, eager to see the long-awaited Mr. Hunt. When they arrived at the alehouse, those able to crowd into the pub promptly ordered libations all around. About one o'clock, Mr. Hunt arrived. Gwynna slipped in behind a burly man, eager to hear the orator up close.

He was most unprepossessing, standing only slightly taller than herself and dressed in the manner of one from the country. He wore spectacles and was losing much of his hair on top. But all else was forgotten when he began to speak in a mesmerizing, melodious baritone.

"We are met here, my fellow laborers, to petition the Prince Regent and the legislature for some relief to those growing miseries, the tale of which would require a month to tell," he began. "Only yesterday I heard of a poor laborer of Spitalfields, who, with a wife and three children, had been heard to pray that some friendly hand would deliver him from his intolerable load." He shook his head and eyed them sadly from big, brown eyes. "What, then, is the cause of this unparalleled and universal distress? Is it, as our enemies had the impudence to promulgate, the indolence and improvidence of the poor? This is the cause assigned by a corrupt and hireling press. But it is untrue. On the face of the earth there are no people so industrious as the people of this country. An Englishman works as much in a week as any other laborer in a month."

"Hear, hear!" came the shouts. "We do, we do!"

He drew himself up to his full height and looked sternly around the room, making eye contact with every man before him.

"What is the cause of the want of employment?" he thundered. "Taxation. What is the cause of taxation? Corruption. It was corruption that enabled the borough-mongers to wage that bloody war against Napoleon, which had for its object the destruction of the liberties of all countries, but principally of our own."

Gwynna gasped. She had never heard the war denounced so roundly.

"Beware of false friends," he continued in an ominous voice, "of wolves in sheep's clothing. Where are they now? They no more dare to appear before our assemblage than my Lord Castlereagh."

The room erupted in laughter, and Mr. Hunt warmed to his subject. "Beware the rich aristocrats in Parliament who profess to be in sympathy with our plight," he continued. "They call us friends but send spies to our midst to create some disturbance which might serve as a pretense for calling out the military.

"Friends," he said, his voice rising in passion, "we know the superiority of mental over physical force. I shall not counsel any resort to the latter unless the former has been found ineffectual. It is our duty to petition, to demonstrate, to call aloud for timely reformation. Those who despise the just demands of the people are the real friends of confusion and bloodshed." There was much applause at this statement, and then a mournful expression settled on his face.

"But if the fatal day should be destined to arrive," he conceded, "I shall not be found concealed behind a counter or sheltering myself in the rear."

Thundering applause greeted this declaration. "We must have relief!" he cried, spurred on by the crowd's approval.

"Everything that concerns our subsistence or comforts is taxed. Is not our beer taxed? Our coats, our shirts? Everything that we eat, drink, wear, and even say?"

"Yes! Hear, hear!" came the answering shouts.

He pulled out a book, which he said was a report prepared by a committee of the House of Commons. He said it contained a list of those gorged and fattened on the backs of the people—royalty and members of the nobility who received pensions or had their taxes forgiven.

"The Prince of Wales is here down for fifty thousand pounds, and the Princess Charlotte of Wales for six thousand, which Parliament has seen fit to expand to sixty thousand pounds to support her own splendor and that of her husband," he said. "Moreover, if the Prince of Cobourg survives his amiable consort, he may draw from our taxes fifty thousand pounds a year, and we are to have the pleasure of paying them."

When the jeers subsided, Mr. Hunt went on: "Here is Lady Grenville down for fifteen hundred pounds, no doubt for her meritorious public services." Loud laughter greeted this comment. "Lady Chatham, three thousand pounds. Lady Stanhope, fifteen hundred." The list seemingly included all parties, whether Whigs or Tories.

Gwynna was appalled, her mind numbed by Mr. Hunt's revelations. Then she heard him call out the Duke of Claremont's title.

"This worthy, by all reckonings one of the wealthiest men in all England, is allotted thirty thousand per annum free of taxes, presumably to assist him in the maintenance of his numerous estates." Gwynna gasped. Mr. Hunt smirked. "It is men like this who fatten themselves at our expense!"

"Hear, hear!"

The voices swelled into a deafening indictment of the duke and of her own foolishness in caring for such a man.

The outcry thundered mercilessly in her ears. Gwynna could not bear to hear more. Silently, her eyes wet with tears, she edged toward the doorway.

His own butler had the temerity to look askance when he discovered his employer standing on the stone steps.

"Your Grace," Adams acknowledged haltingly.

Gideon frowned. Had the women so taken over his abode that his presence here was something to be remarked upon, even by his own butler? Perhaps he should have sent advance word of his visit, but he had wanted the element of surprise in order to judge for himself whether the ladies were ready for their introduction to society next week. It was not Elizabeth who concerned him. Respectability and poise was bred in her to the bone. *She* would make no missteps. It was Gwynna he needed to see, to ascertain for himself whether Elizabeth and Mrs. Biddingham had properly prepared her for her debut. Otherwise, it would surely be a disaster.

With a reproving arch of his brow, Gideon handed his gloves and chapeau to the butler. He had the satisfaction of seeing the august servant blanch at his silent reprimand.

"I shall take sherry in the drawing room," Gideon announced peremptorily. Adams's eyes shot in alarm to the closed drawing room door. Gideon frowned impatiently. "Good God, man. Have the ladies so addled your brain that you have forgotten how to perform your duties? Sherry at once, please. Then send the ladies to me."

The butler bowed as Gideon strode to the drawing room and threw open the door. Two people were sitting close together on the loveseat, hand in hand. Instantly their heads bobbed up, and their startled eyes widened in horror.

Gideon blinked. "Elizabeth! And—" He frowned at the young man next to her. "You are . . . ?"

"Dr. Youngblood, Gideon," Elizabeth supplied quickly as she rose, her face a deep red. "Perhaps you met in the convalescent home. He has been visiting in London and was kind enough to come around to check on me."

The young man so introduced rose, his face no less red than his patient's. "Your Grace," he acknowledged, stammering. "I am happy to find Lady Elizabeth in such good health."

"No doubt." Gideon's eyes narrowed as he surveyed them. Elizabeth was staring down at her feet, but the doctor was making a valiant effort to hold his gaze. "Actually my fiancée looks a little feverish," Gideon observed dryly. "Elizabeth, may I inquire as to the whereabouts of Mrs. Biddingham? You *do* remember the chaperon I engaged?"

Elizabeth looked up quickly. "She is napping, I believe," she murmured.

The elegant brows rose higher. "I see. And Miss Owen?"

"She is about." Now Elizabeth's eyes were indignant. "I do not know what you are implying, Gideon, but I assure you that there is nothing amiss in my spending a bit of private time with James. Dr. Youngblood, that is. He *is* my doctor."

"Of course," Gideon replied with a thin smile. "And I am the Queen's lady in waiting." Just then the butler entered, bearing a tray with three glasses of sherry. "Ah, here is Adams, and with just the correct number of glasses. Most efficient."

With that, Gideon sat in a wing chair of claret leather and drained his glass. The others sat awkwardly as the butler quickly refilled Gideon's glass. "And now, Adams," Gideon said in an ominous voice, "you will please send Miss Owen to join our little gathering." The butler bowed stiffly and left.

The young doctor wore a most earnest expression,

Gideon noted. Another moment and he would drop to his knees and declare himself before them all. Gideon felt a surge of anger—not, amazingly, at the fact that Elizabeth was obviously besotted with this young pup, but at the fact that their illicit courtship had evidently occurred with the collusion of the entire household. And perhaps, he thought with dawning suspicions, with the active assistance of one particular member of it.

"How nice that you could drop by, Gideon," a familiar feminine voice said from the doorway. "One would think that you had forgotten us completely. But then, I suppose a man in your position has many demands upon his time." Gwynna Owen smiled sweetly at him.

Gideon rose. "Yes, I can see that my absence has been quite a hardship," he drawled. "Good afternoon, Miss Owen."

She sailed into the room, a vision in a gown of jonquil silk that brought out the dazzling blue of her eyes and set off the splendor of her red hair. Gideon had not realized it would grow so fast. It was long enough, in fact, to be swept into a knot at the back of her neck, but even the yellow ribbon could not restrain the errant tendrils that framed her face in a haphazard and enchanting fashion. Gideon felt a familiar knot in his stomach, a tightening in his loins. These weeks apart had not, as he had hoped, made him indifferent to her.

"Have you come to inspect the finished product, Your Grace?" she asked. "I have been most diligent in my lessons, I assure you. Mrs. Biddingham has seen to it that I have been instructed in proper manners, conversational skills, and the latest dances. I do not believe I will disgrace you. Or your class."

Gideon eyed her consideringly. Her transformation was amazing. She was no longer the little hellion from Wales, but a beautiful woman obviously perfectly at home in his house. "You are now a member of my class, Miss Owen," he said pointedly. "I would advise you not to forget that."

He could tell that a biting retort hovered at her lips, but she merely inclined her head in silent disdain. She *had* learned a few lessons since he had last laid eyes on her. He crossed the room to the mantelpiece and leaned against it.

They were watching his every move, he noted in satisfaction. He calmly took another sip of sherry. Elizabeth was wringing her hands nervously, while that doctor of hers was obviously forcing himself not to pat her shoulder comfortingly. Gwynna looked satisfied but guilty, in the way of a cat who has just polished off the family canary. He eyed them over the rim of his glass, his brows arched in patient skepticism as he waited for an explanation. He said nothing, merely continued to study them, allowing the unnatural silence to take its toll on their guilty consciences. Not that he expected Gwynna to succumb to such tactics, but he was gratified to see that it was not long before Elizabeth jumped to her feet, tears streaming down her face.

"Gideon," she cried, "I am dreadfully sorry, but I cannot marry you." She whirled toward Youngblood. "I have fallen in love with another man."

Gideon allowed one brow to furrow in surprise. "You shock me, Elizabeth."

The good doctor had also risen to his feet. "Do not be harsh with Elizabeth," he said, obviously in deep anguish. "It is my fault. I should never have come here or stayed so long. I knew she was promised to you. I have behaved dishonorably. I expect you will want to call me out. It will take me a few days to round up my seconds. You see, I do not know many people in town . . ." He broke off mournfully.

"A duel!" Elizabeth cried. "Oh, Gideon, you shall never be so cruel!"

"As to demand satisfaction from a man who has stolen my fiancée, a woman I have for the last year considered to be my wife?" Disdain dripped from his words. "Come now, Elizabeth. You cannot be such a ninny as to think I would let such an insult go unanswered."

Elizabeth ran to the mantel and grabbed his arm. "Gideon, please! Do not kill him. I shall marry you, if you will but spare his life!"

"Elizabeth!" It was the young man. So he had some spunk after all. "I should never allow you to do such a thing! His Grace is right to demand satisfaction, and though I know nothing of the art of weaponry, I shall not let you stand between me and a bullet." His voice broke. "I love you too much to let you go to another man." He met Gideon's gaze. "Forgive me, Your Grace, for committing such a breach of honor. But as long as it is done, you must know that I will fight to the death for Elizabeth."

"How touching," Gideon drawled. "But that will not be necessary." At their surprised faces, he added dryly, "You see before you, Youngblood, a man with a surfeit of obligations to the parson's noose." They looked at him in confusion. Gideon took another sip of sherry. "If you can assure me that Elizabeth's happiness is your desire," he continued quietly, "I shall release her from her commitment to me and take no offense from your actions."

Elizabeth gasped and threw herself into Youngblood's arms. The young doctor frowned. "I do not understand," he said. "How can you do this?"

"It is quite simple," Gideon said, draining the last of his sherry. "Since my marriage to Elizabeth is not to be formalized and our mutual obligation to be relinquished, I am now obliged to marry Miss Owen."

He had the extreme satisfaction of seeing Gwynna's expression of complacent scorn vanish abruptly. Instead she looked at him, aghast. And, for once, utterly speechless.

"And now," he said calmly, "I believe it is time for dinner. Youngblood, I trust you will join us?"

The doctor nodded numbly. Gideon smiled. "Splendid," he said. "Simply splendid."

CHAPTER 17

"DISGRACEFUL. UTTERLY DISGRACEFUL."

At Mrs. Biddingham's declaration, several pairs of eyes looked up guiltily, but the chaperon was too immersed in recounting her disturbing news to notice.

"Such outrage!" She buttered a roll. "They beat a poor patrolman, too. All because he tried to stop the looting. 'Tis a sorry pass when such lawlessness is tolerated."

Gwynna's appetite had long since vanished in the turmoil before dinner, and she listened to Mrs. Biddingham's chatter with half an ear.

"What rampage, ma'am?" Elizabeth asked politely.

Mrs. Biddingham looked at them in surprise. "Why, have you not heard?" She smiled. "Oh, I suppose you young people have other things to do besides reading the newspapers. I always manage to do so just before my afternoon nap. Then I drift off to sleep. Gwynna, it was most considerate of you to suggest that I retire each afternoon. I declare my energy has increased tenfold!"

Gwynna colored but managed to ignore Gideon's sardonic expression. "You were speaking of some disturbance, I believe, ma'am?" she prodded, eager to leave the subject of her chaperon's afternoon naps behind.

"Oh, goodness me, yes," Mrs. Biddingham replied. "The *Times* reports that a mob at Spafields rampaged through the east end of town yesterday. It was most disgraceful."

"Mob?" Gwynna's pulse quickened. "How unfortunate. Was there any damage done?"

"I should say so. They broke several shop windows in the Strand and King Street and did the most dreadful looting! There was a general melee after the Bow Street officers and patrol arrived. One patrolman was beaten, and several officers were hurt."

"My goodness!" This from a shocked Elizabeth.

"Yes, indeed," Mrs. Biddingham clucked.

"Whatever were they about?" asked Dr. Youngblood.

Gideon took a sip of wine. "All these mobs are the same," he declared in a bored tone. "They profess some lofty-sounding goal, such as feeding the poor and reforming Parliament, but in the end they are all rogues and thieves. Rioting is all they know."

"That is not so!" Gwynna declared hotly. "Violence is not their preference. They are decent men who seek worthy reform, something you could never begin to understand."

His brows rose. "Oh? Whyever not, Miss Owen?"

"Because you are concerned only with your own welfare and with increasing your own wealth at the expense of the people."

"Gwynna!" Mrs. Biddingham was aghast.

"You turn your back on the poor," Gwynna continued scornfully, "preferring to spend your money on fripperies that proclaim your consequence."

"Gwynna!" Elizabeth said, shocked.

Gwynna ignored them. Every grievance, every inconvenience, every slight she had suffered at his hands came to the fore. He was everything she despised.

"You care nothing for the plight of others," she rushed on. "You are so consumed by your own vanity, your own consequence, your own stupid whims, that no one and nothing matters to you in the least." Her chest was heaving with emotion. "You—"

"Enough."

That single word, delivered in a quiet but unmistakably authoritative tone, stopped her mid-sentence. He said nothing more for a moment, content to eye her under haughtily arched brows. Then he smiled.

"It is fortunate that my future wife possesses such an accurate judgment of my character," he said. "I daresay we shall never misunderstand each other."

He turned to the doctor. "Now, Youngblood, you were speaking earlier of a promising new treatment for the megrims. I think it would behoove me to pay closer attention. Continue, if you please."

"Oh!" Gwynna's outraged exclamation provoked not the slightest reaction from Gideon. She rose, intent on leaving. But before she could clear the doorway, his voice met her ears.

"I shall expect you in my study at precisely ten o'clock, Miss Owen."

With an infuriated cry, she stamped out of the room.

GIDEON SURVEYED THE PETITE FIREBRAND before him. She had clearly spent the time since dinner girding for this confrontation. Her cheeks, inflamed by anger, glowed deep amber in the candlelight. The bodice of her jonquil gown rose and fell rapidly as she sought to control her fury. The flickering blaze in the hearth cast the dress in hues of yellow fire; she looked as volatile as the flames.

"I see that your disposition has not improved in the weeks since our last meeting, Miss Owen," he observed, not bothering to rise from his desk to greet her. There was no need to add that the interval had done nothing for his mood, either.

"I shall not marry you."

He merely arched a brow at this declaration, then lifted the decanter and poured some of its contents into a glass. He savored the warmth as the liquid trickled down his throat. His eyes flicked over her form, which was rigid with emotion.

"I do not recall having asked you, my dear," he replied in a silky voice.

The delicate features of her face furrowed in consternation. "But you told Dr. Youngblood that you were obliged to marry me."

"Quite true. Alas, you are the second woman I have compromised in a year's time. Now that Elizabeth's future is happily settled, I have no other choice but to see an honorable resolution of matters between us."

"I do not understand. You had said you would find me a husband. Is that not an honorable resolution?"

"Come, Miss Owen," he said, frowning. "Do you think that I would allow a child of mine to be raised as another man's if there were another option?"

She looked at him in confusion. "Child?" Her brow cleared. "There is no child. I am not breeding."

Gideon received this news without flinching, although he was aware of an odd surge of disappointment. "That does not matter. I am obliged to marry you, if for no other reason than my behavior on the island." He paused, and for the first time looked away from that sapphire gaze. "And on our journey here," he added softly.

"But," she stammered, flushing, "it was I who came to you that night."

"That is of no importance." He cleared his throat. "As a gentleman, I am obliged to resist such blandishments from a lady in my charge, even when she is persistent in the extreme."

As he watched the rosy blush spread over her face, he found himself wondering, not for the first time, what it would be like to have her in his bed night after night. He frowned as he realized his thoughts were taking him far afield. "At all events, we shall proceed with the wedding," he said briskly. "The fact that there is to be no child removes some of the urgency, of course. We shall take a few months to accustom you to your future duties as a duchess, but no more. I mean for us to wed before spring."

She shook her fist at him. "I shall never agree to this!"

Calmly he drained his glass. "Oh, yes, you will," he said, setting it down with a thump. "For after we are married, you shall have any sum you wish for that island of yours. Think of all the starving people you can save." He smiled, knowing that it made him look insufferably smug.

It was fortunate that his reflexes were still quite excellent, for he was able to dodge the fist that suddenly came at him, narrowly missing his nose. Instantly he leapt from behind the desk and grabbed her hands.

"Miss Owen," he said through gritted teeth, "your manners are sadly wanting."

She struggled to free herself from his grip. "I shall not be your wife and I shall not take your tainted money!" she cried.

He tightened his arms around her wriggling form. "Tainted? What are you talking about?" His eyes narrowed. "My money is accepted by everyone," he added dryly, "even the most discriminating tradesmen."

"Nonsense," she retorted. "They are merely dependent on your business for their survival. Do you think they admire you for profiting on the backs of the poor? For maneuvering out of the taxes that oppress everyone else?"

He glared at her, incredulous. "*Where* are you getting this drivel?"

"You are on Mr. Hunt's list. Along with half the *ton*, not to mention the Prince and Princess Charlotte, and . . ."

"Hunt?" he echoed, his expression thunderous. "Are you speaking of *Henry* Hunt?"

"So you have heard the name." She eyed him disdainfully. "No doubt it is a subject of great sport at those clubs of yours. Well, he is twice the man you are, *Your Grace*. And he is onto your tricks. Thirty thousand pounds, tax free, indeed! Simply for being born to privilege."

A horrible suspicion rose to his mind, only to become a blinding certainty. Instantly he released her. "Were you with that mob in Spafields yesterday?"

"What if I was, Englishman?" she replied defiantly. "You are not my keeper."

God. The woman was thoroughly mad. "Do you have any idea how dangerous that was?" he demanded, barely restraining his fury. "They are a lawless, ruthless lot. Is it not clear by their activities how little respect they have for another man's property or person?"

"They do not seek out violence," she insisted. "I would wager that the disturbance was provoked by one of the government's spies. When I left the alehouse, Mr. Hunt was counseling peaceful means of reform."

"Alehouse?" He was incredulous. "Do you mean to say that you were at a public house with that man?"

She hesitated. "I was in disguise," she added hastily. "As a boy. The way I traveled to Cheshire from Wales. And I had my dagger."

He stared at her for one long, speechless moment. Then he sank into his chair. "Has anyone ever told you, Gwynna Owens," he said slowly, "that your disguise is so thoroughly inadequate . . ."

"You did once, I believe," she interrupted angrily.

"That in the middle of the day in one of the worst parts of London . . ."

"They were decent people," she insisted.

"Any one-eyed idiot could see through it . . ."

"No one noticed." She crossed her arms defiantly.

"And that your dagger couldn't stop a London scape-gallows if your life depended on it."

"Which it did not." She glared at him.

The fury suddenly left him. He felt utterly drained. "You were extraordinarily lucky," he said at last, reaching for the decanter. He poured himself another drink and downed it. "I have changed my mind about our wedding."

She clapped her hands together. "Wonderful! I knew you would never force me to—"

"We shall be married as soon as possible. It is the only way I can return to my house, keep an eye on you, and prevent further such foolishness."

She gasped. "Why, you . . . you . . ." She broke off, unable to continue.

"Splendid," he drawled. "At long last Miss Gwynna Owen is at a loss for words."

THE FLOWERS ARRIVED the very next day. Not an enormous arrangement like those Gwynna had seen in parlors on her morning calls, but a nosegay of blue wildflowers that could have been plucked from the lush meadows of Anglesey. She could not imagine where he had found them at this time of year. The card bore his bold scrawl: "I should be honored if you would drive with me this afternoon. Claremont."

He presented himself at a quarter before five, the epitome of elegance and grace in his gold-buttoned blue coat, leather breeches, and claret top boots. As he handed her into his green-and-black curricle, pulled by a pair of perfectly matched bays, his eyes radiated approval of her fashionable forester's green dress and Yorkshire tan gloves. If his gaze faltered a bit at the yellow dyed ostrich plume that extended from her bonnet, he made no comment.

Their drive was surprisingly amiable, with all sorts of equally fashionable people stopping to greet them. Some of the women Gwynna had met during calls with Elizabeth, but the men were all strangers to her. They engaged in good-natured banter with Gideon, although she noticed that their eyes kept returning to her. Gideon patted her hand reassuringly during these exchanges, as if he feared she would feel awkward or nervous. Oddly, with him at her side, she felt no awkwardness at all.

He was obviously trying to be charming. His smile was lazy and intimate, and his hazel eyes met hers in a way that was positively intoxicating. Disconcerted at his unexpected attention, Gwynna found that she could barely recall their heated exchange of last night, or any of their previous strife. The new harmony between them was as delightful as it was alarming. After a half hour, he drove to a less crowded area of the park and suggested that they walk a bit. She felt oddly shy as he helped her out of the carriage.

"I daresay I shall never remember any of those names," she said with a nervous laugh.

"You do not have to, my dear," he replied lightly. "Your new acquaintances will be only too happy to re-introduce themselves, I imagine, especially the gentlemen. I daresay you will find your dance card full at Lady Forsythe's ball next week. Everyone wishes to know about the mysterious duke's daughter from Wales who has captured my undivided attention."

She stared at him in confusion. "But they already know that I am simply your ward."

He put his hand at her waist to guide her around a puddle in the path. "They may make more of it than that, my dear.

Never underestimate the *ton*'s capacity for intrigue and matchmaking. I can almost hear the tabbies' tongues wagging now." He gave her a sidelong look. "Nothing about you is simple, incidentally; at least, nothing that I have found."

Gwynna blushed. She could not imagine why she felt so tongue-tied. Here was a man with whom she had shared the most amazing intimacies, yet he had never before looked at her in quite that way. It made her heart do somersaults.

"I wish to thank you for the flowers," she said, hoping her voice sounded normal. "They were quite lovely. However did you find them?"

He smiled. "An obscure country florist with a penchant for bluebottles—I believe that is what he called them."

"We call them cornflowers on Anglesey," she said, smiling. "They are beautiful."

"They suit you." Copper fire radiated from his gaze. "They are the color of your eyes."

Gwynna flushed anew. She could not bring herself to look away from that mesmerizing gaze. Was it her imagination, or was his face flushed as well? She shook her head. She had best be careful; whatever game he was playing, she was no match for his charm and expertise.

"Why did you bring me here?" she asked, a note of suspicion in her voice. "I suspect it has something to do with your plan to force me to marry you."

He arched a brow in surprise. "Force? I assure you, I have no such plans."

She walked over to a bench and sat down. "Of course not—that is not your way, is it, Englishman?" She eyed him speculatively. "Then I suppose you are trying to charm me into marriage."

He joined her on the bench. "You see through me, imp," he said with a disarming smile. "I cannot pull the wool over

your eyes, can I?" His expression was enigmatic. "I suppose
it is unthinkable that I would merely enjoy your company."

Gwynna eyed him warily. He frowned in mock dismay.

"Is it unthinkable that I would simply welcome an opportunity to feast my eyes on your loveliness?" he asked airily.
"Or to admire the way you wear those fetching new clothes?
The way your eyes shine in delight when the wind whips
your cheeks? The manner in which your extraordinary hair
refuses to stay tucked under that silly hat?"

Her mouth fell open in stunned amazement.

"No," he said with an exaggerated sigh. "It is too much to
imagine. I suppose you would rather us be at daggers
drawn."

"Of course not," she said indignantly.

His brows rose, and he leaned over to whisper in her ear.
"You cannot image how that delights me, Miss Owen." His
warm breath tickled her earlobe and sent the most extraordinary sensations rippling down her spine. As she pondered
this unsettling development, he rose and pulled her to her
feet. Gwynna could not tear her gaze away from the
mischievous gleam in his eyes.

"What are you about, Englishman?" she said, nearly
dying of mortification when the words emerged in a husky
tone that did not sound at all like her voice.

He merely grinned. Then, with gentlemanly aplomb, he
escorted her back to the carriage. During the drive back to
the house, when she was conscious only of his devastating
nearness, he merely rattled on at length about the weather.

The next day he took her to the tower zoo. The following
day it was Astley's and the Elgin marbles. One day they
drove out to Richmond with Elizabeth and Dr. Youngblood
to thread their way through a winding maze. The man was
maddening. If his arms occasionally lingered overlong at
her waist as he helped her from the carriage, it seemed the

merest accident. If he occasionally leaned close to whisper an observation in her ear, it was only because there were too many people about. He did not so much as steal a kiss when they found themselves temporarily lost in the maze. His behavior was most proper and excruciatingly baffling.

In this manner they passed much of the week. Gwynna told herself that he was merely playing some new game, trying to manipulate her with his wit and charm. Yet there was nothing false about the gleam in his eyes when he looked at her, and the glow she felt in his presence was all too real. The air of pleasant amiability between them kept her constantly off balance; the intriguing promise in those hazel eyes vanished mischievously almost as soon as she noticed it. All in all, it was an extremely frustrating week, and her nights were spent in wonder and yearning as she tossed restlessly in her featherbed. Finally, on the day before the ball, a small package was delivered to the town house. Inside she found a small sprig of mistletoe.

"A gift," the card read, "that requires no sacrifice."

Gwynna clasped the treasure in wonder; when a tear rolled down her cheek and onto her hand, she raced up the stairs and shut herself in her room. That night she dreamed of a golden-haired Welsh warrior with hazel eyes.

"In view of recent events, we are reestablishing the secret committee, Claremont. The Home Secretary would like you to serve on it."

She had done something to her hair. It was swept artfully off her face, with only a few errant tendrils to frame the delicate features. He had never imagined she could look so elegant. The silver-blue confection she wore ignited the brilliant sapphire of her eyes. He had seen that blue every night in his dreams for the last week.

"We are preparing for a general uprising. Our informers

tell us that the time is ripe. It is imperative that we consider the internal state of the country. Claremont, are you listening?"

Every man in the room had noticed her; he was sure of it. He never imagined that she would fit so perfectly in this setting, and at her first ball, too. Her vibrancy radiated from the center of the room, where she and Elizabeth were gaily holding court before a bevy of admirers. He had spent a heady week in her company in what he thought was a rather clever plan to charm his prickly fiancée. It had worked superbly—he knew he had her off balance and yearning for him. But the week had had an unforeseen similar effect on him. Tonight he had forced himself to keep his distance; the surge of jealousy he felt at the sight of those mushrooms fawning over her made him dangerously unstable.

"Emergency measures will be necessary. It is only a question of what. In view of the rioting by that Spafields mob, I—"

"Spafields?" Gideon's attention was suddenly caught. "What is that you are saying, Fairchild?"

Lord Fairchild sighed heavily. Just why the Home Secretary had any desire to have the Duke of Claremont contribute anything to this endeavor was beyond him. Why, the man—

"Come on, Fairchild," Gideon said impatiently. "Speak up. What about Spafields?"

Fairchild stared at him. He had never before seen that keen expression on Claremont's face.

"The mob that marched on the Strand last week," he replied. "Our spies say it was that Hunt fellow who whipped them up into a righteous frenzy. We think there will be more such meetings. And violence. We want to be prepared."

Gideon eyed him assessingly. "What spies, Fairchild?"

Lord Fairchild coughed delicately. "Come now, Clare-

mont. You know we have spies planted with the revolutionaries. Your friend Lord Westbrook oversees them."

"Drew?" Gideon asked in amazement.

"I fail to see why this is such a surprise to you, Claremont,"
Lord Fairchild said peevishly. "You are quite familiar with
Lord Westbrook's skills."

"Yes." Gideon's expression was suddenly grim.

"As a former agent yourself, you must realize the necessity
of such a tactic," Lord Fairchild continued. "The government
has to be prepared."

"I suppose you pay them well. For information on
'revolutionary' activities."

"Of course," Lord Fairchild snapped impatiently. "What
is your point, Claremont?"

Gideon's eyes narrowed. "Just that when a man is paid to
provide information on a certain type of activity, it is in his
interest to find that activity—whether or not it exists. How
do you know the rioting was not provoked by someone
other than Hunt?"

Lord Fairchild was indignant. "Preposterous! You sound
precisely like Hunt."

Gideon arched a brow. "Oratory is not my style, Fairchild," he drawled.

"Yes. Well." Lord Fairchild cleared his throat. "As I was
saying, the Home Secretary wishes you to serve on the
committee."

"Committee?"

"The secret Parliamentary committee," Fairchild said
with the forced patience of one who believes he is talking to
a madman. "We had one in 1812, when General Ludd ran
amok. I suppose you were too involved in the war to notice.
The committee will receive reports from our spies and
recommend a course of action."

Gideon eyed him thoughtfully. "And you wish me to serve on this committee?"

"The Home Secretary seems to think your service during the war equips you with special insight in these matters," Fairchild replied carefully.

Gideon smiled thinly. "But you do not agree?" he asked.

Lord Fairchild coughed awkwardly. "It is not for me to agree or disagree—" he began.

"Never mind, Fairchild," Gideon interrupted. "I am well aware of your opinion of me. There is no need to put on a show. I shall be pleased to serve on your committee."

"Now, Claremont, there is no need— What?" Lord Fairchild stared at him in amazement.

Gideon casually buffed an imaginary speck of dust from his lapel. His eyes slid lazily across the room to where Gwynna was being led out on the dance floor by a fawning young buck in an excruciatingly vivid parrot-green-and-yellow waistcoat. The idiot was positively drooling over her.

"I said that I shall be pleased to serve, Fairchild," Gideon drawled. "And now, if you will excuse me, I must rescue a young lady from her exquisitely bad taste."

THE MAN WAS INSUFFERABLE. His flattering attentions of last week were clearly a subterfuge, for tonight he was nowhere to be seen. It was bad enough that she had to endure her first ball with all of these people staring at her and with only Elizabeth for support. He was probably hoping she would fail. Well, she had not. The first hour had even gone tolerably well. She had managed to turn aside the more impertinent queries, somehow conveying the notion that as she was William Traherne's daughter, very little else needed to be said. She had even received some very flattering comments from several gentlemen, although of course it was mere flummery. She had acquitted herself fairly well on the dance floor, too, despite the fact that she could scarcely distinguish a quadrille from the cotillion.

To think that she had been so distracted by his attentions this week that she had allowed herself to forget about Mr. Hunt's revelations! Why, she had even allowed herself to envision a future for them, to think that her love might somehow induce Gideon to give his money to the poor and selflessly devote himself to worthy causes.

Tonight had been a flight back to reality. He had showed his true colors, ignoring her most of the evening, then suddenly appearing to whisk her imperially off the dance floor, leaving her stunned partner quaking for fear of having displeased the great Claremont.

He could at least have offered to dance with her, Gwynna thought glumly. She could well imagine the figure he cut on the dance floor. He was looking especially handsome tonight in black superfine, a white damask waistcoat, and a solitary sapphire stickpin in his snowy cravat. But he had not asked her to dance. Instead he had abruptly appeared to take her outside to the garden, despite the fact that the weather was clearly threatening.

"The *trone d'amour*," he said languidly as they stepped into the stone courtyard.

Gwynna stared at him blankly, as thunder rumbled nearby.

"The 'throne of love,'" he explained helpfully. "You were admiring my cravat, I believe? That is the name of the style."

"Why—" Gwynna broke off. "You are an exasperating man," she said at last.

"Ah." The hazel eyes gleamed. "Then we are well matched."

Gwynna eyed him scornfully, but he merely smiled and

led her away from the lanterns at the edge of the courtyard and onto a path that wound away from the house. The slight pressure from his arm as he guided her was most unsettling.

"Should we not remain with the other guests?" Gwynna asked nervously.

"Our absence, if it is noted, will probably delight our hostess," he said, stopping near a small tree. "Lady Forsythe is said to have quite a nose for gossip."

She frowned. "And you wish to be the subject of gossip? I do not understand."

"It will make our hasty wedding all the more plausible," he explained lightly. "'Twill be said it was a love match, that I could not wait to bring you to my bed. You will be the talk of London for capturing the heart of the *ton*'s most eligible bachelor."

"Your modesty is most becoming," Gwynna retorted, trying to ignore the copper fire that suddenly blazed in his eyes. "Have you forgotten, Englishman, that I have not agreed to marry you?"

"That," he murmured, drawing her close, "is only a formality."

"What do you mean?" she asked. Her pulse hammered as his lips brushed hers.

"I obtained the special license yesterday," he whispered, nuzzling her hair.

"You conceited man!" But her heart thrilled to the news, even as butterflies fluttered in her stomach.

He began to rain kisses over her neck and shoulders. Goose bumps rippled her spine. Gwynna was mortified as she felt her knees start to buckle, but his strong arms supported her. She had an irresistible urge to lean into them, to rely on his strength. He *was* strong, she realized; beneath that elegant facade and casual air was a man with the steel of a Welsh prince. She supposed he felt little else for her but this fierce, relentless desire that leapt between them. Still, she sensed that he would—if she let him—take care of her for all time.

It was tempting to allow him to do so. He had already captured her heart—though she would never allow him the satisfaction of knowing. It was frustrating, this seesawing between loathing him and wanting him. Despite his arrogance, his hypocrisy, his disdain for her ways and for people less fortunate, she still loved him. But in this magical week in his company, she had forgotten that the differences between them were so great. That was a mistake, for while Gideon might offer his gold to ease the plight of the islanders, he would never lift a finger to help them himself. He did not believe in her causes; his soul was not in it, nor would he let it be touched. She would have to fight her own battles. Yet as he held her in his arms, their differences seemed to disappear, and she found herself yearning to spend a lifetime with him.

"Marry me, Gwynna," he murmured, his warm breath tickling the inside of her ear.

She stared into the seductive copper fire, finding a spark in its depths that ignited her very soul. Thunder crackled overhead. Owen's disapproval, no doubt.

Wisdom warred with instinct. She wanted this man too much. She was helpless to fight him.

"Yes," she said breathlessly, knowing that she had utterly lost her mind. "I will."

They scarcely noticed when the first raindrops fell. It was only when the sky unleashed a torrent that they raced back to the house, laughing and disheveled. His laughter was magical, a deep, full-throated sound that made her smile like some love-struck ninny.

Curious looks greeted them as they entered the ballroom. Even with a mild wetting, the duke was the picture of elegant aplomb. But her hair was a mess, and her gown was damp and rumpled; she knew she looked like an utter wanton.

"A *duke's* daughter?" Gwynna heard one incredulous tabby observe. "I declare, she looks more like a Covent Garden strumpet."

Daughter of Sin. Gwynna sighed forlornly. It was no more than the truth.

Chapter 18

THIS WAS IN EARNEST. NO DEMONIC CLERGYMAN SMIRKED AT THE door. No clothing had to be hastily adjusted in a darkened cave in order to deny a guilty passion.

This time when he married Gwynna Owen there would be no shrugging off his vows.

Gideon surveyed his reflection in the glass. His buff breeches, silk stockings, gold-buttoned blue coat, and white damask waistcoat bespoke Weston at his most subdued best. He fixed the diamond-and-gold stickpin in his white cravat, which he had fashioned in a simple style for his wedding day. He did not think the man who married Gwynna Owen should be sporting something as intricately ornate as the Maharatta.

His wedding day. With Elizabeth standing not at his side but at Gwynna's, as her attendant. It was amazing how topsy-turvy his world had become since he had chanced upon an impertinent scamp fending off two thugs on a Cheshire moor.

There was no reason to think that marriage to Gwynna would be any less turbulent. She would turn his house upside down with her fierce Welsh ways. He would never have chosen such a course had he not so thoroughly compromised her. No man in his right mind would willingly yoke himself to a woman who disdained everything he represented, who could scarcely look at him without falling into a temper. They would constantly be at loggerheads.

Except when the fire between them consumed their differences in its delicious, desperate heat. The look in her eyes when their bodies moved in sweet harmony was almost more than he could stand. At such times, when she dropped her prickly armor, he glimpsed the beauty of her soul in all its fierce courage, honor, and purity. At such times, he knew that a life with Gwynna Owen was worth any price. He swallowed hard.

"It is always nice to see the groom smiling as he is about to face his doom."

Gideon looked up to see the Earl of Westbrook languishing in the doorway, an amused look on his face. His expression darkened. "You need not look so pleased, Drew. You married men seem to take perverse delight in seeing the noose tighten around another suffering bachelor." He buffed his nails on his coat sleeve and yawned. "I hope you enjoy the spectacle."

The earl eyed him assessingly. "Your careless airs do not fool me for one moment," he said calmly. "I can see what is written on your face so plainly that if you have not seen it, you are not the man I thought."

Gideon arched a repressive brow. "I do not pretend to guess what nonsense you are babbling about," he drawled. "You know the circumstances that have brought me to this pass as well as anyone."

"Perhaps better," the earl murmured enigmatically. He ignored Gideon's glower and handed him a glass of champagne. "Here. There will be more of this after the ceremony, but I thought a prenuptial toast was in order." He closed the door. "Besides, it is the only time we have to speak privately."

Gideon accepted the glass. "If you mean to prattle on in this vein," he said in a bored voice, "I cannot think what we have to talk about."

"The threats against Prinny's life."

Gideon's brows arched eloquently.

"I thought that would get your attention," Drew said, taking a seat. "As you know, there is much distress at the highest levels over the recent disturbances."

"I assume you are referring to the riots in town?" Gideon's voice was carefully neutral. He had known when Fairchild revealed Drew's involvement in the intelligence effort that things were indeed serious. And while he had been proud to serve in Drew's elite spying network during the war, now he eyed his friend with a sinking feeling.

"And in the country," Drew responded. "There is much hysteria in the Home Office about the possibility of revolution. Unfortunately most of our informers are an unsavory lot, as suspect as the people they are being paid to watch. It is not as it was when you and I were in this business." He smiled ruefully.

Gideon sipped his champagne. "I assume that you will eventually explain how this concerns me," he said lightly, although he already had a fairly good notion.

The earl appeared to be preoccupied with the bubbles in his glass. "I do not agree with the prevailing view that we may soon be facing a general uprising," he said. "The people in the country are more concerned about the price of bread and the Corn Laws. But this group in town is most worrisome. Their Mr. Hunt is a very clever man. He talks of peaceful reform, but apparently his minions are out secretly fanning the fires of true rebellion. And now we have word of a plot against the Prince."

"Despicable, to be sure," Gideon commented. "But surely such threats are not unheard of." He fixed the earl with a bland gaze. "Come, Drew. This is my wedding day. I have other things to think about at the moment."

The earl studied a speck on the rim of his glass. "I know

that you are on the committee. These matters must of
necessity be your concern now." He shifted awkwardly in
his chair.

Gideon sighed. Drew looked exceedingly uncomfortable.
He deserved to be put out of his misery. After all, the man
was merely doing his job. "Of course," Gideon agreed
dryly. "But perhaps what you really wish me to know is that
those spies of yours, those estimable knaves whose jobs it is
to gather evidence of rebellion, are quite skilled at ferreting
out the identities of Mr. Hunt's supporters."

Drew met his gaze evenly. "One of them was intrigued by
a young woman masquerading as a boy at the Spafields
meeting."

Gideon downed the rest of his champagne. "I see."

"He followed her home." Drew rose. "Fortunately the
man is not a blackmailer, although I imagine he was
tempted. But when he discovered that his prey was con-
nected to such a powerful personage as a duke, I expect he
thought better of the notion. He came straight to me with his
information. No one else knows."

"You are not by any chance implying that my future wife
is a traitor?" Gideon asked casually.

His light tone did not deceive the earl. "Of course not,"
Drew said quickly. "From what you have told me, Miss
Owen does seem to be an independent and rather eccentric
young woman with certain radical notions. Not at all the
type to find it easy going in the *ton,* but not necessarily a
traitor. At all events, she is soon to be a duchess, so I
imagine she will shortly be hailed as an original."

"If she does not fall into some nefarious plot before then,"
Gideon added morosely.

The earl laughed. "I know that you will make certain she
does not. I have the highest regard for your skills. I have no
doubt you will keep her in line."

except for some gold piping at the edge. She felt ridiculous in her tissue-thin nightgown, so transparent it made her feel like a harlot.

He continued to look at her in unnerving silence as she sat before the vanity. Finally he placed his hands on her shoulders and began to knead them gently. A warmth spread over her neck, down her spine, and into the pit of her stomach. Her breathing grew more rapid as his fingers wandered down her front, grazing the tips of her breasts. As he knelt to kiss the back of her neck, his hand slipped under the gauzy fabric and cupped her breast.

Gwynna could only sit in mesmerized silence as his hands brought her to a state of breathless longing. Suddenly, however, he left her side.

"Gideon," she cried in protest.

But he had only gone to put out the candles, all except one on the dressing table. Its golden glow reflected the copper fire in his eyes as he pulled her to her feet.

"I like hearing you say my name," he said softly. "It is ever so much nicer than 'Englishman.'"

Gwynna stared at him, wondering how it was that she had come to love this man so much. She wondered what he was thinking. Could he ever come to feel as she did? She opened her mouth to speak, but the words would not come out.

"Mine," she finally murmured incoherently.

His brow furrowed, then cleared in understanding. "Gwynna," he whispered, and she thrilled as his voice caressed her name.

He kissed her then, and Gwynna glowed in the warmth of his embrace. After a moment, though, he drew back to study her. Her body began to tremble as he subjected her to intense scrutiny; all the while his fingers were making light, maddening circles on her back. She wanted to reach for him, to plead with him to make love to her, but his steady gaze

kept her immobile. He seemed strangely withdrawn, and
there was a flicker of uncertainty in his eyes. She had the
strangest feeling that he suddenly wanted to be anywhere
but in this room with her. She closed her eyes in pain.

"Please," she whispered at last, wondering if he could see
her shaking.

He eyed her assessingly. "You are afraid."

Gwynna nodded.

"Of what?" he asked softly.

"Everything. Nothing. I-I do not know," she said, feeling
wretched. How could she explain her fear that losing him
would be like losing her soul? "I should not have married
you," she said at last. "I do not fit in your world."

"I know."

So he felt it, too. Gwynna's pulse hammered in her ears.
He was going to send her away. But he merely continued to
look at her with those keenly intelligent eyes. How had she
ever thought that gaze fatuous and empty?

"I take it that Owen does not approve of me," he said
lightly. "Or is it the ancients?"

Gwynna's forehead wrinkled in confusion. "What?"

He smiled. "How else to account for the fact that my
fierce Welsh warrior is suddenly so apprehensive? Have the
spirits condemned us?"

She shook her head. "It is just that I fear I have been too
impulsive. We are so different. I do not see how we can live
together as husband and wife. We shall bring each other
grief."

"No doubt." He toyed with the ends of her hair. "It was
the reception, was it not?" he asked quietly. "You do not like
my painted friends?"

"I do not fit in," she said morosely. "That is painfully
clear."

"Perhaps it is the other way around," he murmured, his

lips touching the top of her head. "At all events, I do not think we should allow a few outlandish pinks to ruin our wedding night. Do you?"

The copper fire in his eyes blazed a gentle challenge. He was right. She wanted nothing so much as to lose herself in his arms, to forget about the war clouds on the horizon.

"Well," she whispered finally, "I suppose there will be time later to fight those battles."

"Spoken like a true Welsh princess," he said, and lifting her into his arms, he carried her to the bed.

When, hours later, the rosy tinge of dawn filtered through the curtains, Gwynna shook her head in wonder. Their night of shared passion had been beyond her wildest imaginings. She was exhausted and happy.

And still afraid.

"THAT MAN IS FOLLOWING US, MARY."

The serving girl eyed her mistress anxiously. She, too, had seen the burly and rather handsome man who had followed them from the milliner's shop on Bond Street. In Picadilly he had kept carefully hidden behind the waiting carriages as he watched them. Now in the park he kept to the cover of trees at the edge of the path.

Mary sighed. If only the duchess did not have this penchant for walking, they would be safely tucked into the duke's carriage, not traipsing through the park like two sitting ducks. "I imagine he will go away, Your Grace, if we ignore him."

Gwynna's eyes narrowed. "The man has followed us all morning, Mary. I wish to know why."

Mary shifted nervously. Her mistress had a few wild hairs in her head, that was for sure. And at the moment, she did not much like the expression on Her Grace's face. "I am sure His Grace will get to the bottom of it, ma'am," she ventured.

"I do not intend to have my husband fight my battles for me, Mary," Gwynna said briskly. "Now, here is what we shall do."

The maid's eyes widened in horror as Gwynna outlined her plan. "Oh, no, ma'am," she said. "I do not think that would be wise at all!"

"Nonsense," replied Gwynna. "We shall have the element of surprise. I bought an extra length of this nice, wide ribbon. It is strong enough, I think. Here. This copse of trees is perfect. No one will interfere."

"Oh, ma'am," the little maid cried in horror. "I do not think—"

"Come, Mary," Gwynna said reassuringly. "I shall protect us both. You must needs have a bit more faith."

The maid closed her eyes. "Yes, ma'am," she said numbly.

Minutes later the man lay flat on his stomach, having tripped on the ribbon the women had pulled taut and low between the trees. In an instant, Gwynna and Mary were sitting on his back, Gwynna's dagger at his neck.

"Now. You will tell us why you are following us," Gwynna commanded.

The man muttered something.

"Speak up, man, or I shall slit your throat," Gwynna declared. "What gives you the right to harass two helpless young women?" She eyed him defiantly. The lout was big enough to toss them both into the bushes if he chose, but he was clearly dumbfounded at finding himself even temporarily at their mercy. The knife helped their cause, of course. Thank goodness that long habit had led her to keep it on her person at all times.

"Helpless? God save us all," the man muttered. "Let me up, ma'am. I mean you no harm."

Gwynna's eyes narrowed. "And just how do I know that you speak the truth, you scapegrace?"

"You can ask the duke," the man said plaintively. "He has known me for nearly ten years."

"What?" Gwynna eyed the man indignantly. "Up this instant, man. I will have the truth!" She rose and pulled a trembling Mary to her feet. The man rolled over and sat up, watching them suspiciously. His eyes strayed to her dagger. "Be quick about it, please," Gwynna said impatiently, "or I shall scream and you can explain to the Watch how you accosted us."

"Accosted *you?*" The man stared at them incredulously. Then he sighed. "Very well, ma'am. I was told by your husband to keep an eye on you."

Gwynna's mouth fell open. "You were hired to follow me? Whatever for?"

The man shifted uncomfortably. "He wanted to make sure you weren't associating with any dangerous types. I was told to report to him on whether you went to any more of those meetings."

"Meetings?" Gwynna's face went rigid. "I see. And how long have you been employed in this manner?"

"Since the day after your wedding, ma'am. Two weeks. But I have been in the duke's employ since the war. If he heard that I let myself be waylaid like this by two women, and one a little mite like yourself, why, I—" He broke off, suddenly realizing he might have offended her.

Gwynna made circles in the dirt with the toe of her kid boots. Mary watched her nervously, and the man cautiously began to brush the grass from his clothing.

"What is your name?" Gwynna asked.

"Jeremy Barker, ma'am."

"I take it you have some experience in clandestine matters?"

"Yes, ma'am. Although after today, I should probably stick to tending horses."

Gwynna smiled. "Do not feel badly, Mr. Barker. After all, it took us two weeks to notice you."

"Thank you, ma'am." He eyed her uncertainly.

Gwynna put her dagger back in its sheath. "Well, then."

"Ma'am?" He shot her a questioning glance.

"I am finished with my errands today, Mr. Barker," she said crisply. "Perhaps you would like to accompany us home. I have a sudden urge to speak with my husband."

CHAPTER 19

HE HAD NEVER LOOKED SO ARISTOCRATIC, GWYNNA THOUGHT dourly. The midnight superfine fit his broad shoulders to perfection. The white silk stockings were from the finest loom, the damask waistcoat was a superb silk-satin. The breeches were the perfect shade of buff, and they showed his muscled calves to singular advantage. His chapeau, which had arrived only yesterday from an elite Bond Street haberdashery, would sit elegantly on that head of stylishly tousled hair. As he deftly completed his evening toilette, Gideon Traherne was the picture of husbandly arrogance.

"You had no right," she insisted furiously.

That he did not so much as pause in the task of constructing his cravat was pure masculine insolence. Perhaps she could manage to deposit a glass of claret upon that snowy cloth later this evening. The thought of the spreading red stain gave her immense satisfaction. She saw that he was watching her in amusement.

"Whatever revenge you are plotting, my dear," he drawled, "I would advise you to leave off. We are not in Wales, where every imaginary grievance is settled at swordpoint."

"Imaginary grievance?" She stared at him in outrage. "You have me followed like a common criminal for a fortnight and you call it an imaginary grievance?"

He shrugged. "As usual, you are engaged in flights of fancy. I did no more than any husband faced with a wife who has been known to consort with revolutionaries and thugs. It is my duty to make certain that you do not get into trouble."

"Once again, Englishman, you display appalling arrogance and ignorance." Her fists were clenched at her sides. "What you call revolution is no more than a worker's honest struggle for fair wages and a decent meal for his family. You and your society friends care only for yourselves and your fat pensions from the Crown. I despise you all!" She whirled toward the door.

"Bloody hell."

In one swift movement he caught her wrists and pinned her against the wall. "Your opinion of me and my set is of no importance," he said coolly, his eyes glinting with anger. "You are my wife. It is my obligation to protect you. I intend to do that, even if I have to lock you in your room and throw away the key."

Gwynna's wrists ached from the wrenching pressure of his hand. "You have no right!" she whispered fiercely, blinking away tears.

"I have every right. It is you who have none in this matter," came the clipped response.

"Damn your English pride," she cried. "The truth is that you fear being disgraced by your baseborn wife. To have me tossed into Newgate would reflect badly upon your noble sensibilities. Appearances are everything to you, are they not, Englishman? I am like that scar you try to cover with fine linen and elegant manners so no one will guess that you were once capable of tender feeling." She eyed him defiantly. "I shall not be silenced by your notion of proper behavior, proper dress, or proper speech. An Owen does not trade principle for a pretty dress."

Abruptly he released her. Without a word he returned to his mirror and completed his cravat, his expression unreadable. Gwynna eyed the sudden transformation in wonder. His forehead was smooth and unlined, his face impassive. No telltale twitch of the jaw so much as hinted at any lingering emotional turmoil. He was as aloof as he had been the first night she had spied him, sitting astride his horse on the moor, elegantly above the fray.

Even anger was preferable to this distant silence, she thought morosely. Well, what had she expected, anyway? Some heated declaration that he could not bear it if something happened to her? Did she expect him to drop to his knees and declare an undying passion? He would laugh to know how wildly she had engaged in such a false hope. His actions had been intended to keep her from disgracing him; she had been wrong to think that they bespoke a deeper impulse.

And so very foolish to hope that her love might be returned.

GIDEON YANKED OFF HIS CRAVAT and threw it on the floor. He could hear her movements through the door between their rooms. It was only a few hours before dawn. That infernal party had taken forever. They had spent an entire evening with smiles pasted on their faces, although it could not be said in Gwynna's case that she had made much of an effort. She was mad as a hornet.

Devil take it. She had not the slightest clue that those revered revolutionaries of hers were plotting to kill the Prince. For her it was all a matter of glorious principle. But Drew's spies had now firmly linked the plot against the Prince to a Mr. Parkes, said to be one of Hunt's people. The man was being closely watched, but Gideon knew that it was only a matter of time before something happened and Gwynna found herself in the middle of it.

The only thing to do was to get her away from London. They would return to Claremont Castle. There, at least, she would be safe. There would be no tattling tabbies, no fatuous dandies, no silly parties that lasted until dawn. Perhaps they could recapture the closeness of their intimate moments, the warmth that seemed to evaporate the moment reality intruded. He wondered what it would be like to have more than Gwynna's passion, to have her wholehearted love. He knew she would be a fiercely loving and loyal helpmeet to the man who could claim her heart.

Gideon grimaced. He had done little tonight to inspire her loyalty. He had played the heavy-handed husband, inviting her disdain. But how could he explain to her the earth-shattering sense of vulnerability that had come to him on their wedding night—the heartsick fear at the pit of his stomach at the thought of losing her? He had not felt like this since the death of his parents.

Was it love? He prayed not. He had loved his parents with all his heart, but it had not saved them. Early in life, he learned not to put his faith in love.

Gideon stared at the door, wondering whether there was some glimmer of hope for them. After all, he was a grown man now, not a boy to be enslaved by a childish fear. He knew Gwynna would never let fear stop *her* from following her heart. He could learn from her.

He smiled as a sense of peace settled over him. He would go to her now and make amends. He would hold her. They would build on that.

Quietly he pushed open the door. She was standing in the center of the room, dressed in her nightrail, as if she had been waiting for him. His heart soared. Perhaps dreams were possible after all.

Then he noticed the small red ring on a silver chain

around her neck. The one that was supposed to ward off diseases. And him. His heart chilled.

"Protection?" he asked, forcing a light tone to his voice.

She lifted her chin defiantly. "Yes."

"Against me?"

"Do you doubt it?"

His chest felt like stone. The hope that had surged in his breast fled before her stark rejection. "As I told you once before," he said quietly, "you have no need to wear an amulet against me. I have no intention of forcing myself upon you."

She fingered the ring uncertainly. "Truly?"

That one heartfelt word ripped through him like a dagger. He would be damned if he'd let her see how she had destroyed him. His lips thinned into a haughty smile, and his brows arched with all of the arrogance of his title and position.

"My dear," he drawled in a voice laced with irony, "you have the word of an Englishman."

THE HOME SECRETARY SHOOK HIS HEAD. "The winter has commenced with a severity almost beyond example," he said ponderously. "The frost and rain have been abysmal. The harvest was a disaster, and the greater proportion of corn is still uncut. In the country the weather is so severe that bodies of men, women, and children are found daily in the snow. I have sufficient disasters to occupy me for weeks. And now you bring word of more trouble in town?" He looked at Drew with a repressive eye.

Drew exchanged a quick glance with Gideon. "Unfortunately, sir, that is the case. We suspect that the meeting at Spafields next week is merely a pretense. Once the people are assembled, Hunt and his followers plan to incite them to march through the city. We expect a repeat of the earlier violence. Perhaps worse." He handed the secretary a hand-bill.

"*Britons to arms!*" it read. "*Break open all gun and sword shops, pawnbrokers, and other likely places to find arms. No rise of bread. No Castlereagh. Off with his head. No national debt. The whole country waits the signal from London to fly to arms. Stand firm, now or never.*"

The secretary blanched as he read the paper. "Insurrection!" he shouted, banging his fist on his desk. "We must meet the threat head-on. I want every delinquent brought to justice. Fairchild, call a meeting of the magistrates and principal officers. I want all patrols increased. Parents must be notified to keep their children out of the area."

"It will be done," Fairchild responded quickly.

Gideon shifted uncomfortably in his chair. An unruly mob concerned him not in the least, but he had a disturbing image of a pixie-like figure in boy's clothing standing in the middle of the fray. He would make certain Gwynna did not take it into her head to dabble in revolution next week. Barker would jump at the chance to redeem himself. And this time the man would have help.

"I want these delinquents clapped in irons," the Home Secretary said. "It is time that we squelch the revolution brewing in this country. I will not tolerate this outrage." Most of the men around the room nodded. Gideon merely yawned. The secretary eyed him sternly. "Well, Claremont? You have not been heard from on this. Do you have any ideas for protecting our citizens?"

Gideon's smile was enigmatic. "Forgive me, Lord Secretary. I was woolgathering."

"About some new style of cravat, I'll wager," Lord Fairchild muttered.

Gideon sighed. "We all have our obsessions, Fairchild."

Lord Fairchild snorted, and the Home Secretary eyed

Gideon in disgust. Gideon merely returned them a distant smile. Only Drew saw the worried look in his eyes.

The two women exchanged tearful hugs.

"You will write often," Gwynna commanded.

Elizabeth smiled. "You need not worry about me, Gwynna. Mrs. Biddingham will stay with me until the wedding. I expect to see you both there in two months. I will have much to do in the meantime, of course. James says the little house is in need of a woman's touch. I cannot wait to see it."

Gwynna shook her head in wonder. Elizabeth had blossomed from the elegant young lady she had once thought fragile into a glowing young woman eager to exchange her coddled life for one as a doctor's wife. Love, it seemed, had worked wonders. For some people, she amended hastily.

"You may stay here as long as you like, Elizabeth," she said.

Elizabeth turned toward the waiting carriage that already held Mrs. Biddingham. "You have been kind to allow me to make my home here until James found us a house," she said. "But it is time that you and Gideon have this place to yourselves. You are nearly a month married, after all." Elizabeth bit her lip, and Gwynna knew she was thinking of the chilly atmosphere that had reigned since she and Gideon had argued. The door between their rooms was always shut now. They scarcely even spoke to each other. The servants walked on tiptoes, for fear of shattering the tense peace. Elizabeth must have jumped in delight when James's letter arrived announcing the purchase of the house.

"Do not worry about us," Gwynna said firmly. "Go on. Your new life is waiting."

Elizabeth hesitated, then stepped tremulously into the carriage. "Good-bye, Gwynna," she said. "Thank you."

Gwynna frowned. "For what?"

Elizabeth smiled. "For throwing James and me together. I know it was your doing. I would never have had the courage. I was not right for Gideon. I know that now. You are the love of his life. I only pray he realizes it."

Gwynna steeled herself against the lump that welled in her throat. If Gideon was in love, it was certainly not with his wife. He was scarcely home at all these days. He had never seemed so remote as he did now.

Well, there was no sense in mourning a foolish fancy. She would be gone soon enough. Anglesey needed her. Now that Elizabeth was leaving, there was no reason to remain in London. She had been foolish to think that she could fit in here. The only time she had felt engaged in something worthwhile was that day at Spafields. At least someone in London was involved in a cause larger than himself. It would be a grand day when Mr. Hunt and his followers set London on its ear.

She waved good-bye to Elizabeth, then adjusted the bonnet on her head and wrapped her cloak around her. The carriage rolled away. Gwynna gestured silently to her maid and began to walk. Blinking nervously, Mary picked up a bandbox and followed with a tremulous step. Three blocks from the house, Gwynna hailed a hackney cab.

She smiled as she settled against the worn leather interior, undaunted by Mary's fearful expression across from her. Gwynna had looked forward to this meeting ever since she had spotted the freshly printed handbills dotting the store-fronts on the Strand. Mr. Hunt and his people knew how to organize. Such skills were needed on Anglesey. She would learn from these people. Then she would go home.

Jeremy Barker hopped quickly into the cab behind the two women, his heart thumping rapidly in his chest. The duke's lady might be a handful, but he would not be outwitted this time. A quarter hour later, he watched, aghast, as the hackney cab rolled past the outskirts of the city and into a side alley near the notorious alehouse known as Merlin's Cave.

SOMETHING WAS WRONG. It was nearly midafternoon and Mr. Hunt was nowhere to be seen, although his presence was eagerly awaited by the crowd. One of the orators, a Mr. Watson, was standing atop a cart urging the group not to wait for its leader but to follow him into town to show displeasure at the Prince's refusal to hear their petition for aid to the poor. There was a rumor that the Prince had fled to Brighton in order to avoid any contact with the protesters and their representatives.

"His Royal Highness and his cowardly ministers need to be taught a lesson," Watson cried, unfurling several flags. "There are five thousand men in this place able and willing to follow me into the city, where we can do just that." The mob surged forward toward the standards.

Behind her, Mary gave a little shriek. "It is all right, Mary," Gwynna said firmly. "Do not panic. We will simply wait here for Mr. Hunt. He will know what to do."

But the throng of burly tradesmen and laborers swept the women along like leaves on the wind. Mary clung to her, weeping, as Gwynna fought to make a path through the myriad arms and legs, but she was waved aside like an insect. At the tavern she had changed into the boy's clothing Mary had brought in the bandbox, and no one paid any attention to a lad and a little maid.

"Goodness!" Gwynna cried, as rough hands pushed her forward. They would surely be trampled to death if they were unfortunate enough to lose their footing. The only thing she could think of was Gideon's cold anger when he learned that his wife had disgraced him by appearing in public in men's clothing and muddy boots.

Gwynna wondered if her dagger was still secured in the waist of her breeches; the crowd was so tightly packed around them that she could not even move her arms to check. As the mob pressed forward under Mr. Watson's colorful standards, Gwynna and Mary were carried toward the front.

"Arms, arms!" someone cried.

Gwynna saw a man point to a gunsmith's shop. A startled customer at the shop entrance spoke to him. "My friend, you are mistaken," he said. "This is not the place for arms."

To her horror, the first man drew a pistol and shot the customer, who fell to the ground. The stunned shopkeeper instantly closed the door. Enraged, the mob surged forward, smashing windows and breaking down the door. Inside they appropriated guns and pistols that they distributed in great glee to those outside.

"Mary!" Gwynna cried. "We must leave this instant!" The little maid clung to her, scarcely able to move. In truth, there was still nowhere to go; a frenzied mass of limbs and burly bodies blocked their path. They were swept past the gunshop and Cheapside, where the men who had stolen the weapons began to fire them into the air. Within minutes they had reached the Royal Exchange. The mob surged through the gates.

"This for the Prince! This for the Lord Mayor!" came the shouts. Some of the men began to fire randomly, jeering and taunting the Lord Mayor and an alderman, who watched in horror from the steps of the building. Suddenly the gates swung shut, trapping the crowd inside. In the next terror-filled moment, Gwynna saw soldiers ring the compound, their weapons trained on the mob. She turned to Mary, but the maid was nowhere to be found.

"Mary!" she cried, but around her was a sea of enraged

rioters, pushing on all sides. Bruised and battered, she had nowhere to go.

Suddenly a pair of arms grabbed her from behind. They lifted her in the air as if she were a feather. "Stop it!" she cried, struggling against the unseen assailant. "Let me go!"

But her captor, whoever he was, took no notice. He threw her over his shoulders like a sack of potatoes and elbowed his way through the sea of bodies with determined ease. Her screams went unnoticed in the melee around them. Gwynna's pulse hammered in her ear as she fought to master her panic. She was powerless to fight her assailant, powerless to do anything other than bounce against his back as he carried her along. In her ignominious position, she could tell little about him other than the fact that his tattered leather coat smelled of the stable. His shoulders were solid and strong, like his arms. She could feel the corded muscles of his back strain as he worked his way through the mob. He seemed to have the strength of ten men.

Gunfire erupted around them as the soldiers began firing on the mob. Held aloft like this, Gwynna knew she would be an easy target. "Put me down!" she cried.

The man made no reply, only hastened his steps. Gwynna's heart pounded in her chest as he carried her up some steps into a building, through a corridor, and outside again. She was completely disoriented, with no notion of where they were. She heard a creaking sound and realized that they had passed through a small gate. From her vantage point, they appeared to be in a dim alleyway beyond the Exchange. There was no crowd, no soldiers. They were completely alone. The ruffian had her at his mercy. Gwynna swallowed hard, hoping that her dagger was still in place. She would not suffer defeat without a fight.

His arms were wrapped around her legs and backside as

he held her over his shoulder; now one of his hands moved insolently to cup her buttocks.

"Put me down!" she demanded, hoping the bluster in her voice covered the unnaturally high note of fear. The hand lingered for a moment on her hip, then trailed leisurely down her leg.

Suddenly he set her on her feet. She stared at the tattered jacket, stained cap, coarse workshirt, and smudged face. Her mouth fell open.

"You!" she cried, thunderstruck.

Cold fury was written on his face. Copper fire blazed from his eyes, but when he spoke, his voice was perfectly controlled.

"Shall we go home, my dear?" he drawled, arching one brow. "I find myself quite weary of these theatrics."

CHAPTER 20

"WHERE IS MARY?"

He did not bother to look at her, but merely gazed idly out the carriage window. "Fainting into Jeremy Barker's willing arms when last I saw her." His voice was devoid of warmth.

Gwynna studied his rigid profile. "You had us followed, then?"

His gaze slid to her long enough for Gwynna to see the cold rage there. In the next instant he casually adjusted a sleeve of his ragged jacket and calmly resumed his study of the passing street scenes. Even in that dilapidated attire, he still radiated arrogance and poise.

"Your brilliance never ceases to amaze me, my dear," he said flatly. "Now, if you do not mind, I prefer to continue this ride in peace."

Despite his icy remoteness, Gwynna felt a sudden need to bridge the distance between them. "I never thought to see you in such clothes," she ventured hesitantly, "though I suppose you must have used similar disguises in the war."

His head whipped violently around. "There are a great many things that you have never thought of, my dear," he said coldly. "Such as the fact that you could have been killed today. Or worse. Did that not cross your mind?"

Gwynna bit her lip. "I *did* have my dagger . . ."

"Enough!" he roared, and the carriage fairly shook with his rage. She took a deep breath but said nothing. He was right. They had been perilously close to disaster. She shuddered to think what might have happened had he not been there. Still, she might have managed to defend them. She lifted her chin defiantly. It was her right to pursue the causes she believed in. She would not allow him to decree otherwise.

They rode in silence after that. When they reached the town house, he stepped from the carriage and lifted her out before she could even put her foot on the steps. Without a word he carried her into the house, past the startled Adams, up the staircase, and into her bedchamber. He dropped her on the bed, where she landed on her back with a resounding thump that nearly took her breath away.

"Give me the dagger," he commanded.

She lifted her chin defiantly. "No."

A muscle moved in his jaw. In the next instant he reached into her breeches and pulled out the weapon.

"You are living in a dream world," he said in a carefully controlled voice, "if you think this piece of tin would have done aught but get you killed in that mob today." He let it drop to the floor with a clatter.

Gwynna bristled. "I am skilled in its use. We Owens have always mastered the sword. Why, Owen himself once—" She broke off as he leaned over her, a murderous expression on his face. His hands went to the pillow on either side of her head.

"I am weary of your Prince Owen and his mighty feats of battle," he thundered in an awful voice. "I am weary of your Welsh superstitions and your foolish belief that anything can be accomplished simply because you wish it so. I am weary of your causes and your Druids and your flights of fancy. I am weary of—"

He got no further. Gwynna smashed her fist into his chest. "*That's* for your fine English arrogance," she cried. "*I* am weary of your cravats and your tailors and your dandies and your silly notions about what is proper behavior! I shall return to Anglesey. At least there I have work to do!"

He seized her hands and pinned them above her head. She wriggled violently, but he brought his body over hers, immobilizing her. "I assume you mean to inspire the entire island to throw off oppression," he jeered, "just as Mr. Henry Hunt and his minions inspired the masses today to destroy the shops and businesses of decent, hardworking people. If that is your idea of reform, you are no better than a common criminal waiting his due at Newgate."

"Protest does not need to end in rioting and violence," she retorted between clenched teeth.

"And just how do you intend to insure that?" he challenged, his brows arching in scorn. "By risking your life for every cause that a clever orator can persuade you is worthwhile? Face it, Gwynna. You are nothing more than a pawn to the clever tongues of evil."

Daughter of Sin. He might as well have said it. Gwynna bit her lip and fought against the tears. She would not give him the satisfaction of knowing that he had wounded her to the quick.

"You are wrong," she said quietly with as much dignity as she could muster. "But I can see that you will not be persuaded. I shall leave in the morning."

Their gazes locked, sapphire steel against hazel ice. For a long moment they stared at each other, motionless, scarcely seeming to breathe. Suddenly the hazel eyes blazed with copper fire. Gwynna watched, mesmerized, as hunger supplanted his rage. Slowly one of his hands drifted downward to toy with the laces of her shirt. The other kept her hands pinned above her head.

"I might lock you in this room," he said lightly, though his voice was oddly husky. "You would be protected, coddled, catered to, given everything your heart desired. Would that tempt you, my dear?"

Gwynna stared at him in confusion. One moment he was raging at her, the next he was speaking romantic nonsense. "No," she said, though her voice did not sound as firm as she wished.

"Ah, so I thought," he said mournfully. "It is my fate to have married the one woman whose principles cannot be corrupted."

His nimble fingers slipped under the fabric of her shirt and touched her skin. Gwynna shivered involuntarily, and he arched a brow.

"Perhaps," he mused, "you are not so thoroughly incorruptible after all. Perhaps I can find other temptations to keep you here." He began to tease one of her nipples.

Gwynna squirmed under his touch. "You are not playing fair," she said reproachfully.

"No," he agreed. "That would be entirely too principled, would it not? Not at all the thing for an English aristocrat."

His mouth descended to her breast. Gwynna stifled a groan. "You promised never to force me," she reminded him breathlessly.

He paused, noting her parted lips and rapid breathing. "I do not believe it will come to that," he murmured, gently unfastening her breeches with his free hand. "An Englishman always keeps his promise," he added softly.

Gwynna tried to muster outrage at his presumptuousness, but her anger was obscured by the desire kindling in the pit of her stomach. His fingers trailed along her skin in a tantalizing promise of things to come. She watched him, helpless to protest further.

Gideon stared at the sapphire eyes, their pupils wide with passion. She could not know what it cost him to restrain himself from ripping those infernal breeches off her. Cautiously he freed her hands and waited for her to lash out at him. Instead she continued to stare at him, her luminous gaze commanding him to proceed. He forced himself to go slowly as he eased the breeches down her legs, depositing kisses along her soft skin. Even as his control was being assaulted by searing desire, his brain was awash with nightmarish thoughts of what might have happened to her in that lawless mob if he had not found her. She could have been shot, or worse as soon as one of those drunken louts discovered her sex. The realization had shaken him as nothing else.

He felt her tremble as his lips found the inside of her thighs. He should have had a complacent bride, someone like Elizabeth who would not defy him at every turn. He should have had the well-ordered existence he had planned, with passion and other unpredictable forces relegated to carefully controlled compartments of his life. He could not believe the display of emotion she had provoked in him today. It was so unlike him. He had always been able to protect that innermost spot that had remained untouched since the death of his parents and the application of William Traherne's cold paternalism.

Gideon heard her moan as his mouth found the center of her desire. His thoughts spun out of control as she drew him into the heat of her passion. She would not allow him to keep her at bay, to keep his feelings inside where they ought to be. No, she must needs risk her life, throwing him into an agony of despair for fear of losing the one thing that had come to mean more to him than life itself.

Her sweet woman's taste overwhelmed his senses, but he fought for one last rational thought. She wanted to leave, and he would let her. He could not face a lifetime with Gwynna Owen. It was too painful, too disruptive. She demanded nothing less than his soul. And that he would not, could not, give her.

She arched upward, moving against him as she laced her fingers in his hair. Gideon felt the first shudders of her climax, and his heart soared at the pleasure he had brought her. Then his own blinding passion took over, and he could no longer think at all. He entered her at last, crooning her name as if it were a magical word that would preserve their union for all eternity.

"Gwynna," he whispered again and again, knowing that he was drowning in her, losing his last grip on the lifeboat that could carry him home. He clung to her, unable to turn back to the safe sands of the shore. Instead he drove on, propelled by an inexorable force toward a foreign horizon that went on and on and on.

"I WISH TO SEE the duke's resting place."

Aloysius Busby shifted uncomfortably before the young woman's demanding gaze. "The former duke is interred in the family mausoleum, Your Grace," he said politely. "It is never opened except to bury the dead. There is nothing to see there, I'm afraid."

Gwynna eyed him haughtily. "Are you refusing my request to see my father's grave, Mr. Busby?"

Mr. Busby sighed. It seemed that the new duchess and her autocratic husband were perfectly matched after all. "No, Your Grace," he said politely. "But we will need assistance. There are several gates that must be unlocked and a heavy stone statue that sits most awkwardly in front of the lock on the last gate . . ."

"Then see to it, Mr. Busby," she commanded.

An hour later, Gwynna, Mr. Busby, and young Jim Crowley were hiking toward the imposing stone structure on a hill above Claremont Castle. Gwynna was not sure why it was suddenly so important to see her father's grave, except that this was the last time she would ever set foot on

Claremont property. Tomorrow she would leave for Anglesey, and the Trahernes would be part of her past.

Gwynna blinked back tears, remembering how she and Gideon had parted the day after he rescued her from the riot. His face rigid, he had handed her into the carriage, then quickly stepped back as if he could not bear to touch her. Obviously he was glad to have her out of his life.

Well, she was glad to be on her way, too. She could not sit around London and endure another moment of the false gaiety and superficiality that was life in the *ton*. She had a name to uphold, a cause to fight for. She was an Owen. Their worlds must forever be separate.

The men were struggling with the gates. She felt a twinge of guilt as Mr. Busby's face grew red with exertion. Finally the last gate swung open, and they stepped inside.

"There," Mr. Busby said, breathing heavily. He held the torch aloft so she could make her way in the dim, ornately carved chamber.

So this was where the dukes of Claremont had their final rest. Stone gargoyles and cherubs looked back at her with blank eyes. Gwynna wondered if all the dukes had been of the same stamp, arrogant and cold like Gideon. Yet Gideon was not like that, not really. The copper fire in his eyes could melt an iceberg, and their lovemaking that last time had been uniquely intense, as if their souls had met on some wondrous level. But then he had withdrawn to his chamber. The next morning, he had quietly let her go.

She tried to concentrate on the name written on the stone crypt. William Edgar Traherne. From the little she knew about him, it appeared that her father had been incapable of love. Even Mr. Busby, loyal retainer that he was, had not painted a warm portrait of the late duke. It was hard to imagine what about the man had captivated her mother. Likely she would never know.

She stared at the tomb, blinking until her eyes were used to the dimness.

"You see, Your Grace?" Mr. Busby ventured hesitantly. "There is really nothing to see."

Gwynna moved closer, running her hands over the letters that had been carved in the stone. How she wished that she had known him. But he had not wanted that. Was it because they had been nothing to him, her mother merely an island wench he bedded in a night of unrestrained lust?

Tears came to her eyes, blurring her vision such that she almost missed the tiny letters chiseled under his name. When at last she saw them, she gasped in amazement. Blinking rapidly, she ran her fingers over the letters one by one.

"Your Grace?" Mr. Busby prodded hesitantly. Gwynna turned toward him, tears streaming down her cheeks. "Your Grace!" he stammered, reaching for a worn handkerchief in his pocket.

"Do you not see, Mr. Busby?" she said haltingly. "The lines inscribed here?"

He squinted and studied the letters. "Why, no, ma'am. I cannot read a single word."

Gwynna smiled through her tears. "Of course. I am sorry, Mr. Busby. It is Welsh. Beautiful, glorious Welsh. Allow me to translate." She cleared her throat and read in a shaky voice: " 'The remembrance of thee, thou golden beam, never passed over me without weeping.' "

The men stared at her, uncomprehending. "It is from a poem by Gruffyth Llwyd," she explained, her voice breaking.

"A *poem*?" Mr. Busby echoed in astonishment. "The duke had a *poem* carved on his tomb?" He frowned. "Forgive me, madam, but that does not sound at all like the duke."

"I am beginning to think that there is much about my father that we do not know," Gwynna said, turning away. It was clear that Mr. Busby had not the least understanding of the significance of the finding. Her father, the man everyone believed incapable of tender feelings, had had carved on his final resting place a poet's soulful lament for a loved one lost. Her heart soared, for she knew without question that those lines expressed his love for her mother and the loss he felt at her death. The final proof was in his choice of this poem, which she knew by heart. It had been written four hundred years ago in praise of Owen Glendowr.

Whatever else William Traherne was, he had loved Megan Owen.

Gwynna closed her eyes against the bittersweet knowledge. Her parents were gone, but however fleetingly, they had crossed the chasm between their two vastly different worlds. Had they struggled, like her and Gideon, before finally driving each other apart? Had they declared their love, only to watch it strain under the force of her family's disapproval? Or had William Traherne saved for his tomb the declaration that he loved his late bride? A declaration that no one, save her, could understand?

She swallowed hard. Their love, whatever it had been, survived in her. But what of her and Gideon? Were they doomed to repeat her parents' mistakes? Faced with this poignant symbol of lost love, she yearned to return to him, no matter how difficult it might be to live in his world. But there was one obstacle she could not overcome: he did not love her. She could not become someone else, living in a world she despised, merely to pretend that he did. She was an Owen. Owens were made of stronger stuff.

This then, was the sacrifice. She understood now. A broken heart to last the rest of her days was the price she would pay for loving Gideon Traherne.

"Mr. Busby," she said softly, "I am ready to return to the castle."

CHAPTER 21

SHE HAD BEEN GONE A FORTNIGHT. TWO WEEKS OF UTTER HELL.

The voices around Gideon blended into a single annoying buzz as he sat, arms crossed, trying to force his attention on them and away from that one stark fact.

"We have found no connection between the riots at Dundee last week and what happened here in London a fortnight ago." It was Drew's voice, forceful and brisk.

"Nonsense." The Home Secretary eyed Drew indignantly. "All seditious acts fuel the general insurgency. We must prepare for revolution."

"The disturbance in Dundee was fueled by the sudden increase in the price of meal," Drew said patiently. "The men saw their survival at stake. They vented their spleen on the corn dealers, especially a Mr. Lindsay, and set his house on fire. Some of them evidently felt remorse, for they extinguished it shortly thereafter."

"Hmmph." The Home Secretary looked skeptical. "If survival is the concern, why attack the dealers? That only makes food scarcer and dearer, since the farmer will simply carry his crop elsewhere, to a dealer who can sell it safely. No, this is not about hunger, Westbrook. Those rioters are plainly revolutionaries."

Revolutionaries. Once he had thought that label applied to Gwynna, and perhaps it did. But she was so much more than the sum of her causes, which in themselves were more about constructive change than sheer destruction. To be sure, she was unsettling in the extreme. The day she left him, he had still been reeling from the previous night's lovemaking, which had finally snapped his rigid control. Profoundly shaken, he could scarcely bring himself to touch her as she entered the carriage, for fear he would disgrace himself by pleading with her to stay.

Had he fought so hard to keep his soul, only to lose it to a red-haired Welsh princess? Gideon shook his head. He was being fanciful. There was nothing the matter with him. He had merely lost a wife, a woman who did not belong with him anyway. He tried to force his attention to the matter at hand.

Drew's face, he saw, was suffused with irritation. "Some of the rioters must subsist on less than one meal a day," his friend pointedly informed the secretary. "The deprivations, scarcity of employment, low wages, and other conditions they must endure only increase the likelihood of disturbance. We do not think these conditions bespeak revolution, only the need to address the root causes."

"Nonsense." This from Lord Fairchild. "Reports are coming in from all over the country. Bolton. Manchester. Stockport. Sheffield. The local authorities have pleaded for immediate military reinforcements. The state of the country is ominous."

And dangerous, Gideon realized. What was he thinking of, allowing her to embark on an arduous, cross-country trip? It was true that he had sent her off with a full escort, eight outriders under the command of Jeremy Barker. She would travel like a duchess—at least to Claremont. But he had a nagging feeling that Gwynna would not wish to arrive on Anglesey in such style. He frowned. Why had he not thought of that? She would doubtless slip her escort and travel on her own, perhaps in that ridiculous disguise of hers. Was she even now making for Anglesey alone? The thought was terrifying. Besides the lawlessness around, the weather was abysmal. A hurricane had struck in the south, and violent snowstorms were raging to the north and west. Even in London, there was talk of the Thames freezing over.

"The local officials are merely panicking," Drew said. "Some of the 'seditious' meetings that cause them such alarm are no more than the normal activities of societies and trade unions."

"Radicals all," declared the Home Secretary. "Friendly Societies, Hampden Clubs, Spencean Societies—it does not matter what they call themselves, they are all promoting riot and mayhem."

"Some are simply conducting their usual business," Drew insisted in exasperation. "We have only rumors of an armed uprising. They have been in no way substantiated."

"What other evidence do you need?" demanded Lord Fairchild. "After Spafields, I should think the proof is overwhelming."

The Home Secretary looked around the room. "Well, gentlemen, it seems we have a difference of opinion. What say you, Claremont?"

Gideon arched his brows. "I think it would have been helpful," he said casually, "had His Royal Highness not fled to Brighton."

The Home Secretary blinked. Lord Fairchild looked nonplussed   eyed him with interest, an expression of wry amusement on his face.

"What nonsense are you babbling, Claremont?" Fairchild demanded.

Gideon rose to his feet, crossed the room to Lord Fairchild, and eyed him assessingly. His lordship shifted nervously in his chair.

"No offense was meant, Claremont," Lord Fairchild said

quickly, but Gideon merely gave him a frosty smile and walked over to the mantelpiece.

"You asked for my opinion, Lord Secretary, and so you shall have it," Gideon said. "You are free to ignore it, of course, as I shall certainly endeavor to forget the ignorance and hysteria I have heard here today."

The Home Secretary frowned. Lord Fairchild cleared his throat, and the other men in the room stared. Gideon carelessly brushed an imaginary speck from his lapel.

"The Prince's timing was abysmal," he said. "He should not have gone to Brighton as his most disgruntled subjects were assembling in Spafields to await his decision on their petition. His flight into the arms of a hurricane signaled his preference to take his chances with the vagaries of nature rather than to consider a heartfelt plea from the people for relief of their misery. His callous attitude is echoed by his ministers, local officials, and indeed, the men in this very room."

He gave each man a searching look as he leaned against the mantelpiece. "There is not one of you who, finding himself in the circumstances of endeavoring to provide for his family with no prospects for the day's meal, would not strike a blow against those whom you perceive as the oppressors. Drew is right: we must go after the root causes of these disturbances. We gain nothing otherwise. We must reform the export laws. And I see nothing amiss with extending the right to vote to all citizens."

There was a stunned silence that lasted for several minutes, during which most of those in the room stared at Gideon in shock. He merely returned them a benign expression.

Finally the Home Secretary spoke. "Are you quite well, Claremont?" he asked hesitantly. "We have heard of your, uh, domestic difficulties. Perhaps that might explain your thoroughly unexpected point of view." He looked hopefully at Gideon.

Gideon's brows arched disdainfully. "I take it, Lord Secretary," he said, "that you have the ill grace to refer publicly to the fact that my wife has seen fit to take herself off on a holiday alone. I did not realize the matter was common knowledge, but since you have broached the subject, allow me to say that my domestic situation has had no effect on my reasoning abilities."

With that, he turned and left the room. Only after the door shut behind him did his composure slip.

"Liar," he bit out, and a startled clerk nearly jumped from his chair. Gideon nodded curtly at the man and strode out into the snow.

GWYNNA KNELT AT THE ENTRANCE to her father's tomb. The first rays of dawn were just filtering through the gray horizon. In a moment it would be time to leave. She must be gone before the castle stirred. But first she would say this prayer. The ancients had always said the prayer of life for the dead, to hasten their spirits heavenward to join the eternal force. She was quite certain that no one had said such a prayer for William Traherne.

She pricked her finger with the dagger and allowed a drop of blood to spill onto the pile of small stones she had assembled at the tomb's outer iron gate. She murmured the ancient words of the obscure prayer. Then she kissed the altar and lifted her arms to the sky.

"William Edgar Traherne," she cried softly, "may your soul live on for all eternity."

A gentle breeze ruffled her hair. A few birds had begun their waking songs. The crimson dawn would soon move westward. Gwynna smiled. Now she could leave in peace.

She turned to go, then hesitated. If only she could have

some memento. Nothing large, to be sure. She had only a small pouch for her things, and the leather jacket she had borrowed from one of the stable lads against the biting cold had only one pocket. But it would not take above a few minutes to return to the castle and choose some small souvenir. She ran down the hill toward the castle.

Slipping inside minutes later, she realized she need not have hurried. Everyone was still abed. In Gideon's absence, no one felt the need to rise early, and she had instructed Rowland not to rouse the staff on her behalf. She crept down a hall toward the library. Perhaps a small book of poems would do.

Gwynna threw open the curtains to allow the sun's fledgling rays to penetrate the darkness. She scanned the shelves. They were filled with the classics, in Greek and Latin, neither of which she could read. She frowned. She did not want some obscure volume of Latin. Recalling the inscription on her father's tomb, she had a sudden inspiration. Might he have some volumes of Welsh poetry?

She looked hurriedly around. There did not seem to be much of a system of organization. Most of the volumes were covered in dust. Finally, in a nook near a large upholstered chair, she spied a tattered little red volume, its binding worn but the gold-leaf letters still visible. She read the author's name with elation.

"Gruffyth Llwyd," she whispered, gingerly turning the pages. The book was in the original Welsh. Had her father managed to learn her mother's language? Or had he simply enjoyed staring at the words, remembering his lost love? Perhaps the two of them had sometimes sat on Anglesey's flat, smooth beaches, her mother reading poetry to her enthralled lover.

Gwynna shook her head impatiently. There would be time to daydream later. For now, it was imperative to take her leave. Hastily she closed the book. A piece of parchment, folded neatly in two, slipped from its pages and wafted to the floor. There was a seal on one yellowed corner. She retrieved the paper and held it up to the sunlight, squinting to make out the words.

"The Archbishop of Bangor," she read. Her eyes widened in wonder as she scrutinized the rest of the document. There, for all to see, were the names of William Edgar Traherne and Megan Glendowr Owen.

Her parents' marriage certificate.

They had crossed the strait to be married in Bangor. The vows had not been said at the tomb, only consummated there. No wonder the records had not been found on the island. They must have felt the need for secrecy, in the face of her grandfather's opposition. But why had the duke left her mother to weather a pregnancy alone? Unless he did not know that she was breeding. Gwynna pondered that possibility. Perhaps he had not known until David Owen wrote to inform him of her mother's death and her birth. But why did the duke not then acknowledge his daughter? Gwynna bit her lip. She knew so little of William Traherne. Perhaps he thought she was better off on the island than in this forbidding castle with an embittered man. Sadly she realized she would never know. Her father had chosen to carry his bitterness and grief to his grave.

Gwynna returned the document to the book. "He has paid the price for his actions, Mother," she said in a hushed voice. "And so have we all."

HE TOOK A LAST LOOK at himself in the foyer mirror. Gwynna would no doubt be irritated by the fact that his curly beaver hat sat at precisely the right angle. And by the fact that his fur-lined cloak was as elegant as anything anyone on Anglesey had ever seen. A tiger could not change his stripes, any more than he could consign his wardrobe to the rag pile because it did not fit his wife's notions of proper revolutionary attire. What mattered was that the cloak would be warm as toast for traveling, although it did, perhaps, look a bit funereal. He smiled. There was nothing funereal about his mood. For the first time in three weeks, Gideon felt an elation of anticipation over the future.

He was going to retrieve his wife.

Well, perhaps not *retrieve* her, precisely—at least not to return here. Gwynna had made her feelings for London clear. They would live at Claremont, where she could rusticate to her heart's content and visit that island of hers whenever she wished. They would remodel the nursery and somehow make that drafty castle livable. Perhaps they would journey to London upon occasion, but he was through with the trappings of society. He would immerse himself in life in the country. She would show him how to commune with the clouds. Perhaps he would learn Welsh. Their worlds did not have to be miles apart.

His butler opened the door for him, and Gideon paused on the threshold to survey the skies. More snow clouds were moving in, but he would be well on the road before they could upset his travel plans. He squinted at a cloud. It seemed to bear her image. Even the wisps curling around it reminded him of the unruly red hair that framed her face. He knew his brain was playing him tricks, but that was all the more reason to be on his way. With a jaunty step, he moved toward his waiting traveling coach.

"I hope you are not leaving," a voice said urgently. "I need your assistance."

Gideon frowned at the figure that blocked his path. "Whatever is it, Drew, it will have to wait. I am leaving, as you can see. I do not know when I shall return."

"This cannot wait," the earl replied tersely.

Gideon arched his brow. "Nonsense. My happiness is at stake, my dear fellow," he drawled. "You would not condemn a man to a life of misery just because the Home Secretary has yet another report of an uprising in the making."

"Someone has just attacked the Prince."

Gideon stood motionless while his carefully constructed fantasy crumbled around him. In the same moment, the cloud bearing Gwynna's image drifted away. He sighed heavily.

"Let us go, then."

"Evans will be furious."

"What difference does it make? He has all the food he needs. We are the ones who will suffer. There is no corn for the rest of the winter."

A woman spoke. "The magistrate says there is not the least cause to anticipate a scarcity."

"Aye, and there are plenty who disagree with him," returned her husband. "I am with Gwynna. We need to take matters into our own hands. The shipments of our food abroad must stop. Otherwise there'll be none for our families."

Ryan Jones shook his head. The room was full of angry miners and Amlwich residents who feared a winter of famine. They were just irate enough to act. Gwynna had ignited a powder keg with her fiery words.

"The mine owners have promised to come to our aid," Ryan interjected, but this set off another round of grumbling. Gwynna looked at him indignantly.

"You know as well as any man in this room, Ryan Jones, that the owners' promises are as empty as our pantries. They have not made good on the loans. Even if they did, I am certain the money would buy only a small amount of inferior corn. They will continue to export the best."

"Yes, but—" Ryan broke off, his words drowned in a sea of angry voices. Somehow he had to prevent Gwynna from getting involved in this crisis. It was too dangerous, and she was too incautious. She would find herself clapped into irons, or worse, if he could not think of something. But he knew that the people were drawn to her as they were drawn to no other. Hers was the first voice they had heard in a long time that rang of hope and action. And, of course, she was an Owen. There was no gainsaying an Owen on Anglesey.

"Now," she was saying, "if we are agreed, here is my plan. The *Wellington* is to sail in three days' time. They have been loading it with oats all week."

Everyone nodded. They had all seen the ship docked in Amlwich harbor.

"Just how do ye plan to stop a ship from sailing, missy?" asked one of the men. "Be ye expecting Owen himself to sweep down from the clouds and stand in its way?"

There was laughter all around. Gwynna eyed him defiantly. "Even you, Duncan Miller, will have to admit that not even the *Wellington* can sail without its rudder." Her eyes gleamed at the sudden interest in the eyes of those around her. "Now. Here is what we shall do."

Ryan listened to her words with growing horror. Slowly the heads in the room began to nod in approval. He put his hands over his face and groaned.

CHAPTER 22

HE COULD NOT WAIT TO SEE HER FACE WHEN HE TOLD HER OF THE violence that her esteemed Mr. Hunt had wrought. No matter that Hunt was disavowing any nefarious intent or association with that fellow Parkes, who had been caught on the spot. Even if Hunt was himself innocent, his clever oratory had set the stage for the assault, and Gideon was fairly sure that even Gwynna would not approve of such a cowardly and disgraceful act. At first it was thought that bullets had shattered the windows of the state carriage as the Prince returned from the opening of Parliament. That the missiles turned out to be rocks hardly lessened the crime. The mob had even assaulted the horses pulling the Prince's carriage. It was a dastardly attack on the very symbol of order, tradition, and authority.

Gideon grimaced. He was beginning to sound like the Lord Secretary. Now *that* was a sobering thought.

He could not imagine where it would all end up. The assault had fueled the government's fears and galvanized even the most recalcitrant members of Parliament to action. The secret committee had met night and day over the last week. Already there was talk of suspending habeas corpus. The poor and the disadvantaged would suffer, as usual. Now where had *that* thought come from? He frowned. He was beginning to sound more like Gwynna every day.

Worst of all, the assault had delayed his departure, and when he arrived at Claremont Castle, it was to discover that all was at sixes and sevens. A horrible fear had torn at his gut when he discovered that she had fled the castle. At least she had not set out on foot—one of the horses was missing. When Gideon arrived, Barker had just returned from searching the countryside unsuccessfully for two days. The man's teeth were chattering so from the cold that it took Gideon several minutes to understand what had happened.

Then there was Aloysius Busby's meandering account of what had transpired at William Traherne's tomb. If any of them had known Welsh, there might have been a clue as to what had so moved his wife. But Gideon was not about to waste time scouring Cheshire for someone to translate the inscription on a dead man's tomb. Not when Gwynna was no doubt in the thick of things elsewhere. Anglesey, if he did not miss his guess.

He made it to the strait in less than a day, only to find that the last ferry to the island had already left and he would have to cool his heels overnight in a Bangor inn. It was not until the next midday that he stepped onto the island, pausing long enough to savor the pungent sea breezes and the beauty of the sprawling beaches. But he was not here to see the sights, so he spurred Captain onward. In a frantic afternoon of searching he discovered that Gwynna was not in her grandfather's house, not at the tombs, not at her cousin Bridget's. The woman had wrung her hands and eyed him nervously for a full half hour before she finally told him what he dreaded to hear: his bride was off leading a revolution at the north end of the island.

"I know it sounds dreadful, Your Grace," she responded at his appalled expression, "but the Owens have always answered the needs of the people."

Some day, Gideon thought grimly, he would avenge himself on Owen Glendowr.

GWYNNA SMILED. The *Wellington's* rudder sat safely in the churchyard. They had surprised the ship's crew and made off with it in a daring assault at dawn. Despite the cold, scores of townsfolk were parading in the streets and down at the harbor. Any moment now and the constables hurriedly sworn in by the magistrate would arrive to take the rudder back. Whatever happened after this, the people had won. They had become a force to be reckoned with. As if to underscore the point, the dark clouds that had hovered all day suddenly cleared, leaving them under sunny, crystal-blue skies.

"We shall not let them have it," Gwynna said firmly, and a dozen heads in the courtyard nodded vigorously. But one man frowned.

"Best let them, Gwynna. If the constables don't succeed, you can be sure that the soldiers will not be far behind."

"Duncan is right." It was Ryan. "Let it go, Gwynna. Else we shall all end up in jail."

Gwynna eyed them steadily. "Anyone who wishes to leave may do so. You all have families who would suffer if you were clapped in irons. But I do not, so I shall stand in your stead."

There was much discussion over this. "If you are arrested, we will rescue you, Gwynna," shouted one young man.

"Thank you, John," she replied with a smile.

Just then a rumbling of horses sounded from out in the street. Suddenly nearly thirty men burst into the courtyard. Stephen Roose, the magistrate, stood at their fore.

"We have come for the rudder," Roose announced.

Gwynna gestured behind her. "There it is, gentlemen," she said calmly. "But you will have to take it by force."

"Now, Gwynna," Roose began placatingly, "there is no need for conflict. We wish a peaceful ending to this disturbance. I shall be forced to call for your arrest if you do not cooperate."

Gwynna nodded. "You must do what you must, Stephen," she said. "But so must I. And I tell you that we cannot stand by any longer while our food is shipped out for the profit of the wealthy few. Our families are going hungry. Our men are unemployed. Those fortunate to have jobs must slave in the mines for abysmal wages that are seldom paid. Get the mine owners down here, Stephen. Get the landowners. Then we will talk about the *Wellington*'s rudder."

Roose glared at her, his face florid. "Damnation, woman, you cannot simply take matters into your own hands like this."

"We can and we have," she replied firmly. "It is our duty to set aside this oppression. You live on this island," she added at his scowl, "as do your constables. You have families. How long are we meant to stand by in the face of approaching famine?"

The constables exchanged glances. Roose eyed them uneasily and shook his head. "There will be no famine. Something will be done to assure that sufficient food remains on the island."

"I have no faith in empty promises, Stephen Roose," Gwynna retorted. "You speak for no one but yourself. Bring the owners, and we will talk."

Roose swore. "I cannot allow you to flout the law, woman," he said angrily. "Will you step aside?"

Gwynna shook her head. "Nay. I will stand firm."

"Men, arrest Miss Owen," Roose ordered angrily. "And seize the *Wellington*'s rudder."

The constables shifted nervously but did not appear to

know how to proceed in an advance upon a solitary woman. The magistrate's face reddened in fury.

"Damnation!" he shouted. "What kind of men are you to be cowed by a slip of a woman with a clever tongue? You were sworn this very day to do your duty!"

Hesitantly the constables moved forward. Gwynna stood facing them, her chin high. With a heavy sigh, Ryan Jones moved to her side. One by one, the other townsfolk in the courtyard moved to stand behind them, shoulder to shoulder in front of the rudder.

Roose was apoplectic at their show of defiance. "Pistols, men!" he shouted. He drew his weapon. After a moment's hesitation, the constables followed suit.

Gwynna took out her dagger. Those behind her pulled out an assortment of weapons. "We do not want to fight you," she said, "but we will if we must." Roose took a step forward, and the phalanx of constables did likewise. Gwynna lifted her dagger skyward.

"Very well, then," she said in a firm, clear voice. "To the day of judgment!" She repeated the words in Welsh. The townsfolk echoed her battle cry, and the air in the courtyard was suddenly electric with tension.

Gwynna's knuckles whitened around her dagger. Her body felt strangely light and nimble in the exhilarating cold. Her mind was clear, although her senses swam in the heady excitement of anticipated battle. She would lose, perhaps, but she would give a good accounting of herself. If her life was meant to join the eternal force today, so be it. She would have no regrets. The image of a pair of burning hazel eyes came before her, but she willed it away. No regrets, she repeated firmly to herself.

The silence in the courtyard was deafening. Roose looked like a madman, his eyes wild and his face dangerously flushed. His rapid breathing produced clouds of vapor from his nostrils. He turned to his men. Gwynna could see his lips move as he barked an order; oddly, she could not hear him. She gripped her dagger with all her might and waited for them to fire.

Now, she thought. *Let it be now.*

"How dreadful," drawled a bored voice. "I do so detest bloodshed."

Gwynna stared in amazement. At the courtyard entrance, an elegant figure sat astride his magnificent roan.

"Gideon!"

He nodded an acknowledgment, though his eyes never left the pistol Roose held in his hand. "I do wish you would consult me before you involve yourself in such matters, my dear," Gideon said. "I believe there are more peaceable ways of deciding the fate of a rusty rudder."

"You do not understand," Gwynna insisted angrily.

"That is where you are wrong," he replied calmly. "I do indeed."

The red-faced Roose finally found his tongue. "Who are you?" he demanded.

Gideon inclined his head. "I am Claremont. Miss Owen's husband, to be precise."

"Claremont?" Roose gaped at him. "The *Duke* of Claremont, the same one who—"

"Not the same one, my good fellow, if you are referring to Miss Owen's father. That was my late relative. A thoroughly infuriating man, to be sure. But let us return to the matter at hand. You see, I am afraid I cannot allow you to put a bullet into my wife, as tempting as that may seem at times. My suggestion is that we adjourn to another place and deal with this matter in a calmer fashion."

Roose shook his head. "I do not seek violence, Claremont. But I must have the rudder. I cannot allow it to remain here."

"And have it you shall," Gideon replied. "But I believe

the people's demands must also be heard. Are you prepared to hear them?"

All eyes turned to Roose, who shifted nervously under the scrutiny. "I have no authority to negotiate any demands," he said in a surly tone. "I am merely here to enforce the law."

"Then I suggest that you send for someone who can address the people's concerns," Gideon said smoothly. "The mine owners, perhaps? And the landowners. As my wife so wisely suggested." Gwynna eyed him in surprise, startled at his support.

Roose weighed this for a moment. The entrance of the Duke of Claremont into the fray changed things enormously. He knew he could not afford to offend this man.

"Very well," he said at last. "I shall send someone forthwith. Shall you be participating in the negotiations, sir?"

"I would not miss them," Gideon murmured.

Roose lowered his weapon. There was a collective sigh of relief among the constables as they followed suit. But just as Gwynna felt the tension begin to flow out of her body, an angry voice boomed across the courtyard.

"Halt in the name of all that is holy!"

Now all heads turned to the newcomer. He stood at the opposite side of the courtyard, a towering figure of rage. He, too, held a pistol, and it was pointed at Gwynna.

"Evans!" she gasped. He was dressed all in black, and the scowl on his face looked to be that of the devil himself.

"See here, Evans," Roose protested.

"Drop your weapon, Roose," Evans commanded, "and have the others do likewise, or I shall shoot her from this very spot."

Stunned, Roose nodded to his men. Their weapons clattered to the ground, as did those of the townsfolk.

"I cannot let this daughter of sin lead my flock astray,"

Evans declared in a thunderous voice. "She is a willful woman who thinks to laugh at the law and its emissaries. She cares not for the ways of righteousness. She twists everything to her own ends, in the way of one who was conceived in sin and cannot but live her life as fruit of that evil seed."

"You are a liar, Evans," Gwynna shouted. "*You* are the one who twists everything. You seek only to make a profit on the backs of the people. We know that you are paid well for the shipments that leave these shores. You hide behind your pious words, but your soul is as black as that of any demon."

"Silence, temptress!" he roared. "You deserve to die for the wages of your sin, and to suffer the torment of the damned for all eternity."

He was mad, Gwynna thought, utterly mad. But she was powerless to move as those coal-black eyes summoned her into their depths. He came toward her, the pistol pointed straight at her heart. Her pulse thundered in her ears. Surely he would not shoot. Even Evans was not depraved enough to kill her before the entire town. No one around them dared to breathe.

"I say, Evans," Gideon drawled, "has your vengeful Welsh soul overcome those lofty Methodist principles of yours?"

The minister glowered, but kept his eyes fixed on Gwynna. "Do not think your clever words or foppish ways can save her, Claremont," he said in a singsong voice. "She is beyond you, beyond all hope. I should have killed her when I had my hands on her. It would have been so easy to snap that slender neck for her sins, for the temptations she offered."

"I offered you nothing, Evans," Gwynna cried. "It was

you who used my grandfather to get to me. You who assaulted me as he lay dying."

"Silence!"

His roar was that of an enraged, wounded animal, and Gwynna watched in horror as he leveled the pistol at her. Everyone in the courtyard stood stunned and motionless. Now she could see her fate as clearly as if it had been laid out from the moment of her birth. At least this time there would be witnesses to make him pay for his crime. He would hang; her death would be avenged. Gwynna bit her lip. That was precious little compensation for a life without Gideon. As those thoughts flashed through her head, she saw Evans's enormous body jerk strangely. She stared, uncomprehending, as he came toward her. But something was wrong. Like a character in a dream, he moved slowly, his limbs not fully in his control. Suddenly he fell heavily at her feet.

In her daze she had not heard the report of the gun that brought him down. But she knew instinctively that it had come from the gleaming silver pistol she had once seen in the finely gloved hand of a rider on a Cheshire moor.

And she knew that Christmas Evans had been shot clean through the heart.

HE FOUND HER at the tomb.

Gideon halted Captain at the edge of the clearing and watched as she approached the ancient earthen mound. She was dressed in her breeches and thin homespun shirt, scant protection against the harsh winter winds. They did not seem to disturb her, however; she looked calm and serene.

She must have risen at dawn, for he had presented himself at her cousin Bridget's door only a little after that. He had scarcely slept. By the time he had settled things last night with that infernal magistrate, someone had already delivered her safely to her cousin's house, and he was forced to take a room at the Bull's Head Inn. When he had arrived this morning to claim his wife, Bridget had haltingly informed him that Gwynna was gone.

In that moment he vowed never to let her out of his sight again.

Now here she was at last, chanting some incomprehensible prayer. He supposed he would never understand these Welsh customs. No doubt it would take a lifetime. He smiled at the thought.

She knelt at the tomb's stone entryway, where she had arranged a pile of small rocks. She pulled out her dagger and put it to her breast.

Good God. Not again.

"I trust you are not planning anything lethal," he said. "I would hate to give Evans's ghost reason to dance in glee."

She started and looked up at him in surprise. Then she smiled shyly. "It is only a small sacrifice. Teuth is feeling generous this morning."

He dismounted, watching her carefully. "Is he?"

She nodded. "He is pleased that bloodshed was averted."

Gideon's brows rose. "Have you forgotten the unfortunate Mr. Evans?"

"No. But it appears that his sacrifice was necessary."

"I see." He sighed. "Gwynna, I confess it is most difficult for me to understand these rituals of yours."

"I know. I am sorry." She paused, then hesitantly added, "I have not thanked you for what you did last night."

He looked at her from hooded eyes. "Did you think I would allow the man to put a bullet into your heart?"

"N-no, I suppose not," she haltingly. "It is just that, well—confound it, Gideon, I never know what to think. You are full of surprises."

"I know the feeling," he replied dryly.

"I also wanted to thank you for the loans you arranged," she rushed on. "They will see the island through the winter. Once the mine owners understood that the wealthy Duke of Claremont was willing to subsidize the plan, they had no reason to hold back. And your idea of putting the men to work on harbor improvements was an inspired notion."

"Thank you."

Gwynna felt strangely shy. He must have come to say good-bye. Had he not just pointed out the differences between them once again? How could a pink of the *ton*, a duke at that, endure having a wife who pricked her flesh in sacrifice to some obscure Druid god? He had once called her barbaric; that was how she would always appear to his world. She rose, not knowing how to proceed. He simply stood there, watching her from those hooded hazel eyes.

"What was it that you discovered at William Traherne's tomb?"

His question caught her by surprise. "That he loved my mother and grieved for her until his death." She lifted her chin defiantly, bracing for his scoffing denial. "I found their marriage lines in a book of Welsh poems in my father's library."

There was a brief pause before he spoke. "I am not surprised."

Her mouth fell open. "What?"

"My cousin was my guardian for a time," he said. "Did you know that?" She shook her head. "The man I knew was cold and arrogant," he continued, looking off at the horizon. "He cared for nothing and no one. He was an empty shell of a man, incapable of love and marriage."

Gwynna frowned. "Then why are you not surprised to learn that they wed?"

"Because now I understand that I knew him afterward, when his soul had already died to his grief. And because," he added ruefully, taking her hand, "if your mother was anything like you, she must have thoroughly shaken his world." He smiled. "I believe William Traherne fell in love for the first and only time in his miserable life."

His expression grew somber. "Perhaps he had second thoughts after they married. Perhaps they argued, as we have done, over the differences in their worlds."

Gwynna flushed.

"Or perhaps he wanted to give her time to accustom her father to the news," he continued. "For whatever reason, he left the island. Too late he realized that he had left the only redeeming piece of him behind. When he learned of her death—and your existence—it must have devastated him. He never recovered."

Tears spilled from her eyes. "Why did he never write to me? Or visit? Or acknowledge me in any way?"

Gently he brushed a tear from her cheek. "Perhaps in his last days he planned to," he replied softly. "We know that he was trying to secure your guardianship. We do not know why he did not do so earlier. Possibly he simply could not get beyond his grief."

Gwynna thought of her grandfather, who had spent so many years in grief. She wanted to weep for the prisons of silence these two men had forced on themselves. She touched Gideon's hand. Instantly he pulled her to him.

"William Traherne could not admit you into his life because you reminded him of what he had lost," he said quietly. "My cousin did not fully learn the lessons of love."

"The lessons?" She eyed him tremulously.

His hands fell to his sides, and he stepped back. "That one has to take chances," he replied in a strained voice. "To risk all, or face losing all."

"What are you saying, Gideon?" Gwynna asked, her heart in her throat.

Copper fire blazed in his eyes. "That I love you, Gwynna, with all my heart. That I should like to spend all my remaining days showing you how much."

"Oh, Gideon," she cried, and threw herself into his arms. Her sudden action cost him his balance, and they toppled to the ground. She gasped as they landed with a thud on the hard earth, although he did his best to cushion her fall. "I am sorry," she said apologetically. "I am too impulsive."

"Much too impulsive," he agreed gravely as his arms stole around her waist. Their gazes held for a long moment.

She bit her lip. "I will embarrass you in front of your friends."

"Then perhaps," he said, settling her against him, "I shall no longer call them friends."

"I will never manage to dress as elegantly as you."

His brows arched in his best hauteur. "Few people do," he said in an exaggerated drawl.

"I could never live in London for very long."

He smiled. "I confess that I have lately developed a fondness for moldy old castles."

"And Anglesey. I could not bear to leave it forever."

"The summers here have much to commend them," Gideon offered, nibbling at her ear. "We might even build on that land your father acquired."

Gwynna stared at him in amazement, scarcely able to believe her ears. "I shall insist on keeping my dagger," she said with a sudden frown.

He eyed her sternly. "Only if you promise to leave off attending riots." She hesitated, then nodded. "I suppose that you will continue chanting gibberish at tombs," he added mischievously as his fingers began to toy with the laces of her shirt.

Gwynna forced herself to ignore the sudden goose bumps

rippling her skin. "It is not gibberish," she said, bristling. "If you would but trouble yourself to learn a little Welsh—"

"Now *that* is an idea," he interjected. His fingers, more purposeful now, slipped under the shirt fabric.

Gwynna tried to maintain her concentration. "I shall insist that you pay your taxes," she said severely.

He arched a brow. "As long as I do not have to suffer Mr. Hunt's presence in our drawing room." At her defiant look, he sighed. "Very well. But do not expect me to make myself amiable for the man. I cannot abide fools. Especially at dinner."

"I love you," Gwynna murmured. Swiftly his mouth covered hers, and she was lost in the sweet oblivion of his embrace. After a moment, however, she raised her head and stared at him uncertainly.

"We are so different, Gideon," she said with a worried frown. "So very, very different. Are not our worlds impossibly far apart?"

He cocked his head consideringly. "They are far enough apart so that I imagine we will often be at loggerheads over issues of style, but perhaps not over those of substance." He looked deep into her luminous eyes. "They are close enough so that I imagine I will sometimes wonder where you leave off and I begin."

"Truly?" she whispered.

"Truly," he murmured, his eyes blazing. "You have invaded my soul, Gwynna Owen," he confessed hoarsely. "All that I have, all of me, is yours, if you will but take it."

Gwynna wrapped her arms around him. "Then forever we shall be joined," she whispered. "It is the will of Teuth."

Gideon pulled her hard against him, murmuring a silent prayer of thanksgiving to Teuth or whatever other gods were listening. Even as his hands touched her, a sudden wind whipped up. Gwynna shivered and burrowed under his cloak. "The spirits are restless," she observed.

"Perhaps they merely wish us elsewhere," he said idly, his hands beginning a slow, warming caress of her body. He closed his eyes and pretended to listen with great concentration. "I sense that one of them wishes us to adjourn to the inn, where we can continue this discussion in more private and intimate detail in my room."

She smiled through chattering teeth. "That would be Owen," she explained. "The Knight of Glyn is a very lusty sort."

"Ah." Gideon pondered that information, then arched one rakish brow. "Perhaps," he drawled, "I shall manage to tolerate the fellow after all."